Won't Go Home
Without You

Also by Cheris Hodges

Just Can't Get Enough

Let's Get It On

More Than He Can Handle

Betting on Love

No Other Lover Will Do

His Sexy Bad Habit

Too Hot for TV

Recipe for Desire

Forces of Nature

Love after War

Strategic Seduction

Tempted at Midnight

The Rumor series

Rumor Has It

I Heard a Rumor

Deadly Rumors

The Richardson Sisters series

Owner of a Broken Heart

Won't Go Home Without You

Won't Go Home Without You

CHERIS HODGES

Kensington Publishing Corp.
www.kensingtonbooks.com

DAFINA BOOKS are published by

Kensington Publishing Corp.
119 West 40th Street
New York, NY 10018

All Kensington Titles, Imprints, and Distributed Lines are available at special quantity discounts for bulk purchases for sales promotions, premiums, fund-raising, and educational or institutional use. Special book excerpts or customized printings can also be created to fit specific needs. For details, write or phone the office of the Kensington special sales manager: Kensington Publishing Corp., 119 West 40th Street, New York, NY 10018, Attn: Special Sales Department, Phone: 1-800-221-2647.

The DAFINA logo is a trademark of Kensington Publishing Corp.

ISBN-13: 978-1-4967-3189-0
ISBN-10: 1-4967-3189-1
First Kensington Mass Market Edition: February 2021

ISBN-13: 978-1-4967-3190-6 (ebook)
ISBN-10: 1-4967-3190-5 (ebook)

10 9 8 7 6 5 4 3 2 1

Printed in the United States of America

Acknowledgments

I want to thank all of the readers who have stuck with me through the years. With your encouraging words and love of my characters, I'm able to keep going on those days when I feel like I want to quit. Writing is a very solitary thing, and without you, I wouldn't be here. So, thank you.

And I also want to thank my sisters, The Destin Divas. When I say I love us, I mean that from my soul. I want to give a special shout-out to Sharina Harris and KD King. Sharina, thank you for introducing me to our wonderful agent, Amanda Leuck.

KD, girl! If you aren't the best friend a person could ever have. Thank you for being my cooking Google, and one day, I'm going to send you that check. One day. (LOL)

To my parents, who have believed in me from day one and supported this dream that has become a career, I could never thank you enough. Always know that it's your love story that gave me wings to write.

Six Months Ago

Robin Richardson-Baptiste closed her eyes and tried to forget what she'd read on the paper in her hand. The words couldn't be real. Her hands shook and tears poured down her cinnamon brown cheeks.

Logan, her husband, was a father. He'd cheated on her. He made a damn baby. She couldn't move, she couldn't speak, all she could do was stand there and cry. After everything that she'd been through. After he said that he was going to be there for her no matter what. This is what was happening? This is what he'd done?

"Robin?" Logan's voice felt like a slap in the face when he walked into the foyer of their house. "Who was at the door?"

She didn't say a word. She couldn't even look at the man she'd promised to love, cherish, and be faithful to. Obviously, she'd been the only one who'd taken their marriage vows seriously.

"Babe, what's going on? Did something happen to Pops?" He closed the space between them and reached out for her. Robin recoiled at his touch, then pressed the paper against his chest.

"Get the fuck out of here!" Anger made her voice deep like a lion's growl.

"Robin? What . . ."

She slapped him, unleashing all of the anger and sadness that had taken over her soul. "I hate you. How could you do this to me?"

Logan read the paternity results and his mouth dropped open. "You can't believe this. Robin, I've never cheated on you and I don't have a child."

She was about to pound his chest with her fists, then she took a step back. "You know, I've seen enough of these test results in family court to know that when someone is ninety-nine-point-nine percent the father that shit is real. Who is she? Who is the mother of your baby?" Robin didn't wait for an answer, which would've been another denial. She punched him in the chest, then ran upstairs to their bedroom. Robin slammed the door and locked it before flinging herself on the bed and sobbing into her pillow.

Dr. Logan Baptiste loved his wife more than life itself and he didn't understand what had just happened. Maybe he was still sleeping and this was a nightmare. But the real paper in his hand wasn't a figment of his imagination. It was a lie. Ten years ago, he married the woman of his dreams. Robin Richardson had been a quiet beauty who made his heart sing every time she walked into a room at Xavier University.

The moment he heard her say hello, he knew he was going to put a ring on it. Winning Robin hadn't been easy. While his charming demeanor and super good looks allowed him to have his choice of women, all he'd ever wanted had been Robin. Double R, he'd called her when he'd gotten into a study group with her.

She'd told the then basketball star that everyone in her group pulled their weight, and if he wasn't there to do the work, he could go ruin someone else's project. He'd been hooked.

Why would she believe that he'd do something so callous to her, when he knew she . . . He couldn't get stuck in the past—he had to get to the bottom of this bullshit and make his wife see the truth.

Logan was shocked and disappointed to see that the paternity test had been performed at the hospital where he worked and that the mother's name had been redacted. Was this just a cruel joke? As one of the lead cardiologists at Richmond Regional Medical Center, Logan took his job and reputation seriously. That had been one of the reasons why he'd started investigating the drug company that he believed was responsible for the death of several transplant patients. The more questions he asked, the fewer surgeries he'd been scheduled to perform. It didn't matter that he was one of the best surgeons on staff.

Now this.

Was he now a source of gossip because of this lie? While part of him knew he should've been pleading his case to Robin, Logan headed out the door and to the hospital. Someone was going to explain this smear job. Was this the way they wanted to move him out of his position? Hell no. He wasn't going to take this bullshit. He was going to go down fighting if he had to.

Chapter 1

Robin knew the last place she needed to be was in Charleston, South Carolina, helping her baby sister, Nina, with her wedding plans. There was so much her sisters didn't know about what was going on in her life and she didn't want to tell them while they were celebrating Nina and her fiancé Clinton's upcoming nuptials.

I can do this, she told herself as she walked into her family's historic bed-and-breakfast. The Richardson Bed and Breakfast had been the place where she learned about love as she watched her mother and father, Sheldon and Nora, live out a fairy tale romance that Disney couldn't reproduce if they tried. Granted, she knew now that there had been some hard times that probably tested their relationship.

But there were no outside babies. Robin gently patted her cheeks to stop her tears from coming. She wanted a family like she had growing up. A loving husband, three or four kids, and happiness.

But even if Logan hadn't cheated, she wouldn't have been able to have a child. Two years ago, Robin had been diagnosed with ovarian cancer. She had a lifesaving hysterectomy. Because she had her husband's support, she'd never shared with her family—especially her sisters—what she'd been through.

She didn't want pity. And she didn't want a reminder that she couldn't have the life she'd dreamed of when she'd said "I do" to Logan.

Obviously, he hadn't planned on taking his vows seriously. That's why he'd gone out and made a baby with that nurse. She'd served him with divorce papers over the summer and he'd had the unmitigated gall not to sign them. He kept sending them back to her attorney with a note: *Not signing until we talk.*

But she didn't want to talk to him, didn't want to see him—she just wanted to be done with him. And Logan wasn't making it easy.

Besides, the last conversation they'd had seemed cruel now. They had been discussing adoption and telling her family about her cancer. That, she'd told him, was going to be hard, because cancer had claimed their mother's life years ago. Back then, it felt safe to talk to him about everything. To share her fears with the man whom she'd thought she would love for the rest of her life. Robin's cancer diagnosis had put so much fear in her heart and soul because her mother didn't survive.

Logan had assuaged her fears, telling her about all of the treatments and advances in surviving cancer since her mother's death. Robin knew her three sisters would've been overly emotional if she had shared her illness with them. That's why she'd valued having Logan's strong shoulders when she was going through it.

But now, it felt as if it had been a charade. A big fucking joke.

Robin had moved out of the house in Richmond because Logan wouldn't leave. Sheldon had come to Virginia and helped her move into a town house in Petersburg. She told her dad the whole story about Logan's infidelity and the baby.

Robin had broken down and revealed her health issue. Of course, Sheldon had been shocked that she hadn't allowed her family to be there for her.

"Daddy, I thought Logan and I could handle this. He said he was going to . . ." Her voice trailed off and tears spilled from her eyes. "He said as long as we had each other, nothing else mattered. We'd make a family our way. Didn't know that meant he'd go drop sperm in a . . ."

"I could kill him. All that Pop *shit and he does this to you?"*

Robin shook her head as her tears fell. Sheldon drew his daughter into his arms and held her. "Robby, I wish I knew what to say to make you feel better."

"Did you and Mommy ever . . ."

"I never cheated on your mother, but we had our ups and downs. All marriages do."

"But how can a man take vows and break them like this? Then he keeps the lie going like I'm some kind of idiot who's going to stick around. That mother . . . Sorry, Daddy."

"No need to apologize this time. I understand that you're upset. But you're going to have to decide if you are ready to let him go and end your marriage."

"Why wouldn't I be? Logan knew I wanted a child—

children actually. He knew how . . . Daddy, this is the worst betrayal. There's no coming back from this."

Sheldon brushed a tender kiss across her forehead. "Make sure that's true. I know you don't want to hear this, but I can't wrap my head around Logan doing this to you. That boy . . ."

"People change and I can't believe you're defending him! Daddy!"

"I'm not defending him and I'm not telling you that you should go back to him, but this doesn't seem like the man who begged me for your hand in marriage and promised me that he'd never hurt you."

"Obviously people change," she said again.

"That's true, but I can't believe there . . . Robby, whatever you need from me, let me know. I'm going to follow your lead. If we have to kick his ass, then we'll do that. But if you ever decide to take him back, then I'm going to support you on that as well."

She dropped her head in her hands because she didn't know what she wanted to do.

Robin opened the door to the suite where her sisters had gathered. Planting a plastic smile on her face, she walked in and gave Nina a big hug.

Logan walked into the house he and Robin had shared for nearly a decade and was still floored by the silence. Six months without his wife had been driving him crazy. What was also making him lose his mind had been the fact that she'd moved out like a thief in the night—with Sheldon's help.

Logan knew his father-in-law was loyal to his daughters, but he thought the older man would've allowed him to plead his case. Nope. The calm and serene Sheldon Richardson actually told him to *fuck off.*

He was still shocked to hear that word come out of Sheldon's mouth. He'd even called his sister-in-law, Alexandria, who'd been a fan of his in the past. But she obviously had his number blocked. The two times he had called, the calls went straight to voice mail.

When the Richardsons closed ranks, there was no getting inside that wall of loyalty.

As much as he wanted to fight for his marriage and prove his innocence, Logan couldn't. Not until he had gotten to the bottom of the deaths that he was sure had been linked to Cooper Drugs, the company the hospital had started using for transplant patients. Then there was his career to consider. Something he'd worked so hard to build.

But is it worth losing your marriage?

The ringing of his cell phone shattered the silence and nearly made him jump out of his skin.

"Dr. Baptiste."

"Logan," a female voice cooed. "It's Danielle."

He rolled his eyes. Why was she calling? He'd just ended a twelve-hour shift and had no plans to go back to the hospital.

"What's up?" he asked the nurse.

"Your patient, Mr. Gary Cooper, there aren't any orders

for his medication this evening and I'd hate for something to go wrong."

Logan groaned, because he knew good and well that he'd left detailed notes on the man's insulin dosages. But he wasn't going to allow anything to go wrong. "I'll be there in fifteen minutes." He ended the call without saying good-bye. It wasn't as if he had anything else to do. Being alone in what had been a dream house was nothing short of a nightmare.

Speeding down the road toward the hospital, Logan thought about the days when heading into work was an exciting time for him.

Then all hell broke loose.

Kamrie Bazal. The nurse, who had assisted him through some of his biggest surgeries at Richmond Medical, had the nerve to accuse him of being her son's father. Bullshit. He'd never slept with that woman.

No matter what a flawed DNA test said. But he'd been hit with divorce papers and a child support lawsuit in a span of six months. Then there was talk of an internal investigation at the hospital about his so-called relationship with Kamrie.

That made him laugh. Outside of the operating room, he had nothing to do with that woman. Though there were plenty of other doctors who couldn't say the same thing. He thought she'd been a friend. He had been nothing but kind to her.

So, why did she pick me? He pulled into his assigned parking spot in the parking garage.

When he got out of the car, his phone rang. Seeing that it was a blocked number, he hit the ignore button.

This day was getting more annoying as the minutes ticked by.

"Logan."

Turning around, he saw Kamrie walking toward him. "What the hell?"

"I'm sorry for the subterfuge. But you won't talk to me and we have to figure this thing out."

"Figure what out?" He folded his arms across his chest. "You mean to tell me that you and Danielle don't have anything better to do than fuck with me after my shift?"

"You could get to know your son and . . . I heard your wife left you. Nothing is stopping us from being a family now."

Logan blinked, then broke into laughter. "Have you lost your mind? How are we going to be a family when that kid of yours isn't mine?"

"We're going to do this. You remember the night of the hurricane. We were all trapped here and . . ."

Logan threw his hand in her face. "You're fucking insane."

"That's not what the DNA test says. Jean is your son and I know for a fact he's going to be the only child you're ever going to have, since your soon-to-be ex couldn't give you a child."

"Watch your mouth. You're not even fit to think about her, much less say a mumbling word about her." Logan clenched his hands into fists. And though he would never strike a woman, Kamrie was a test.

"Logan, we can have the family I know you want. Jean should meet his father and have a relationship with you."

He took a huge step back. "You don't know shit about me."

She smiled, reminding him of The Grinch on Christmas day. "You keep acting as if you've forgotten that I know every inch of that amazing body. Especially . . ." She nodded toward his crotch. "Stop denying it. We're a family and you should come home, where you belong."

Logan crossed over to his car and slammed inside. He wondered if he could order a seventy-two-hour hold for that crazy bitch. *Calm down*, he thought as he pulled out of the parking garage. Logan knew he needed to find his wife. She hadn't taken his calls and her lawyer wasn't forthcoming with where he could find Robin.

Of course, going to her office was an option but it was going to be his last resort. He didn't want to cause a public scene this close to the holidays. Hell, he didn't want to cause a scene, period.

But he had to find her and they needed to talk. Robin was more than likely in Charleston, South Carolina, with her family. Maybe it was time for him to listen to the human resources director and take some time off.

All he wanted for Christmas was to win his wife back and get his life back on track. And he was going to do whatever he had to do to prove his love to Robin. That meant that he was going to have to get Kamrie to come clean about the father of her son.

Logan couldn't live without Robin and this lie wasn't going to destroy them. All he could do was pray that he wasn't too late.

Chapter 2

Robin tried to keep a brave face on for her sister. Nina looked so beautiful in her white gown. The older the youngest Richardson sister got, the more she looked like their mother, Nora. Especially when she smiled.

She was smiling a lot these days. Young love was a beautiful thing. But Robin hoped Nina would never face the kind of pain that Logan had caused her. It would've been different if the son of a bitch had been honest and owned up to what he did. It was his constant denials that kept her angry. She couldn't believe her prince charming had become the average Joe.

When caught, deny and lie. Logan—her man—was supposed to be better than that. He'd promised her that he'd never lie or hurt her. That bastard did both. Logan knew how much she wanted to have a family of her own. But that was never going to happen. Her family didn't know why she and Logan hadn't had children, and, thankfully, her sisters weren't the type of women who thought the key to a happy marriage meant a house full of kids. But Robin wanted children and wanted to have the kind of family that she'd grown up with.

Cancer changed that.

She thought that it wasn't going to change her marriage. Logan had promised her that it wouldn't. He'd even said that he didn't want children. He'd said they could spend their lives traveling and enjoying each other. She believed him. Believed that she alone was enough for her husband.

After her surgery and the fact that she would never be able to have a child, Logan swore that they could make a family any way they wanted to. Adoption, foster parents, volunteering at schools or Boys & Girls Clubs.

"Family," he'd said, *"is what we make it."*

Then I guess he made it with that woman. Wonder if he's going to claim his kid now?

Alexandria, Robin's oldest sister, touched her shoulder. "What's going on with you?"

"Huh?"

"You keep staring off into space and this isn't like you. You normally have some magical story to tell about your wedding."

Robin waved her hand. "I'm fine. The last thing I want to do is take away from Nina's day and Christmas."

"But you don't have to suffer in silence. I know something serious is going on. Let's go grab a drink, and if you want to talk, we can. Otherwise, we can drink and eat chicken wings."

"I'm vegan now."

Alex rolled her eyes. "Vegan? Why?" She looked her sister up and down. "It can't be for vanity's sake. You look amazing. A little too thin, if I'm honest."

"I'm doing it for my health." Robin smiled. "But I'm glad you think I look good."

"Yeah, well, you have a lot working in your favor. We share the same DNA."

Robin pinched her sister's arm. "Modest much?"

"Let's get out of here. Yolanda and Nina are going to be flipping through fabric swatches and ignoring us for the next few hours and you need to talk to me."

Robin dropped her head and fought back the hot tears welling up in her eyes. Alex wrapped her arms around her sister's shoulders. "I'll happily kick his ass."

"Now you sound like Yolanda." Robin laughed and wiped a tear away. "There's more to this than just Logan cheating."

Alex furrowed her eyebrows. "What's really going on?"

Robin tried to usher Alex out of the room before Nina or Yolanda saw her tears. Too late.

"Robin!" Nina and Yolanda were by her side in a flash. "Why are you crying?" Nina asked.

"I told you something was going on over here," Yolanda said. "Spill it."

"Leave her alone," Alex warned. "Don't y'all have stuff to do?"

"Yeah," Nina said. "And at the moment, I'm going to hug my sister."

Nina drew Robin into her arms and gave her a tight hug. She wished that she hadn't told her little sister about Logan. But, since Yolanda knew, Robin had to share the sad news. "Do you know how much I love you for being here right now? I know it has to be hard for you to remember your wedding when your marriage is falling apart."

Robin sighed and ran her hand across her face. "I wish it was just that. Nina, I am beyond happy for you and Clinton. This isn't just about my marriage ending."

Yolanda nodded. "Start talking, Robin."

"We're going to need a few bottles of wine for this," Robin said. "Let's go and have a few drinks."

"Wait," Nina said as she looked down at the slip she was wearing. "I need to change."

"We'll be at the bar across the street," Robin said as she and Alex left. Yolanda stayed behind with Nina.

The drive to Charleston seemed to take forever. Six hours turned into eight because of the holiday traffic on the interstates. And there were a few moments when Logan almost turned around. What if he arrived in Charleston and Robin wasn't there? Suppose Sheldon decided to have him arrested for trespassing?

Logan wasn't stupid enough to believe that he could plead his case to his father-in-law and have him on his side. Robin was his daughter and though Sheldon was a fair man, nothing was stronger than the love he had for his daughters.

Still, he had to get Robin to hear him out. Logan knew he couldn't live without her. And this lie was going to be the death of him. Especially if she continued to believe it. *Why would she think that I'd want another woman when she has been the only one I've ever needed?*

Logan slowed down as the person in the car in front of him abruptly slammed on the brakes. Switching into the right lane, he wondered if the accident in front of him was a sign. When he arrived in Charleston, was his marriage going to really crash and burn like the Prius that had hit the deer? He didn't look at the carnage in the other lane as he pressed forward. If he was going to fight, then he couldn't be a punk ass.

It was after three a.m. before he arrived in Charleston, and it didn't dawn on him until he pulled into the parking lot of a no-name motel that it was Christmas Eve. Christmas just didn't mean a thing to him without Robin. After parking his car, Logan walked into the lobby and wasn't surprised to find the front desk clerk asleep.

He tapped the desk and smiled as the man opened his eyes. "Sorry to wake you," Logan said.

"My bad. It's been a long day. You need a room?"

Logan nodded. "Got any king-sized beds?"

"Nope. Queen or twin."

"I'll take a queen." Logan sighed and pulled out his wallet. "Don't hit me on the head with the cost for one night, though."

"Don't tell the boss that I was sleeping and I'll let you stay for fifty dollars."

Logan pulled out his credit card and nodded. "My lips are sealed."

After getting checked in, Logan walked into a room that smelled a lot like mildew. He shook his head, thinking about how stellar things had always been at the Richardson B&B.

In college, Robin talked about her father's hotel and made it sound like some fairy tale castle. When she'd taken him to Charleston in their junior year at Xavier, he saw that she was right. The history of the place in the face of Southern discrimination, how he raised his daughters surrounded by such beauty and privilege, yet they were some of the most gracious women ever. Even if Alexandria tried to act like she was a hard ass. Clearly, she wasn't. Alex had a protective nature over her family but knew that Sheldon wore the pants. He had been pleasantly surprised by the wedding toast she'd given all of those years ago.

"To the man who will love my sister to the moon and back. And to my sister, who found her Creole prince charming, may God bless your union. And may you teach my sister how to make jambalaya."

He wondered if Alex would listen to him and help him win his wife back. It took him about three seconds to realize that he was foolish to think that any one of those sisters would listen to a word he had to say.

Even if he hadn't done anything wrong. Kamrie had been spreading this lie about them sleeping together and that child being his. He had to stop it and that meant he needed a real DNA test. That would mean giving credence to the rumors Kamrie flaunted. Logan stupidly had hoped this thing would disappear. He wanted to keep his marriage and his reputation intact. As the rumbles in the rumor mill grew and grew, Logan couldn't ignore it anymore. He needed to clear his name. But not just for his career. He had to do whatever he needed to do to win his wife back.

He could understand why Robin was so devastated by this. She'd been the one who wanted a big family. Three children, all boys. Logan smiled as he thought about the days they'd lain in the grass on the quad and planned their life.

"What do you see in that cloud?" she asked as she pointed to a puffy white cloud.

"A big chance that we're going to be all wet real soon," Logan replied with a laugh.

She grabbed his hand and placed it on her thigh. "Who says I'm not wet already."

"Now, Robin, you know you can't play with me like that."

She licked her bottom lip. "I don't play. But I got some studying to do."

"All work and no play makes a dull girl."

Robin rolled her eyes and eased closer to him. "I made a promise to my mother and I have to keep it."

"What promise was that?"

"To be focused. And as amazing as you are, Mr. Baptiste, you're not taking my focus off my future."

"Nah, that's not what I'm doing. We're going to be a team. So, if you need to study, then get to it."

She looked down at his arm, which hadn't left her waist. "You're going to let me go or no?"

"Do I have to?"

Robin raised her right eyebrow. "Aren't you in my study group?"

He nodded. "But I'm skipping tonight. Guess who has a chance to go and cut open a human heart tonight."

Robin shook her head and moved his arm. "The fact that you're so excited about that really makes me believe you're going to be a great doctor or a serial killer one day."

"Stop watching those true crime channels, attorney."

The couple rose to their feet and held each other just as the first drops of rain started falling. Logan leaned in and kissed her while they were drenched.

"Looks like I'm going to have to dry you off after all." Logan scooped Robin into his arms and ran to his dorm.

She held on to him so tightly. But it was the smile on her full lips that made him realize she was the woman he'd spend the rest of his life with.

No matter what he had to do, Logan was going to get his wife back.

When the sun slashed through the windows, Robin was sure that she'd been asleep for only fifteen minutes. How many bottles of wine did she and her sisters go through last night as she told them about the demise of her marriage, her cancer, and Logan's refusal to end things? Robin didn't always share her failures with her sisters. She'd only told them that she and Logan had grown apart.

Two whites and one red. And Robin was sure that she'd drunk all of the merlot. Of course, Alex and Yolanda had been pissed that she hadn't told them about her cancer and the surgery she had had to remove her uterus.

Nina had just cried. And Robin pointed to that reaction as to why she'd never told them. But deep inside, she knew she didn't tell her family because Logan had taken such good care of her that she hadn't needed her sisters. He had been her emotional support. He'd taken a leave from work as she'd gone through treatment and ultimately the surgery. Logan had been able to ask the doctor questions that Robin would've never thought to ask.

She'd been so grateful for him and his medical knowledge. And he'd comforted her so much when it sunk in that she wouldn't have the three children they'd always dreamed about.

Robin walked into Whole Foods with Logan. One of the changes they'd been making in their lifestyle had been to eat more clean meals. Robin had been reading about vegan meals and their healing properties.

Logan was happy to go along with it as long as he could sneak a steak every now and then. She leaned against his shoulder as he pushed the green cart. "I think we should start with vegan mac and cheese tonight. I saw a really easy recipe that uses cauliflower noodles."

"I'm sure it tastes better than it sounds," he replied, then stroked her cheek. "Glad you wanted to get out of the house today."

She released a heavy sigh. "I think I've been in bed long enough."

"Babe, if you need more time or to call one of your sisters . . ."

Robin shook her head. "If I call one, they all will come and I can't . . ."

He stroked her cheek again and kissed her. "Understood. You just let me know what you need and I'll make sure you have it." Logan pointed to a display of vegan cheese. "And there is the fake cheese."

She pinched his side. "You're funny. We're going to need almond milk, some pepper. Umm, what is the vegan substitute for eggs?"

"I don't think there is one, Rob." As Logan walked

over to the display to grab the cheese, a little girl who'd been running from her flustered mother grabbed his leg.

"Dada!"

Robin's knees quaked as she watched Logan set the cheese aside and pick the little girl up to stop her from outrunning her mom.

"I'm so sorry," the woman said breathlessly as she reached for her daughter. But the little girl wrapped her tiny arms around Logan's neck.

"Dada!"

"Baby, no. This isn't Dada." The woman shook her head. "She learned that word two days ago. Now, every man in Richmond is 'dada.'"

Robin dropped her head in her hand and tried not to cry. But how could she not? Logan would never have a child of his own to call him daddy. She wouldn't have a precious little girl to chase around the market.

The tears came as she watched Logan force the little girl back into her mother's arms. He rushed to her side and pulled Robin into his arms. Her sobs made her body shake. Logan held her tighter. "Shh, shh."

"That-that was so sweet of you to hold that little g-girl. I'm so sorry that I won't be able . . ."

"I'm holding everything I ever need right here." Logan stroked the back of her neck.

"B-but . . . We dreamed about a family and now . . ."

"Robin. You are enough. We can make a family any way we want when we're ready." He held her out in front of him and wiped her tears with his thumbs. "You want to go home and order takeout?"

Robin brought her hands to her face as she shook her

head. *"No. I can't cry every time I see a child. I know I'm blessed to be alive."*

"And I'm blessed to have my wife. Robin, you're all I need. And down the road, we can look at options, but right now, we need to focus on you and your healing."

She nodded. "It's time for me to see that therapist. Will you go with me?"

"You don't even have to ask." Logan brushed his lips against hers. "Whatever you need, I got you."

Robin took a deep breath and wondered what made him let her go. Swinging her legs over the side of the bed, Robin knew she needed to put on a brave face and meet her family for breakfast.

Nina's wedding, along with Christmas, was tomorrow and she didn't want to be the Grinch. Nor did she want anyone feeling as if they needed to hide their happiness. So, Robin decided that she was going to fake it and hope the spirit would bring some happiness into her heart before the new year.

Before she could open the door, Nina burst into her room. Her little sister's red-rimmed eyes gave her pause.

"Nina, what's wrong?"

She wrapped her arms around her sister and squeezed her tightly. "Nothing's wrong. I was just thinking about you all night and . . ."

"Don't do this," Robin said as she stroked her sister's hair. "I'm fine, Nina."

"But we almost lost you and you didn't even let us help."

"Because I knew this was going to be the reaction. I

don't need your tears, sis. Not when you're this close to your wedding day." She held her index finger inches from her thumb. "I'm here to celebrate your wedding. Not make you cry."

Nina leaned her head on Robin's shoulder. "But I can't help but wonder how I can make a marriage work if a man like Logan couldn't be faithful to you and he hurt . . ."

"Stop it. What happened to me has nothing to do with your future."

"You and Logan were my relationship goals. How could he do this to you?"

Robin shrugged, being that she had struggled with understanding it herself. He promised that she was enough. Promised that he loved her and he broke that vow to her in the worst way.

"I'll get over it," she said as she let Nina go. "Now, we need to get some breakfast and put this behind us. We need to get you ready for your wedding."

Nina's smile lit her face. "Yes. Clinton is joining us for lunch and he's cooking."

"Oh, I didn't know he could cook. I'm feeling better about your future with him more and more! You guys won't starve. God knows you can't cook to save your life."

Nina sucked her teeth. "Ha, ha. He's actually helping me with my cooking abilities."

Robin burst out into laughter. Just thinking about Nina in the kitchen was enough to brighten her spirits. "I hope the first thing you learn is how to make grits that you can eat with a fork."

Nina rolled her eyes. "Clinton is not marrying me for my grits."

"Thank God. Because that wedding would never happen. Now get out of my room so I can get dressed."

"Okay. But, Robin, don't ever hide something that important from us again."

"Hopefully, I'll never have to. Now, go, Nina." She shooed her sister out of the room.

Robin took a quick shower, then dressed in a pair of knit pants and a ruffle top. After slipping into her leather loafers, she headed into the dining room to meet her family. Robin's heart nearly stopped when she saw Logan standing there surrounded by her angry sisters.

"You got a fucking nerve!" Yolanda yelled. "Why is your cheating ass here?"

"You really should leave," Alex chimed in with an angry hiss.

"Guys," Robin said. "Let me handle this."

"Oh, hell no," Nina said. "We're handling this together and if that means Logan gets the beatdown he deserves, then . . ."

"Y'all!" Robin growled. "I said I got this. Get out."

Alex nodded toward her sisters. "Come on."

"We're going to be right outside the door," Nina said. "You scream, we are coming in hot."

Robin hid her smile because her sisters were crazy. Once she and Logan were alone, she gave him a slow once-over and he looked like shit.

His face had stubble and Logan always kept his ebony face clean shaven. His eyes looked tired, red rimmed, and vacant.

"My sisters had the right question—why are you here?"

"Because I want to prove to you that everything you've believed over these last six months has been a lie."

"That DNA test wasn't a lie. The only lies have been flowing out of your mouth." She folded her arms across her chest and closed her eyes. Why did she want him to take her into his arms? Why did she want to tell him that this was all a nightmare and he really hadn't cheated on her?

But she couldn't. She saw the test results. Science was fact.

"Robin, I swear, I didn't sleep with Kamrie. That DNA test could've been faked, and if you can't believe that, then what have we been doing all of these years? You are the only woman I've ever loved."

Tears threatened to spill from her eyes, but she'd be damned if she'd let him see her cry. "My sister is getting married tomorrow. You don't need to be here; you don't need to show her what happens when a man doesn't honor his vows."

"Damn it! I'm not that man, Robin!"

It didn't take long for her sisters to burst into the dining room. "What's with the yelling?" Alex demanded as she hopped in Logan's face. "You did this to our sister and . . ."

Logan held his hands up. "I didn't come here to start trouble, but I'm here to get my wife back. You all love your sister and I've always respected that, but this isn't your concern."

Yolanda lunged at Logan and it took all of Nina's strength to keep her sister from reaching him. "Were you thinking about my sister when you were sticking your dirty dick in that other woman?"

"Yolanda!" Alex and Robin exclaimed.

Nina let her sister go. "She has a point."

"I'm going to tell y'all the same thing I've been telling Robin. I never slept with that woman and her son isn't mine," Logan said. "And I'm not leaving until my wife believes me."

"Logan, just stop it," Robin said. "Stop it. Sign the fucking divorce papers and end this insanity. Why would anyone go to these lengths to make you believe you're the father of this child if there wasn't a chance that it could be?"

He stepped closer to her and though Robin wanted to move, her feet were rooted to the floor. "Do you still love me?" His voice was barely above a whisper. "Do you still believe I'm the man you said 'I do' to?"

She blinked rapidly and almost said yes. "Don't do this, Logan."

"I'm going to fight for us. And I don't care how long or how hard I have to carry on this battle. Robin, I'm not letting you go."

"Boy, you'd better get your black ass off my property," Sheldon Richardson boomed.

Everything in the room went still.

Logan knew he was in for the fight of his life when he turned around and looked at the people whom he'd once considered family. Hate was etched on every Richardson face that stared back at him. Robin had a wall. He was going to have to break it down piece by piece. But there was something about the way Robin looked at him that made him believe there was a chance for them. He wasn't going to give up. Not with this lie looming over his head.

"I'll leave, but I'm not giving up on my wife," he said as he sidestepped his angry in-laws.

Sheldon gave him a look that he couldn't read. Was his father-in-law ready to fight him or stand aside and allow him and Robin to work this thing out? Nope, he wasn't going to worry about what was going on around him. He had one mission and that was getting Robin back into his life.

Chapter 3

Robin's appetite was gone when she and her sisters finally sat down to eat breakfast. Something about seeing Logan threw her off kilter. It would be so much easier had he just signed the papers and let her move on with her life. Why wouldn't he? He could be with his child and the woman he'd obviously felt comfortable enough with to have sex without a condom. A woman who he had the nerve to say was simply a friend. Kam.

That's what he'd called her when he'd told stories about her. At first, Robin thought she was a dude. Then she'd met the buxom nurse. Tall, brown skinned, with long, wavy hair and piercing brown eyes. When she'd jokingly asked Logan if she should be jealous, she'd believed him when he said no.

She snorted as she stabbed her cold eggs. Why was she even pretending to eat eggs? Robin dropped her fork and looked at her sisters, who were looking right back at her.

"So, we're just going to act like he wasn't here?" Yolanda asked as she broke a piece of bacon in half.

"I don't want to talk about it."

Sheldon cleared his throat. "I believe I told y'all to mind your business and let Robin and Logan handle their marriage problems alone."

Nina raised her right eyebrow at her dad but didn't say anything.

Alex expelled a sigh. "We know what you said, Daddy. But Logan being here makes it our business."

Yolanda and Nina exchanged shocked looks. Alexandria Richardson didn't talk back to their father. Ever.

"It isn't a family affair," Robin said. "Whatever Logan and I decide to do, we're going to make that decision on our own."

Alex drummed her fingers on the table as Sheldon nodded. "Excuse me, but that's bullshit," Alex said. "Knowing what you've been through and the fact . . ."

"Alex, please," Robin exclaimed. "I don't need you to act like this is some mess for you to clean up."

"Robin, you didn't let us help you when you . . ." Yolanda stopped talking when Robin stood up.

"This is why I don't like to tell y'all anything. We're not a gang. I can handle myself and my cheating husband. If I needed all of your posturing and bullshit, I would've called a long time ago." As she stormed out of the room, she heard her father telling her sisters that he told them to mind their business.

Robin needed to clear her head and started walking toward the beach. "Robin."

Turning around, she wasn't surprised to see Logan standing there. When they would visit, they walked on the beach after breakfast and before dinner. Back then it had been because they wanted to make out.

"Logan, why are you still here? If you don't have the

signed divorce papers with you, what's there to talk about?"

"There's a lot for us to talk about. I can't understand why you think I would cheat on you."

"Umm, because of the baby!" She pushed against his chest. "I'm not surprised that you and *Kam* had this affair."

"I was never with that woman. You can't believe that I would want someone else other than you."

"Again! The baby says it all."

"That's not my child. Robin, knowing how much a child meant to you, do you think I'm that much of an ass-hole? Do you?" He placed his hands on her shoulders and forced her to look into his eyes.

"I don't . . . . But why would she say this and pass her child off as yours? Did anything ever happen between you and that woman?"

"No, I thought Kam was a friend. We worked together on many surgeries. Why would I have introduced you to her if I was sleeping with her?"

"That's the million-dollar question. Maybe you thought if I met her that I'd ignore your little affair. Or maybe you thought that I'd join in or sign off on it?" Robin rolled her eyes and started walking toward the water. "Logan, let's just end this." The water lapped her loafers and she bounced back, not realizing that Logan was standing so close to her. But she fell into his arms. She missed his arms. Strong. Warm. She leaned her head against his chest and closed her eyes. How could she still love him after he'd . . . Robin pulled away from him and shook her head. This wasn't the quad at Xavier

University and he wasn't the cocky basketball player who'd stolen her heart.

"Rob, I'm going to prove the truth to you one way or another. But you can best believe that I'm not signing those papers. So, you can tell your attorney to stop calling, texting, and e-mailing me."

"If it's that simple to prove this isn't your child, then why haven't you gotten another DNA test? Why haven't you gone to court to prove it?"

Logan nodded. "For one, I don't want this lie to become public knowledge. If the hospital thinks that I've had an inappropriate relationship with her, my career . . ."

"Damn your career, Logan! What's more important, me or your job?"

"You know you're the most important part of my life, but do you really want me to give up what I spent years building for a lie?"

"Are you serious right now?" she snapped.

Logan folded his arms across his chest. "Yes, I am. I worked too damned hard to lose everything because she wants to play the victim."

"Oh, but it's okay to sacrifice your marriage. Got it." Robin stomped away from him as tears stung her eyes.

Logan took off after her and grasped her elbow. "Robin, please. You know how much it means for me to be a doctor. Please don't pretend that I'm choosing anything over you."

She glared at him, willing her body not to betray her and melt against him. "I can't tell. Just sign the papers. I don't want to deal with this and I don't have to. You made this mess with your wayward dick and I'm not cleaning it up. So, fuck you. Your career and this marriage."

Robin sprinted away from him and didn't look back. She had to face the fact that her marriage was over. If only her heart would listen.

Logan stood in the cold sand watching his wife run away from him. Why did he say that bullshit? He wanted nothing more than to have his wife back, but he had to clear up this lie. The last thing he wanted was to be around Kamrie and try to pry the truth out of her, but what choice did he have?

One thing was for sure, he wasn't leaving Charleston without knowing that he and Robin had a chance of reconciliation.

"Logan," he heard Sheldon call out. Looking up at his father-in-law, he wasn't sure if he should run or stay put to find out what the man wanted.

"Yes, sir?"

"I'm not happy that you're here, but I have questions and we need to talk, man to man."

"Pops, I'm a little talked out right now. This all looks really bad, but you have to know that I . . ."

"We're not doing this out here. Come with me to my office. Got a single malt scotch that we can share. I've always thought of you as my son, and I just want to make sure that if I'm writing you out of my life I have all the facts."

Robin wanted to be left alone, but as soon as she walked into the bed-and-breakfast, her sisters were right in her face. Instead of asking questions, they offered her food. She knew this trick. Hell, Robin invented it. Two chocolate chip cookies and Nina would spill all the secrets. Yolanda was a cake square snitch, and Alex, well, there had to be a whole meal.

She was not falling for it.

"You sure you don't want some hot blueberry muffins?" Alex asked as she held one of the oversized muffins out to her. She had to give it to her sister, she played this game well and was holding her kryptonite.

Robin took the muffin from Alex. "I'm going to eat this, but I don't want to talk about Logan." She turned to Nina. "Where is Clinton?"

"In his office, why?"

"I'm going to say hello to my future brother-in-law and y'all need to do something with your lives that doesn't include harassing me."

"Wait," Yolanda said as she placed her hand on Robin's shoulder. "I'm not going to act like I didn't see y'all outside. Robin, are you sure it's over?"

No, I don't know what I'm sure of right now. But instead of answering her sister, Robin nibbled at her muffin.

"Leave her alone," Nina said. "She told us that this is her business."

Yolanda shot Nina a cold look. "When has that ever stopped you?"

"Guys," Alex said. "We should listen to Dad and let Robin and Logan handle their marriage. We're not giving her peace with the arguing."

Robin nodded toward Alex. "What's going on with these two?"

Alex shrugged and shook her head. "We all have dress

fittings this afternoon, so I hope we can remember that we're here for Nina."

All Robin could think about was how she wanted Christmas to be over sooner, rather than later.

Sheldon slid another shot of scotch to Logan and he accepted it but didn't down it right away. After three shots of the scotch, Logan had been at his limit.

"So," Sheldon said as he leaned back in his seat, breaking the silence they'd been sitting in. "Did you cheat on Robin and break her heart?"

"No. I would never do that to her, not after what we've been through. Pops, I love her so much."

"Then why does this DNA test say you are the father?"

Logan shook his head. "That's what I'm trying to figure out. The results are wrong."

"You work in a hospital. How often are those results wrong?"

He dropped his head. The more he told this story, the more outlandish it seemed. But being that he worked in the hospital, Logan imagined that the results could have been tampered with. Were there people at the hospital who were that unscrupulous? Why would anyone want to do this to him? Had he made himself a target because of his position at the hospital and his disagreement with upper management on some of the drug experiments that he wouldn't sign off on?

That had to be the case. "Maybe this isn't even about Rob and me. It could just be a way to come after me by someone higher up the food chain at the hospital."

Sheldon took a sip of his scotch. "Health care can be

a ruthless business; it doesn't sound too far-fetched. Are you working on something that people want? I know you'd been talking about doing some research and people like big pharma don't want to see advancements that will hurt their bottom line."

"No, but I have been getting under the skin of some of the executives who want to turn the hospital into a testing facility for drugs. I'm not trying to have another Tuskegee project going on. We're a teaching hospital and I don't like the lessons."

"And you really think someone would go this far to bring you down?"

Logan shrugged and toyed with his glass of liquor before taking a small sip. "Pops, it has to be something because there is no way I'd betray Robin like this."

"You need to figure out what's going on and fast, because I've never seen my lady bird this angry. And you'd better be telling the truth."

Logan downed the strong liquor and nodded. "Wouldn't lie to Robin or you."

Richmond, Virginia

Kamrie walked into the doctor's offices suite of the hospital wondering if Logan had returned yet. She hadn't seen him in days and they needed to talk. The time for him avoiding her and their son was over. Jean-Louis Baptiste needed to meet his father.

"Nurse Bazal?" Dr. Kelly Andrews asked when she spotted Kamrie outside of Logan's office. "Everything all right?"

"I was just looking for Dr. Baptiste. Haven't seen him in a few days and . . ."

"Is this about a patient? I've taken over for him for the near future. He's taken some time off for some family issues."

Kamrie raised her right eyebrow. "Is that so?"

Kelly chuckled. "You're really going to play this game? The rumors are swirling about you, Logan, and your son. Pretty sure his wife isn't happy at all."

Kamrie ran her hand across her smooth brown face. "So, you listen to gossip now?"

"Is it really gossip when you're spreading it?" Kelly shook her head and started down the corridor. "If you have any information on patients, let me know."

Kamrie seethed as the doctor walked away; her plan wasn't working at all. Logan's marriage should've been beyond repair. She knew about Robin Baptiste's medical issue and the fact that she couldn't have a child. The fact that she and Logan had a son should've sent Robin running to a divorce lawyer.

Clearly something had happened since she sent the DNA test to her six months ago. She hadn't seen the comely lawyer popping up at the hospital with impromptu lunches or dinners. Logan's mood had been shitty, to say the least.

She'd expected that he would've fallen into her arms and lamented the end of his marriage. Then they would've raised her son together. She'd have the status of being a doctor's wife and the money to do what she wanted.

Kamrie knew what it was like to suffer through not having enough money to make ends meet. Her mother worked three jobs after her father dropped her for a younger woman. Pretty didn't pay the bills, she'd learned at an early age. But her good looks would be enough to get the attention of men with money.

It had worked in Atlanta, until it didn't.

She headed down to the cardiac unit to start her shift. She'd find out what was going on with Logan soon enough. Even if that meant she'd have to officially go public with the news about their son.

Chapter 4

Robin didn't feel like a matron of honor as she slipped into her silver gown. It was a beautiful dress and fit her perfectly. But being on the cusp of a divorce from a man she still loved with all of her heart made her feel less than honorable.

"You look amazing," Alex said as she joined Robin at the mirror in her bridesmaid gown. The deep red color made Alex glow and Robin wondered if they should switch roles.

"Thanks, and you are just glowing in that red." Robin wiped her eyes. "Alex, is it wrong that I still love him?"

Alex wrapped her arm around Robin's shoulder. "Who am I to judge? But this is really hard to swallow."

Robin wiped away a tear. "Tell me about it. And you know what he's concerned with right now?"

"The division of y'all's assets?"

Robin almost laughed at her sister. Of course, business-minded Alex would think that. "No. His reputation. He claims he and Kamrie never had an affair and if he pushes too hard to get another DNA test or go to court he's going to lose what he's worked for at the hospital."

Alex took a slight step away from her sister. "Well, Robin, he's not completely wrong."

Robin shot her a questioning look. "Are you serious? I think our marriage is more . . ."

Alex held her hand up. "Listen to me, Logan worked too hard to become a doctor, you even sacrificed for his career. Why wouldn't he want to protect that from this bitch?"

"Did you just curse?"

"Maybe I'm in denial, but I don't believe Logan did this. An affair?" Alex shrugged. "He doesn't seem like the kind of man who would do that. Not when he came here while you two were in undergrad and asked Dad for your hand in marriage."

"He did that?"

Alex folded her arms across her chest. "You're telling me that you didn't know about it?"

She shook her head.

Xavier University's basketball team was one of the historically black colleges playing in a basketball tournament at the TD Arena. After the first round, XU had been eliminated. Logan had some free time and he decided to visit the Richardson Bed and Breakfast. Alex and Sheldon had met Robin's boyfriend a few months earlier when the two visited on spring break.

Sheldon was impressed with the young man who loved

basketball but had an eye on becoming a doctor and not putting his eggs in the NBA basket.

When he appeared in the lobby of the bed-and-breakfast, Alex had been looking for Robin to be there as well.

"Logan. What are you doing here?" she asked as she walked over to him.

"Clearly not winning the basketball tournament," he said with a laugh. "How are you, Alexandria?"

"Call me Alex. And I'm good. Is Robin here too?"

He shook his head. "She had a huge project at school that she needed to get done. I was wondering if Mr. Richardson is around."

Alex raised her right eyebrow. "You better not be here to tell my dad that you got Robin pregnant."

Logan waved his hands as if he were landing a jet. "No! Come on, man! I'd let Rob do that on her own," he quipped.

Alex relaxed. "Dad's actually in a meeting right now. But what's going on?"

Logan placed his hand on her shoulder. "You are nosey, huh?"

"It's called concern." Alex walked over to the desk and placed a RETURN SOON sign up. "You know, I like you, Logan. Don't mess it up."

"That is the last thing I want to do. Where's the little one?"

"If Nina heard you call her that, she'd try to fight you. I think Nina is at the school doing something with the newspaper staff. This writing thing is probably going to be more than a passing fad for her."

"So, you're the only one who's sticking with the family business?"

Alex shrugged. "Maybe Yolanda will decide to be my partner one day."

The two headed toward Sheldon's office and made it in good timing. His meeting with some potential investors had just ended. When Randall Birmingham blew past Alex, she muttered a string of curse words that shocked Logan and Sheldon.

"Daddy, that man is a snake. Why was he here?"

Sheldon waved his hand. "I've dealt with worse, but it's nice to watch people play their hand." Looking at Logan, Sheldon smiled. "To what do I owe the pleasure of this visit?"

Logan extended his trembling hand to Sheldon. "Well, Mr. Richardson, I wanted to talk to you about something important."

Sheldon rocked back on his heels. "The next words out of your mouth better not be Robin is pregnant."

"No, no! Not until we get our degrees and careers going. Mr. Richardson, I love your daughter. And with your permission, I'd like to marry her."

Alex released an excited squeal. Sheldon pulled Logan into a big bear hug. "As long as you promise to love my daughter and treat her right for the rest of her life, you have my blessing."

Robin wiped her eyes as she listened to Alex's story. "I can't believe he did that." She remembered that the week after the basketball tournament Logan proposed.

"That's why all of this is hard to believe."

"Yet, you were so sure Clinton was using Nina to steal the bed-and-breakfast from Dad."

"Totally different. That was business and I was wrong. I don't think I'm wrong about Logan."

Robin reached for the zipper on the side of her gown and hoped that her sister was right. "Maybe I should meet with him and try to talk about what's going on. But I still can't wrap my mind around a woman telling this big of a lie without a ring of truth being in it."

Alex was about to speak when Yolanda walked over to them. "Oh, we might outshine the bride, y'all." She spun around, then looked at the serious expressions on her sisters' faces.

"What's going on, and if either of you say nothing, I'm going to scream."

"Yolanda, stop being so dramatic," Alex said. "We were talking about our baby sister about to walk down the aisle."

Yolanda sucked her teeth. "Bullshit."

Robin shrugged. "I'm going to meet with Logan and talk about things."

"Like the fact that he cheated on you and made a baby with some bitch?"

Alex pinched Yolanda. "Shh. People are staring and you're out of line."

Yolanda snatched away from her big sister and turned to Robin. "Listen, he doesn't deserve your forgiveness."

"This is why no one likes to tell you anything. Stop jumping to conclusions," Alex said as Robin walked away.

"If a DNA test isn't a conclusion then . . ."

"Why don't all of you shut up?!" Robin exclaimed. "Damn." She ducked into a dressing room and removed her gown.

After the fitting, Robin allowed her bickering sisters to head back to the bed-and-breakfast without her. She walked around Charleston Harbor and thought about the good times she and Logan spent there. An hour passed before she pulled out her phone and called him.

"Rob?"

"We should talk. Are you still in Charleston?"

"Yes. Robin, what I said on the beach . . ."

"I want us to be alone when we talk and that means away from the bed-and-breakfast."

"Where are you now?"

Robin sighed. Did she really want him to come to a place that had so many warm memories for them? What choice did she have? Robin had such a head full of steam that if she saw Logan, it would be ugly. "I'm at the Charleston Harbor."

"I'll be right there. Give me ten minutes."

"All right. There's a café on the corner and I'll be there."

Logan probably should've told Robin that Sheldon had given him a room at the bed-and-breakfast—even though he had no intentions of staying there—but he was so happy that his wife wanted to talk to him that he just wanted to get to her before she changed her mind.

Their last conversation hadn't ended well and to have a do-over was a blessing. And he was definitely going to play beat the GPS today. His phone said he'd arrive at the Charleston Harbor in twenty minutes, but Logan got there in fifteen. He looked for the café Robin said she'd be in and found it quickly. He was happy to find a parking spot close to the door. Walking in, he saw his wife sitting at a table near the entrance.

"Robin," he said as he crossed over to her.

She started to stand but didn't. "Do you want a coffee? I ordered you one, just in case."

"Thank you," he said as he took a seat across from her.

She seemed to study his face as they sat in silence for a few moments. Robin broke the silence. "Why didn't you tell me about your trip to Charleston to ask my dad for permission to marry me?"

"What?"

"Alex told me about it. How could you love me that much and then let this happen?"

"Listen to me, Robin. Nothing happened and I don't know what I have to do to get to the truth."

Robin folded her arms across her chest. "You and that woman were friends. How friendly did it get? Because I can't wrap my mind around the fact that she'd pretend to have your baby if she didn't sleep with you at least once."

"I didn't. Since the day we got married and I took my vows, I've never wanted another woman."

"Guess you had enough in college," she sniped.

Logan shook his head and tried not to laugh. He had to admit that his romance with Robin had had a rocky start. But the moment he'd looked into her eyes and seen them sparkle, he'd known she was all he needed.

"You're really going to go there?"

"Maybe you haven't changed from that cocky basketball player who could have his pick of women." Her laugh eased his nerves. "At least you thought you could."

"You've always been the only woman I wanted. The only one I knew I couldn't live without." He took her hands in his and began to sing New Edition's "Candy Girl" off-key.

Robin burst into laughter, just as she'd done when he'd serenaded her that day at Xavier.

Robin had decided that Logan Baptiste was an asshole, and if he thought she was going to be one of those airhead groupies who followed him around campus like a lovesick puppy, he was wrong.

She had options. And she didn't have to go out on a date with him. And she should've told him no. But here she was waiting for him to show up.

I'm just going to leave. Robin stood up and headed for the restaurant's exit when she heard New Edition blasting. She stopped still and watched Logan dance into the restaurant, dressed in a black Members Only jacket and leather hat. He took Robin into his arms and spun her around.

"My girl's like candy, a candy treat."

Robin laughed and placed her hand over his mouth. "You're lucky that you are smart and can move the ball down the court. Singing is not *your thing."*

Logan kissed her palm. "But you're my candy girl, now and forever."

"What about Tasha Taylor?" Robin raised her right

eyebrow. "She was happy to tell me that she could have you back anytime she wanted."

"You're the only one who can have me anytime she wants. Trust me on that." He pulled her against his chest. "Be my candy girl."

"I'll be your only girl. Because I don't share."

He kissed her forehead and she melted. "Why don't we take our food to go? I want my dessert first."

"And just what do you plan to have for dessert?"

Logan offered her a wily smile. "You."

"Let's do it."

When Logan met Robin's glance, it was as if they were sharing the same thought. "Rob, please believe me."

She dropped her head. "It's so hard. Logan, I'm hurting so much thinking about you having a family with that woman and . . ."

"There is no family with her or anyone else. You are all that I need."

Tears filled her eyes and Logan's heart broke. The last thing he wanted was to see Robin cry behind a lie. He'd wiped her tears when the doctor said cancer. He'd held her as she sobbed when she was told that her ovaries had to be removed. He'd kissed her tears away when she saw that little girl in his arms at Whole Foods.

"Robin, please believe me. That isn't my child."

"Then why? Can you explain away the DNA test?"

He dropped her hands. "I can't, but I can tell you the truth. You are the only woman I've been with for a decade. The only woman I've craved and loved."

"Then why is this happening?"

"I don't know."

She leaned back in her seat and shot him a cold look. "That sounds like such bullshit."

"But it's the truth. Ask yourself, have I ever lied to you? Why would I start now, Rob?"

She inhaled sharply. "That's what I can't figure out."

Logan's heart dropped. Losing Robin's trust was a price he would never accept. But being this close to her and feeling her softness reminded him how much he missed her.

He lifted her chin, forcing her to look directly into his eyes. "Robin, I love you."

"I-I love you too." She stroked his cheek and sighed. "What are we going to do?"

"Let's take this coffee and go talk in private. I have a room . . . ."

Robin shook her head. "You know if we leave together, we're not going to do much talking."

"If that's what you want, then we can not talk."

"I don't want to talk. I want you."

Logan had never heard sweeter words.

Chapter 5

Robin held Logan's hand as they walked out of the café. She couldn't explain why she all of a sudden wanted to be with her husband. Maybe it was hearing the story about him coming to town when they were dating to ask for her father's permission to marry her. Maybe it was the memories of their romance or the fact that she missed him more than she wanted to admit. There was a part of her that didn't believe her husband had cheated on her. But that DNA test didn't lie. And if he wasn't Kamrie's child's father, then why was she doing this to them?

"Are you all right?" Logan asked as they approached his car.

"I-I was just thinking. My God, Logan . . ."

"What? Robin?"

"Let's just go."

"Babe, if you're having second thoughts, it's fine."

She offered him a half smile. "Not having second thoughts, but I'm having all kinds of thoughts."

"You want to go back inside and have dessert? I don't want you to . . ."

She pressed her body against his and brushed her

finger across his lips. "Watching my sister get ready to be a wife reminds me why I did it. But I'm . . ."

"Do you regret being my wife now?"

"Should I?" She raised her right eyebrow.

"No, and I don't know how many ways I can tell you. I love you now just like I did the first moment I set eyes on you."

"Double R."

Logan laughed and nodded. "Double R. You have always been something."

"And I was not a rough rider. You just thought I gave you a hard time because I wasn't falling all over your Nikes."

"True."

"I just knew how to hide it better." She thrust her hips into his. "Your ego was big enough without me adding to it."

"But I backed it up, right?" Logan brought his lips down on top of Robin's. She reveled in the soft sweetness of his lips. Allowed her body to melt into his and savor his touch as his hands roamed her back.

Breaking the kiss, she smiled at him. "Yes, you did."

"We'd better go before things get really out of control." Logan released her, then opened the door for her. Robin slid into the car and watched her husband walk over to the driver's side. She'd missed him more than she wanted to admit. But what would happen if he wasn't telling the truth about him and Kamrie?

She turned and looked out of the window. Couldn't she just take his word about everything, tear up the divorce papers, and move on with her life?

Her mind flashed back to the doctor's office, her

diagnosis and how he stood by her. Was that something a cheater would do?

If you don't trust him, what are you doing? Robin turned to Logan as he drove. He gripped the steering wheel so tightly that his knuckles ashened. What was he thinking? Was he feeling guilty?

"You okay over there?" he asked after a beat passed.

"I'm good. How are you? Holding that wheel kind of tight."

"Feel like I've been driving for two days. The trip to Charleston never seemed that long when you were riding shotgun with me." He shot a quick glance her way. "You and your NPR."

"That was to stop you from singing."

"Cold, so cold."

"Boo, you can't sing. You need to accept that." Robin laughed and felt her defenses weaken.

"Do your sisters know where you are?"

Robin rolled her eyes. "I told them to mind their business, but Yolanda is really mad."

"I saw that." Logan slowed for a red light. "Robin, I know when we were on the beach earlier everything I said sounded like a million excuses. But you have to understand that you're the most important thing to me in the world. I just worked so hard to become a doctor and now to be the . . . I don't want to be a stereotype."

"What do you mean?"

"The big black buck who can't control his dick. I've been trying to be discreet about everything because I know how this turns out. The media and everyone will jump on the scandal but ignore the truth."

"Logan."

"I need you to know this," he said as he turned into the parking lot of the hotel where he'd been staying. "I'm willing to do anything to save our marriage."

"But how can I ask you to give up your career? I know how much being a doctor means to you." What she didn't say was she knew how many doctors got divorces because of having affairs with nurses. That was the stereotype he should've been worried about.

"I don't think that I made it clear enough, but you are the most important thing to me and I don't care what I have to do to prove it to you."

She shivered. Everything he said made her want to believe in him and in their love. But in the back of her mind, she saw him kissing her. Holding her. Making love to her.

"Logan, I don't know what to do."

"Can you just trust me?"

"I want to. I really want to but this doesn't make sense, Logan. It doesn't make sense at all."

He pulled the car into a spot in the parking lot, then shut the car off and turned to Robin. "I can't put this together and I can't make sense of it either. But the one thing you don't ever have to question is how much I love you."

"People make mistakes and still love the other person. If you did that, then just tell me. Maybe we can . . ."

"That's not what happened and I don't know what else I can do to prove to you that I didn't sleep with that woman."

Robin closed her eyes and sighed. "All right."

Logan hopped out of the car and rounded the car and opened the door for Robin. He extended his hand to her and she grabbed it. That electricity, the excitement and passion that she'd always felt when he touched her, jolted her system. Her body hummed with need. Rising to her feet, she smiled at her husband.

"Robin, I need you. Tell me you feel the same."

"I do," she breathed.

Logan captured her quivering lips in a heated kiss. She pressed her body against his, feeling his arousal.

His tongue was sweeter than she remembered as the kiss deepened. Logan pulled back from her and ran his thumb across her full bottom lip. "We'd better take this inside."

Robin nodded, unable to speak. He led her into the hotel room and closed the door. Robin looked around the room and tried not to judge, but it wasn't anything like the rooms at her father's place. Didn't feel like home.

"Just stopped at the first place you saw, huh?" she quipped.

"It's Christmas, there aren't many vacancies, and I was pretty sure my regular spot wasn't going to let me in when I arrived."

"Did you drive all night to get here?"

He nodded. "Do you realize the hell my life has been without you for the last six months? Robin, I miss you more than you could ever know."

She didn't want to cry. The amount of tears she'd shed over the last six months probably accounted for 50 percent of the weight loss her sisters had noticed. So, she leaned in with a kiss. Hoping he knew she'd been in the same hell. It started off sweet, then Logan slipped his hand between her thighs and she was soaking wet.

"Robin, I want you so bad."

"Take me."

He lifted her into his arms and crossed over to the bed. Laying her against the pillows, Logan seemed to drink in her tantalizing image. Robin brought her fingers up to the buttons on her blouse. She unbuttoned the top three buttons before Logan took over and pushed the shirt from her shoulders.

"So beautiful," he moaned.

"Love me," Robin cried as she wrapped her arms around his neck. He brought his lips down on top of hers as he slipped his hand between her thighs. Robin was happy she'd worn a skirt when she felt his fingers touch her love-starved body.

Did he touch her like this? Robin opened her eyes and froze in place. Logan broke the kiss and looked down at her.

"What's wrong?" he asked.

"I can't do this," she said as she pushed him off her. Robin sat up in the bed and exhaled. "Logan, I want to believe you but I keep seeing you with her. Thinking about the things that just don't add up to me."

"So, you're not going to try? You're going with the story that I cheated on you?"

"What would you do, Logan?"

He placed his hand on her bare shoulder. "Trust my wife."

"It's pretty clear that I won't be bringing a baby home, Logan. But . . ."

"You think I did?"

She hopped off the bed and glared at him. "Until you prove that DNA test is false, what am I supposed to believe? Can you just take me back to my car? I can't do this."

"No—sure, because I don't want you to be anywhere you don't want to be." He ran his hand across his face.

Robin wanted to explain what she was really feeling, but how many times did she have to explain her hurt? Her disbelief of this situation. That DNA test told her everything she didn't want to believe.

Robin buttoned her shirt and headed for the door. "I wish it didn't hurt to be with you. I can call an Uber."

"No, I'm not going to let some stranger take you home. I'll drop you off and leave."

"Listen, I'm here for Nina and her wedding anyway. I need to focus on that. Let's just figure this out when I get home."

"Are you going to come home?" He closed the space between them and Robin struggled not to fall into his arms.

"Yes. I'll come home and we can try to figure this out."

Logan nodded. "Thank you."

The ride back to the Charleston Harbor felt like a silent torture. Neither of them said a word. Logan didn't even hum along to his favorite ballad on the radio. Robin stared out of the window, not wanting to look at Logan because she was afraid her eyes would reveal her tumult of emotions.

"Robin," Logan said as he pulled into the café's parking lot. "I'm sorry if I put a cloud over Nina's wedding, but I wanted to . . . Know that I love you."

Her emotions wedged in her throat and she nodded as she opened the door. Looking over her shoulder, she noticed Logan's eyes glistening with tears. Was he crying because he got caught or was he hurting as much as she was? Robin hopped out of the car and rushed over to her own.

Robin sped back to the bed-and-breakfast, tears nearly blinding her as she drove. All she wanted was to wake up from this nightmare. She wanted to be able to make love to her husband and not think of another woman.

But she couldn't. And that hurt.

Arriving at the bed-and-breakfast, Robin hoped that she'd be able to get to her room without running into her sisters and their questions. Her hopes were in vain. Robin ran into Alex before she could make it to her room.

"Slow down! Someone stopped by to see you." The smile on Alex's face was a bit unnerving.

"Not in the mood for company right now."

"Oh, I think you're going to want to see this person." Alex linked arms with her sister and ignored Robin's muted protest.

When they walked into the dining room, Robin's knees went weak. "Terell Warren?" she exclaimed when she saw her old flame from high school. How many years had it been since she'd seen him? And it looked as if time had been kind to him. His coffee brown skin was just as smooth as it had ever been. He was bald now, but it looked as if it had been by choice. Then there were those piercing brown eyes.

"Robin Richardson. I knew you weren't going to let your sister get married and you not be here."

Robin shrugged as he crossed over to her and gave her a hug. "I'm sorry," he said. "You're not a Richardson anymore. You broke my heart and got married."

She pushed out of his embrace. "That wasn't funny the last time I saw you and you said that. Still not funny."

"No matter how many ex-wives I rack up, you will always be the one who got away."

Robin shook her head and turned her back to him. This was a hot mess she didn't need. "Home for the holidays?"

"Taking care of some business. My mother finally decided to leave Charleston and I'm going to make sure our house and other businesses are in order."

"Still a math whiz, huh?" She nudged him and remembered Alex was in the room. "So, Alex, where did Yolanda and Nina go?"

"In the kitchen. Well, Yolanda is. Nina's trying to figure out if it is bad luck to see Clinton before the wedding."

"She has one day before the wedding, I don't . . ." She stopped talking as if she knew Nina was trying to keep all the good luck she could after seeing what she and Logan were going through.

"Where's your ball and chain, Robin?" Terell asked.

"Um, work."

Alex coughed and Robin wanted to toss one of the mints from the table at her. Her sisters had better not be spreading her marital woes.

"I guess even at Christmas people are still going to get sick. He's a doctor, right?"

"Yes."

Yolanda walked into the room carrying a tray of eggnog. "Hey, hey. It wouldn't be Christmas without my special take on eggnog."

Robin dropped her head and laughed. "Why are you trying to get people drunk?"

Yolanda set the tray in the middle of the table and looked around the room. "Why are we all standing up? Sit down."

"I guess that's my sister's way of saying we're going to drink this stuff whether we like it or not," Alex said as she sat down and took a mug from the tray. "Where's your shadow?"

"Hopefully, he's disappeared," Yolanda mumbled as she grabbed her own mug and took a huge sip.

Terell laughed and sat down. "I see the only thing that has changed about you guys is that you've gotten prettier over the years. But y'all are still crazy."

Alex rolled her eyes at him. "I'm going to let that slide for now because it's been so long since I've seen you."

He threw his hands up and laughed. "My bad, sis." Terell grabbed his mug.

"You know," Yolanda said as she drummed her fingers against the table, "I always thought you and Mr. T were going to end up together."

"Here we go," Alex said. "How many of these did you have before you came out here?"

Yolanda leaned back in her chair. "Leave me alone."

"This is going to get ugly," Robin said. "Want to go talk in the sitting room?"

Terell nodded and the two ducked out of the room as Alex and Yolanda began to argue.

"Those two are still oil and water, huh?" Terell said as he and Robin sat down with their drinks.

"Some things will never change."

"Like you still being the prettiest girl in Charleston County."

"I'm a grown woman, Rel. But thanks."

He took a sip of his drink and nodded. "No offense, but sitting here feels like high school all over again. Do I need to look over my shoulder for your dad?"

"We're not sneaking kisses, so I think you're good, Mr. Wall Street."

Terell laughed at the memory. "When he walked in that room and cleared his throat, I thought I was going to pee my pants."

"Are you sure that you didn't?"

He placed his hand on her knee and Robin recoiled. After all, she was a married woman and going down memory lane with her ex wasn't right. But why did it feel so good?

"Sorry," he said when he noticed her reaction. "You're a married woman and I respect that. But I look at you and feel eighteen again."

"Oh please. You wanted to get to New York so fast, you wouldn't even consider Xavier University."

"A big mistake on my part. That's where you met him, right?"

Robin blinked, hoping that she wouldn't burst into tears. "Yeah. Didn't you meet one of your wives at NYU?"

Terell chuckled. "A dude from South Carolina wasn't that popular in the big city. Until they learned I knew how to make money."

"You make it sound like you were surrounded by gold diggers."

"New York was different, but you learn how to adjust. And I did. Fell in love with the fast life and fast women."

"Fast women? What is this, the nineteen fifties?"

"I'm a runner. Joined a group of Kenyans in the marathon my sophomore year. The best runners were the women."

She gave him a deep side eye, then finished her drink. "I bet they were."

Terell laughed. "You got me there. My first wife and I got married and realized that we loved running and stocks more than we loved each other. Good thing we found that out and finalized the divorce before I made my first million in the stock market."

Robin pinched him on the arm. "You're terrible."

"Don't worry, the second wife was able to get her fair share in the divorce."

"How many times have you been married?" she asked.

"Twice. They say the third time is the charm, but I'm never taking that chance unless. . ."

"Never say never. You might luck up and find the right one before you can blink."

Terell leaned into her. "She's already taken."

Before Robin could respond or back away, they heard Sheldon's booming voice from the doorway.

"If it isn't Terell Warren, still trying to steal kisses on my sofa."

"No, sir, not at all," Terell said as he rose to his feet to shake hands with Sheldon. Robin laughed and remembered why it had been so easy to get over Terell: The man was too afraid of her father. Respect was one thing, but this was ridiculous.

Robin was about to duck out of the room and grab

some more eggnog when Terell touched her elbow. "It was good seeing you, Robin. I'm going to head out. Maybe I'll see you around before the holidays are over."

"It's going to be pretty busy around here with Nina's wedding and all. But we'll see," she said as she brushed past him and Sheldon.

Robin wasn't surprised to see that Alex and Yolanda were still sitting in the dining room arguing about something. When they noticed her, Yolanda shot her a questioning look. "I thought you were flirting with Terell and on the verge of having a rebound affair?"

"This is one time I actually agree with your foul-mouthed sister," Alex quipped.

"Clearly hell has frozen over," Robin said as she reached for another eggnog. "Have both of you forgotten that I'm married?"

Yolanda opened her mouth and Alex slapped her hand over it. "I don't know what you were going to say, but don't."

Robin nodded her thanks as she sipped her drink.

"Now," Alex continued. "You have filed for divorce, so there's nothing wrong with lining up dates for when it's final."

"Please stop," Robin said. "I don't need either of you telling me how to live my life."

"No one is trying to do that," Yolanda said once Alex dropped her hand.

"What if I decide to fight for my marriage?"

Yolanda shook her head. "After what he did to you? What are you fighting for?"

Robin sighed and gave her sisters a thoughtful glance. "Logan said he didn't sleep with her."

"And you believe that?" Alex shook her head. "Robin, what do you expect him to say—to a lawyer?"

She slammed her mug on the table. "I swear, if Nina's wedding wasn't around the corner, I'd leave right now. I love Logan and I don't expect either of you to understand. Just leave me the hell alone."

Alex threw her hands up and walked out of the room. Yolanda started to follow Alex, but she felt a hand on her elbow. Turning around, she glared at her bodyguard, Charles Morris.

As much as Yolanda had been in her business, Robin noticed how her younger sisters were tight lipped about why Yolanda had a bodyguard. Robin hadn't even been able to bribe Nina with cookies to get the tea. One thing she knew for sure, Yolanda didn't like having him around. And that wasn't a surprise to Robin. Here was a man who seemed immune to Yolanda's charms. Maybe that's why she was mad every time he walked in the same space she was in.

Sensing a brewing blowup, Robin took her mug and left the room. She'd made her decision about her marriage and her sisters would have to deal with it.

Heading to her room, Robin almost wanted to call Logan and invite him to Nina's wedding, just to piss her sisters off. But that would only confuse everything. She and Logan needed to work things out without her sisters sticking their noses in her business. And she couldn't just turn her heart off to Logan.

She'd tried that for the last six months and it hadn't worked. Seeing Terell made her realize that Logan was the only man she wanted. But how could she be sure that her husband hadn't betrayed her?

Kamrie had been a guest at their house for cookouts and Robin had thought she had been friendly and nice. Then she started calling Logan her *work husband*. Robin remembered how she'd balked at that stupid nickname.

"Work husband?" Robin asked as she and Logan loaded a platter full of grilled corn on the cob.

"It doesn't mean anything."

"Oh, it's inappropriate as hell, Logan. You know what she said to me?"

Logan sprinkled pepper on the buttery cobs. "What did she say?"

"It's nice to meet you, sister wife. In my own damn house." Robin shook her head and crossed over to the refrigerator. She grabbed two bottles of wine and set them on the counter.

"She didn't mean anything by it. Kam and I have spent a lot of time together in the operating room."

Robin grabbed the corkscrew. "That better be the only damn room y'all spend time in."

Logan placed the platter on the edge of the marble island. Crossing over to his wife, he pulled her into his arms. "You don't have to worry about me being in another room other than the operating room with another woman. Because when I come home, you're the one I want in my kitchen."

"Excuse me?"

He brushed his lips against her neck. "You remember how we broke in that island that you had to have? Best meal ever."

Robin blushed as she turned around and faced her husband. "So, the kitchen is the only place you want me?"

"Oh no. I remember the game room."

"When can we kick them out and play?" She ran her tongue across his bottom lip.

"If you do that again, they can go now."

"Hey," Kamrie said from the doorway. "Where's the food?"

Robin rolled her eyes and wanted to tell her what she could eat came in a sack. But instead she shot Logan an icy look.

"Give us a minute," Logan said as he fanned her away and then kissed Robin until her knees went weak.

Robin wiped moisture from her eyes. Had she been a fool to believe him? That woman was in her house. Maybe that was why it had been so easy for her to walk away from their place. A safe haven where the world wasn't supposed to touch them. Yet that bitch had breached her peace and Logan let it happen.

Did he? What if he is telling the truth?

Chapter 6

Logan didn't rush to drive back to Richmond. And because everyone else in the world was tucked in with family and loved ones, he had the highway to himself. What he wanted more than anything else was to have his wife in his arms while they danced at Nina's reception. He wanted to lift a glass of champagne and toast his little sister's happiness. He'd always had a special relationship with Nina because she loved sports and they'd talk about them all. Robin had always left the room when those two sat down and watched *SportsCenter*. Now he wondered if Robin would keep her word and fight for their marriage. Listen to what he had to say about Kamrie's lie and help him recover his reputation.

He couldn't hold Robin responsible for the last part. If he was honest with himself, he'd seen signs that Kamrie was a little off. It was strange that she was always in on most of his major surgeries. Since she was a skilled surgical nurse, he hadn't had a problem with it at first. Then they saved their first patient together during the power outage during the hurricane. And she kissed him. He'd never told Robin about it because he'd brushed it off. Maybe that had been where she'd gotten the idea that she had a chance with him.

Things got stranger, but he still ignored it. Then she was pregnant. How she had a healthy premature birth didn't add up, but neither did Kamrie claiming he was the father. At first, he laughed it off as a joke.

Then the DNA test showed up and his life had been shit ever since. But seeing Robin and hearing her say she'd fight for their marriage had him looking forward to the new year. But he needed some sort of proof to have for his wife before she came home. Logan sighed. He was going to have to talk to Kamrie and see if he could make heads or tails of what she was trying to pull.

By the time Logan made it to his house in Richmond, he was restless. The only person he could call this late was his best buddy, Liam Jones. The twice divorced former marine was the only person he knew who hated all holidays, especially Christmas.

"Baptiste," Liam said when he answered. "This call must mean your trip to Charleston didn't win Double R back."

"She said we're going to make this thing right after the holidays. Her sister is about to get married so . . ."

"Cool, I got scotch or whiskey, what am I bringing over?"

"Both and I'll order some wings." Logan looked at his watch and realized that he was going to have to cook wings, which meant more work than he wanted to do at this hour.

"I know you're not going to order anything—just make sure you season the chicken real good before you put it in the smoker."

Logan laughed. His buddy knew him too well. Heading into the house, he noticed a package on the steps. Thinking it was the yearly gift from the hospital, he picked it up and took it inside. After dropping it in the foyer, he headed to the kitchen and pulled a package of wings from the freezer. He started seasoning the wings and heated up the smoker. Looking around the kitchen, Logan realized that he was missing Robin with a vengeance. One of their favorite things had been cooking. Her low-country style mixed with his creole cuisine made for some amazing meals. And some great love. He glanced at the marble island and smiled.

Making love to Robin was one of his life's joys. How could she think that he would ever want another woman? No one else held his heart and soul the way his wife did. What was it going to take to make her see that?

Logan was so deep in his thoughts that he almost didn't hear the doorbell ring. Wiping his hands, he bounded to the front door, expecting to see Liam and the liquor. Seeing who was standing on his front steps made him wish he'd stayed in his dank Charleston hotel room.

Logan opened the door and stepped outside. "What in the hell are you doing here, Kamrie?"

"It's Christmastime and I know you aren't going to allow Jean to spend his first holiday without his father."

"When you find his father, have this conversation with him. Now, get the hell off my property before I call the police."

Kamrie smiled. "Is this little act for your soon-to-be ex-wife? Logan, I'm offering you a life that she can never give you. A child. Your child is waiting for you. Did you get our gift?" She took a step closer to him. Logan held his hand out to keep her at bay.

"Don't come here again."

"Okay, if this is how you want to play this, then you're going to regret it. How do you think people at the hospital are going to look at you, knowing what a fucking deadbeat dad you are?"

Logan clenched his jaw and was about to tell her the quickest way she could go to hell when he heard Liam's booming voice.

"I didn't know it was a party over here." He bounded up the steps and looked at the angry scowls on Logan's and Kamrie's faces. "Is there a problem here?"

"Nah," Logan said in a calm voice that belied his anger. "She's leaving."

Liam shook his head and walked in the house. "Yo, Robin," he called out. Logan knew he was putting on a show for Kamrie and he wasn't mad at all.

"This isn't over, Logan." Her voice was a bitter hiss.

"Oh, it is and you're going to stop this lie."

"What lie?" She sauntered off the porch and Logan wanted to scream.

Walking into his house, he saw Liam was already in the kitchen mixing drinks. "What the hell was all of that?"

Logan shrugged. "I keep telling you that woman is out of her mind. Now she's showing up here like she has a reason."

Liam took a big sip of whatever he'd mixed in his glass. Then he gave Logan a questioning look. "I have to ask, is there something going on with you and that woman?"

"Hell no."

"Ever?"

"Nothing has ever happened with me and Kamrie. Well, there was a kiss." Logan grabbed his drink and took two huge gulps. That was a mistake. The strong cocktail burned his throat like a thousand fires.

"What the hell is this?" Logan exclaimed.

"I call it truth serum. Scotch, whiskey, and bourbon with a dash of club soda."

Logan blinked. "Shit. A dash is right."

"Listen, I want to believe that you haven't slept with that crazy bitch, but she sent DNA papers to your house."

"What are you trying to say?"

"I'm asking if you're being honest. If all you did was kiss her, now she's claiming you're the father of her son . . . ."

"You want these wings or not?" Logan snapped. "I'm not defending myself to you when I never cheated on Robin and that kid isn't my son."

Liam threw his hands up. "So, why is she doing all this extra shit?"

"That's the million-dollar question. I can't wrap my mind around any of this. Kissing doesn't make children. Even if my mother tried to use that logic on me when I was in middle school."

"That must have been a Southern thing. After my first wet dream, Moms bought me a box of condoms and said she wasn't raising no more kids." Liam laughed and Logan walked over to the smoker and dropped the semi-thawed wings in.

About an hour later, Logan and Liam were sitting in front of the TV eating wings and drinking more of Liam's strong brew.

"You know what, I'm going to get you a Christmas gift," Liam said as he polished off another wing. "I'm going to run a background check on that broad and find out who she really is and see if this is a habit with her."

"You're getting soft over there, FBI man?" Logan teased.

"First of all it's former FBI man. And I'm just drunk. But I want you and Robin to make it. She's beautiful, and God knows your ugly ass can't do any better."

"I'd take my food back if you weren't telling the truth. Robin is the love of my life and I'd do whatever it takes to get her back."

"Good to know, because I'm going to do everything I can to make it happen." Liam laughed. "Being that you kicked my ass across the campus of Xavier because you saw me talking to her, I'm here to make this marriage work."

"You got what you deserved." Logan laughed.

"Whatever. Never saw you get that serious about a chick, so I knew Robin was special."

Logan nodded. "She is."

Robin woke up in a cold sweat. Her dream had scared her more than anything she had ever seen in real life. Logan and Kamrie holding their son and taking pictures in a field of sunflowers. She'd called his name and Logan leaned in to kiss the little boy. Tears burned her eyes and she dropped to the floor as the little boy laughed and said, "Daddy."

Blinking, she drank in her surroundings. She was in

Charleston, in her childhood bedroom. Robin picked up her phone. It was Nina's wedding day, Christmas Day. And yesterday, she'd sent her husband back to Richmond. Did he run into that other woman's arms? Or had he been telling the truth about this all being a lie?

Robin sat up in the bed, realizing that she couldn't dwell on what-ifs. She was here for Nina, and after seeing her sister say "I do" she could deal with her reality.

Robin wiped her tears with the back of her hand just as she heard a knock at the door.

"Come in," she said as she forced a smile on her face. When Nina walked in, she was glad for her fake smile.

Robin rose from the bed and hugged her sister. "You're up early."

"I know. I just wanted to talk to you alone."

"What's up?"

"Well, I just wanted to make sure you're okay."

"Nina, you're getting married later today. You don't need to worry about me."

"Are you sure? I know you saw Logan and . . ."

"Nina, my marriage has nothing to do with what you are about to do. Clinton loves you and you love him. I'm not going to tell you that this is going to be easy, but you can't look at me and think this is your future."

Nina reached out and hugged her sister. "Robin, I'm scared. If you and Logan . . ."

"Nina, we are all different and you just need to focus on your love. You and Clinton will be fine."

Her sister smiled and Robin knew she had to keep a brave face. "I love you, Robin," Nina said. "And I hope you and Logan can find your way back to each other."

"So do I," Robin said in a moment of honesty. "I still love my husband and I'm not ready to give up."

"And you shouldn't. Robin, I don't know what happened, but I don't believe Logan would do this to you. Maybe he should be here."

"From your lips to God's ears. But we're not going to worry about Logan. You and Clinton are about to get married. And that's what we're focusing on. Logan is fine where he is."

"I hear you. And I love you, but . . ."

"No buts, Nina. We're celebrating your wedding and that's it."

Before Nina could respond, Alex and Yolanda walked into the room. "You two good in here?" Alex asked.

"We're fine and I think y'all should start knocking," Robin quipped.

Yolanda fanned her hand. "Whatever. We're just making sure there is going to be a wedding this evening and we don't have to go . . ."

"Anyway," Alex said. "Breakfast is ready and Daddy is waiting for us. Are y'all good?"

Nina and Robin smiled at each other. "We're good," Robin said. "Let's go eat."

The women headed for the dining room and joined their father for breakfast. Just like the good old days, there was French toast, strawberries, eggs with cheese, grits, and crispy bacon.

"Oh, this smells so good," Robin said as she crossed over to her father and gave him a hug.

"It's been a long time since I had all of my girls here for Christmas, so I thought we should have a classic Christmas breakfast."

Alex and Robin exchanged smiles. "Just like Mom used to make," Alex said as she walked over to her father and gave him a kiss on the cheek. Sheldon glanced at his younger daughters and saw a wave of sadness.

Robin and Alex had more memories of their mother, Nora, who passed away after a battle with cancer when Yolanda and Nina were super young. But Yolanda and Nina did have some memories of their mother from childhood. Christmas had been the time when Sheldon and Nora focused on the girls. And it all started with breakfast.

"Come on over here, you two," Sheldon said. "There are chocolate chip pancakes coming out."

Nina and Yolanda smiled, then joined their sisters hugging their father. Robin wished that she could've shared Christmas breakfast with Logan. He'd been a big part of these breakfasts over the years and she missed him.

She wanted to be passing him his plate of French toast and small gift. That was their tradition, small gifts Christmas morning and big gifts around the family that afternoon and making love all Christmas night.

What if he decided that he was going to accept his family this Christmas? What would she return to Virginia and find? Did she have a reason to go back? She shook those thoughts from her head. Today was about her family. And at this moment, that didn't include Logan Baptiste.

Logan had been up since five a.m., despite all the drinking he and Liam had done the night before.

He'd dreamed of making love to Robin, kissing her

and hearing her say that she believed him. But when he woke up alone in their bed, he knew it had been just a dream. And despite the fact that she told him to come home and they would fix things later, he couldn't imagine spending Christmas without her. He rose from the bed, still hungover from the night before, but he wasn't going back to sleep. Logan had to pull his life together and figure out how he was going to get his wife back.

He headed for the shower and decided that going back to Charleston was going to be too much of a distraction. Nina was getting married and he didn't want to take away from her day. It was times like this when he missed his family. Losing his parents during his senior year of high school changed his life. Logan had been withdrawn and lonely, but then his high school basketball coach took him under his wing. He'd helped Logan deal with his grief and turn his life around.

Logan knew how important family was and the thought of losing his was killing him. Running his hand across his face, he knew that he had to do something, but the problem was knowing what he had to do.

After a quick shower, Logan headed downstairs and wasn't surprised to find Liam snoring on the sofa. He tapped his friend's foot.

"Don't you have people at home waiting for you?"

Liam grunted and turned over on his side. "That's why I'm here."

"You'd better go see your people. I'm spending Christmas alone because I have no choice."

Liam sat up and ran his hand across his face. "I just took on a new case, yours. So, stop trying to guilt me into going home to hear my sister and her kids whining about everything that's going wrong and make some breakfast."

"You're real demanding."

"After what I found out last night, you owe me breakfast." Liam pulled his tablet out from underneath a throw pillow. "You are dealing with a stone-cold lunatic."

Logan folded his arms across his chest. "What do you mean?"

"Do you know why she left that hospital in Atlanta?"

Logan shrugged. "I'm not involved with hiring folks."

"Kamrie was released from her job because of an affair with a hospital administrator. His wife, who is connected in Atlanta, made it happen. I'm going to go down there and talk to them."

Logan shook his head. "This is unbelievable. Why wouldn't this have shown up in the background check?"

"Cover-up, maybe? Think about it, a high-profile couple in the medical field wouldn't want to tell the world about a woman like Kamrie. So, they ship her off to another state. And here you are with your drama."

"You got proof of this?" Logan asked, thinking about what he'd need to show Robin.

"That's why I'm going to Atlanta tomorrow."

"The day after Christmas?"

Liam nodded. "You want your wife back or nah? Listen, if this woman is trying to ruin your life, then we have to see if this is a pattern."

Logan nodded. "I get it. Let's do it."

"But first, you got to feed me."

"Bacon and eggs?" Logan said as he headed to the kitchen.

Chapter 7

Watching Nina and Clinton exchange their vows tugged at Robin's heartstrings, and she prayed that her sister would never feel the pain of betrayal that she was suffering through.

Though she wished that she could've skipped the reception, Robin attended the party and tried to put on a brave face. The champagne helped.

"Robin," Terell said as he walked over to her. "You almost upstaged the bride."

"What are you doing here?" she asked as she set her glass on the bar.

"Well, this was a huge event and I wanted to see you again."

"Not a huge event, but wasn't Nina a beautiful bride?"

"I don't know. I couldn't keep my eyes off you."

Robin snorted and reached for her glass of champagne. "You sure it was me and not my father who had your attention?"

"Ha. It was totally you, Robin. What are you doing later?"

She closed her eyes. Robin wanted to go home, kiss

her husband, and wake up from this six-month nightmare. But that wasn't an option. "I'm here until tomorrow. No plans."

"Want to hang out and catch up?"

Before she could answer, Yolanda crossed over to her and wrapped her arms around her sister. "It's toast time. Are you ready?"

"I guess," Robin said. "Terell, I have to go."

Yolanda led her tipsy sister to the dais. "What was that all about?"

"Leave me alone. I was probably on my way to making a bad decision."

Yolanda faced her sister and stroked her cheek. "You know what, I'll do the toast for you because tears aren't going to work here."

Robin touched her damp cheek, unaware that she had been crying. "Yolanda, I can do this. I just . . . Am I ruining Nina's day with my bullshit?"

She shook her head. "No. You've been hiding it." Yolanda pointed at Nina and Clinton as they kissed. "They are happy. I want you to be happy again, too."

"What about you, Yo-Yo? Why do you have a body-guard?"

Yolanda rolled her eyes. "Who is going to do this toast, me or you?"

Robin looked at her baby sister as she stroked her new husband's face. "I got this."

"All right." Yolanda squeezed Robin's hand. "You sure you're okay?"

Robin took a deep breath. "It's not about me today, this is Nina's day." Walking up to the dais, Robin blew kisses to her sister and brother-in-law, then tapped her champagne flute. "Everyone, if I could have your attention for a moment. Today, we're celebrating love and happiness. Nina and Clinton, when I look at you, I see so much love and a bright future for you. Marriage isn't always going to be easy, but . . ." Her voice caught as tears welled up in her eyes. "As long as you have love, it's not going to be hard to make it through the tough times. As long as you have trust, you will have everything you ever need. Don't let anything or anyone else's story make you think love isn't enough. God bless your union." Robin forced herself to smile instead of crying. Everyone in the audience clinked their glasses and Robin took the opportunity to take a seat. Alex grabbed her hand and squeezed it.

"You did good, sis," she whispered.

"Think I'd be missed if I left?" Robin wiped her eyes and glanced over at Nina and Clinton as they shared a kiss.

"I'll cover for you."

Robin leaned in to her sister and gave her a hug. "Thank you." While everyone toasted and cheered the newlyweds, Robin headed for the exit.

"Where are you going?" Terell asked as he followed her outside.

"I just need some air."

"I thought you'd be cheering for your sister all night." Terell smirked. "What's going on with you?"

"My marriage is falling apart and I don't want to bring this negative energy to my sister's big day."

He held his arms out to her and, despite herself,

Robin fell into his embrace. "I'm sorry you're going through this." Terell stroked her back. "You want to go somewhere and talk? Away from all of this?"

She looked up at him and part of her wanted to get a measure of revenge on Logan for breaking her heart. But what would cheating on him change? She'd said she was willing to fight for her marriage, so what in the hell was she doing right now?

"I can't. I should go home."

"Aren't you at home now? Or are you talking about going back to your husband?"

Robin shook her head and pushed out of his arms. "I really need to go." She looked down at her hands and her bare left ring finger seemed to be a stark reminder of why she needed to leave. Robin missed her husband and she was tired of feeling like a storm cloud. Though she tried to hide her pain, Robin knew when she walked in the room she sucked the joy out of everyone's happiness.

Maybe the long drive back to Virginia would give her time to think if she wanted to save her marriage. Wasn't the love she just spoke about the same thing she and Logan were supposed to have?

Then why did he cheat on me? Robin thought coldly.

"But what if he didn't?" she muttered as she walked with no direction outside in the parking lot. Maybe it was time to stop burying her head in the sand and fight for her marriage.

Crossing over to the family wing of the bed-and-breakfast, she decided that she'd leave a note with Alex and let her tell everyone what was going on. She didn't want to argue with her sisters about her decision. After all, it was her marriage.

It took Robin about twenty minutes to change out of her dress and gather her belongings. The sooner she left, the less of a chance she'd have to change her mind. Just as she was about to head to her car, she heard Sheldon call her name.

"Hey, Daddy," she said as she slammed her trunk. "What are you doing here?"

"When one of my daughters goes missing these days, I have to check it out."

"Well, I don't need a bodyguard, but I do have to go."

"Tonight?" He wrapped his arm around Robin's shoulder. "I don't know why you girls like to drive up and down the road like you all are truck drivers."

"If I don't go now, I don't think I'll go at all," she said. "I'm going home. Back to my house and I'm going to see if . . ."

"You're going to give your marriage another chance? I'm not surprised, Robin."

She studied her father's face. "Do you think I'm doing the right thing?"

Sheldon patted her shoulder. "That's not for me to say. I know you're hurting and I also know how much you love Logan. If this is what you want, I'll support you."

"Would—did you and Mommy ever . . ."

Sheldon sighed. "All marriages are different and I don't want you to do anything you don't want to do. Your mother and I had our issues. We worked through them our way, just like you and Logan will. Now, you call me when you get home. And you'd better go before your sisters come around here and try to talk you out of leaving."

Robin kissed her father's cheek. "I love you, Daddy."

"Love you too, baby. Drive safe."

Logan paced the house for the fifth time in an hour. He'd cleaned everything from top to bottom, done the laundry, and even ironed his shirts. Now, he was bored. Logan wished that he hadn't taken leave from the hospital, but going there would add to his stress. By now, the rumors about him and Kamrie had to be at a fevered pitch. But he was concerned about other things at that hospital. The overwhelming number of experimental drugs that some doctors were being paid to use were killing people. The more Logan complained about it, the more crazy shit started happening to him.

Maybe that's what this thing with Kamrie was all about. Someone wanted to silence him and what better way to do it than with a sex scandal? Yes, his reputation was going to take a huge hit, but he had to get his wife back. And that meant fighting this allegation—publicly. Robin was his whole life and he would give anything to have her back in his life. It didn't feel like Christmas being in the house alone. Plopping down on the sofa, he closed his eyes and remembered the first Christmas he and Robin spent together in New Orleans.

Logan looked around his apartment and felt like a cornball. He had a too tall Christmas tree in the corner that had more lights on it than the law should've allowed.

And then there was the fake snow. What did he know about snow? It didn't snow in Baton Rouge and he was sure that it didn't snow in Charleston. What if Robin didn't like snow? When he took a deep breath, he knew he'd sprayed way too much of that fake pine-scented air freshener. His place smelt like an overgrown swamp in the middle of a Florida summer.

And he hoped that when Robin walked through the door she wouldn't regret skipping Christmas with her family to be there with him. The basketball team had a tournament and lost in the first round. Robin had decided that she was going to follow the team to cheer her man on. To say Logan had been surprised by her decision would've been the understatement of the century. Robin loved her family and Christmas.

That's why this day had to be special. And already he felt as if he had fucked it up. The timer on the stove buzzed and Logan dashed into the kitchen to check on the oysters Rockefeller stuffing that his coach's wife had given him the recipe for. The last thing he needed to do was burn dinner.

At least he wouldn't be eating fast food for Christmas this year. Logan pulled the dish from the oven and it was perfection. Now, he had to make sure the Cornish hens were going to be juicy and crisp. And it looked as if they were. So, if Robin could look past the corny decorations, she was going to have a great meal.

Logan was used to women cooking for him, making sure he was satisfied. But Robin was different. Double R wasn't with him because he was a basketball star. She actually saw past that and made him work to earn her heart. It was a mission he'd taken on headfirst. Logan knew this was the kind of woman he wanted to spend the rest of his life with.

When he heard a knock on the door, he thought that he was going to pass out. She was here and he had to act like he hadn't been obsessing over her visit. Crossing over to the door, he took a deep breath and then opened it.

"Merry Christmas!" Robin said as she held up two bags with Black Santa faces on them.

"Merry Christmas," Logan replied. This was a side of Robin he hadn't seen before. She was excited like a kid.

"So," she said as she walked in and kicked off her shoes. "I know you probably didn't want to be here today and . . ." She turned toward the Christmas tree. "Oh my goodness. That tree is awesome."

Logan hid his laughter as she dropped the bags and crossed over to the tree. "When I was little, my mama used to get a super big tree and put too many lights on it." As she stood in front of the tree with a huge smile on her face, Logan crossed over to her and wrapped his arms around her waist.

"And I was thinking that you were going to think I was the corniest man in Louisiana."

She leaned back against him and smiled. "I thought I was going to walk in here and find you super depressed about the tournament."

Logan spun her around. "The minute you said you would spend Christmas with me, I didn't really care about losing in that tournament."

Robin brushed her lips against his. "Then we are going to have a merry Christmas. But what is that smell?"

"What smell?"

"Is something burning?"

"Shit! The hens." Logan let her go and ran into the kitchen. His perfect hens were now a crispy mess. He slammed the pan on the stove and shook his head.

"It could be worse," Robin said from the doorway. "You could've burnt something that I was looking forward to eating."

He tilted his head to the side. "You're telling me that I did all of this for nothing?" He fanned his hand across the pan of dressing, the collard greens, and macaroni and cheese.

"Wow, you have been busy. I love a man who knows his way around the kitchen and likes big trees." Robin licked her lips as she closed the space between them.

"Big trees, huh? That's all I needed to make this day special for you?"

She wrapped her arms around his neck and brushed her lips across his. Logan devoured her mouth with a passionate kiss. Her lips tasted sweeter than honey, and when she moaned as his tongue grazed hers, Logan wasn't worried about dinner.

He wanted to feast on Robin. This would be the first time he made love to her and it had to be special. Especially since he'd messed up dinner royally. Pulling back from her, he had another surprise to offer her.

"Robin, you could've spent Christmas with your family and probably would've had a better dinner. But you stayed here with me, even after we lost the game."

"I'm where I want to be." She stroked his cheek and smiled.

"Glad you're here because I really want to be with you."

"Me too." She thrust her hips into his and his body was on fire. "I'm ready."

"Are you sure?"

She tugged at the zipper on his jeans. "Let me show you how sure I am."

Before he could reply or whisk her off to his bedroom, where there were more twinkling Christmas lights, Robin dropped to her knees and had his pants around his ankles. When she gripped his hardness, Logan moaned in anticipation of her next move.

He wasn't ready when she took him inside her hot mouth. Lick. Suck. Suck. Lick.

Logan had no idea that the brainiac he'd fallen for was so good with her lips and tongue. One more deep suck and he'd be done. But he was powerless to stop her as she darted her tongue across the head of his dick. Then she licked the length of him and Logan's knees quaked. No matter how good it felt, he had to pull back.

"Damn, girl," he moaned as he helped her to her feet. "That was unexpected."

"I hope you didn't think that I was all work and no play." Her smirk made his dick jump.

"Come with me," he said as he held her hand. In that moment, Robin was the most beautiful woman he'd ever known. She was a goddess. Beauty mixed with innocence and snark. He took her to his bedroom. Donny Hathaway's melodic voice greeted them as they walked in. He glanced at Robin, who looked as if she was about to cry.

"Babe, what's wrong?"

She shook her head, then wiped her eyes. "This was my mom's song. She'd play this while we decorated the tree and then sneak kisses with my dad."

"I can turn it off," he said.

"No, it's sweet. I love this song and this season."

She reached up and stroked his cheek. Logan drank in her image, realizing for the first time that she was wearing a slinky red dress with a white fur collar. Oh, yeah, she loved the season. But as cute as the dress was, Logan longed to see what was underneath it.

"Mrs. Claus has nothing on you, babe," he said as he reached for the zipper.

"Glad you finally noticed," she said with a wink.

He slid the dress off her shoulders, her brown skin glowing underneath the twinkling Christmas lights he had placed on the ceiling. The farther he slid the dress down, the more of her exquisite body he revealed. Perky breasts with rock hard nipples.

A heart-shaped tattoo on her hip. That was a shocker. "Who knew you had a rebellious side?" He ran his finger across her ink, then eased her onto the bed.

"Not too many people know about this. Consider yourself blessed to see it."

Logan chuckled. There was that sharp tongue that had pierced his heart. Easing down her body, he kissed her tattoo. "I need to be the last person to get this blessing."

"Then you need to make it worth it." She stroked his neck as he traced the heart with his tongue. Logan slipped his hand between her thighs and fingered her wetness. Robin's moans were like music to his ears. He'd waited for this moment since their first kiss.

Logan pulled back from her and lifted her into his arms as he leaned back on the bed. Robin smiled as she straddled his body. Her hand snaked down his taut body and gripped his erection.

"Damn," he moaned, turning to jelly in her hands. "I've wanted this for so long."

"Then you should've spoken up sooner." She stroked
him long and hard. Chills danced up and down his spine.
If she kept this up, Logan wasn't sure if he'd be any good
when she wrapped those thighs around him.

"R-Robin," he groaned. Logan felt the heat radiating
from her body as she ran her hand down the center of
his chest. The irresponsible and horny side of him wanted
to dive into her wetness without protection and drown in
her heat.

The last thing he wanted was to become that guy. Getting a girl pregnant in college, making her take a backseat to his dreams. Besides, he and Robin had law school
and medical school in their futures.

"Protection," he said as he reached underneath the
pillow and retrieved a condom. When Robin took it from
his fingers and tore the package open, Logan knew she
was going to be full of surprises.

She spread her thighs and slid him inside. Logan cried
out in delight as she rode him slowly. He held on to her
waist as she ground against him. They found each other's
rhythm after a few strokes, then fell into a dance that
made them both feel insane pleasure. Robin threw her
head back and called his name as he thrust deeper and
deeper inside her.

When he found her spot, Robin let him know as she
bounced harder and screamed louder. Her pleasure
made him inch closer and closer to a climax of his own.

"Robin, Robin, Robin," he repeated like a prayer, then
exploded. She fell against his chest and quivered.

"Wow," she moaned as she rolled over onto her side.
Logan wrapped his arms around her, keeping her close.

"Merry Christmas, baby."

"Merry Christmas, indeed." She kissed his sweaty shoulder.

"I'm glad you decided to spend the holiday with me. Never thought that we were going to be like this."

"Then you didn't notice my dress when I walked in?"

"Your smile distracted me. Made me stop breathing for a minute."

Robin laughed. "So, what are we going to do for an encore?"

Logan slipped his hand between her thighs. "Well, I know what I'd like to do."

"What about all that food that you cooked? Shouldn't we eat it?" she quipped.

"You know I have a microwave."

She placed her hand on top of his. "Good. Because I'm really not hungry."

Logan smiled at the memory, realizing that he missed being with his wife more than anything today. Christmas was their time. A holiday he looked forward to. After the family time was over, he and Robin would spend the next three days in bed.

She used to say that she wanted a Christmas baby. Then the unthinkable happened and they knew having their own Christmas baby wouldn't happen. Before Kamrie's lie, Logan had been willing to look into adoption. Robin was adamant about being a mother and he understood why. She grew up around a lot of love and she wanted to give that to a child or children of her own. After the cancer, Logan told her that there were many other ways to have a family.

In May, they had started the process of choosing the right agency to handle the adoption. Robin wanted an infant, but Logan had been open to an older child. Then she had the bright idea of adopting three kids at once. Maybe a group of siblings. Logan needed a little more convincing on that idea.

Glancing at his watch, he wondered how Nina's wedding had been. Robin was probably the most beautiful matron of honor ever—especially if she wore her hair up. She always looked regal in a gown with an updo.

Some of their best times as adults had been going to hospital galas and watching Robin charm the crowd with her beauty. Then when no one was watching, he'd kiss her on her royal neck.

Damn it, he missed his wife. He missed his life and . . . Was somebody at the door? How long had he been vegging out on the sofa? Figuring that it was Liam, he crossed over to the door and opened it.

"Robin?"

Chapter 8

Robin didn't understand why she expected the house to look different. It did not. But she didn't get a warm feeling standing in the doorway. She wasn't happy to be home, she just felt that she had to be there. The fact that she'd considered being with Terell gave her pause.

"I-I needed to be here," she said. "My sister and her husband should celebrate their day without my tears."

"I never wanted to make you cry."

She pushed past him and walked inside. It was still hard to think that this was her house. When she left six months ago, she had no plans to return. Her husband was a cheater with a baby and she wasn't about to stay there and be his fool.

But she was back. Still unsure if she was a fool or not. "No decorations?" she asked as the uncomfortable silence seemed to suffocate them.

"What do I have to celebrate? How long have you been on the road? Are you hungry?"

She shook her head, but then her stomach rumbled, exposing her lie. Logan laughed. "Okay, fine, I could eat."

"Got some leftover chicken from last night. If you want something quick."

"I haven't changed my mind about being vegan, well, vegetarian. I've fallen down the cheese hole."

Logan clasped his hands together. "I can make you a sandwich, salad, and a cup of soup."

"Tomato?"

He nodded as he walked into the kitchen. Robin couldn't help but stare at her husband in those gray sweatpants. They hugged his hips, highlighted his tight ass, which he'd developed playing ball and kept tight with daily workouts.

How many times had she playfully smacked his booty while they cooked together in the kitchen?

I wonder if Kamrie grabbed his ass when they made their son? She closed her eyes tightly, willing herself not to think about that.

"Robin? You all right?"

She opened her eyes. "Huh?"

"I was having a whole conversation with myself. But the main takeaway was, do you want cheddar or Pepper Jack cheese on your sandwich?"

"Ooh, both." She walked into the kitchen and took her standard seat at the breakfast bar. Logan grabbed the ingredients for her salad and sandwich out of the refrigerator, then set them on the marble bar.

"I didn't expect you today," he said. "Figured you and the rest of the family would be having a big party for Nina and Clinton."

"My plan wasn't to dip out on my family and drive here, but . . ." She stopped short of mentioning Terell.

"I'm glad you're here and safe. H-how was the wedding?"

Robin smiled sardonically. "Beautiful. Nina is so happy and Clinton is over the moon. I hope they keep that feeling forever." She stroked her arms and dropped her head.

Logan reached for a knife from the knife block and started chopping the cucumber. "Robin, I hate that we're here. In this situation where you are . . ."

"Can you just make my food? I'm too tired to get into this right now." She closed her eyes and thought about the kiss she and Terell almost had. She almost wished she hadn't tuned out the temptation to get Terell back. But what would that have accomplished if she wanted to work on her marriage? She opened her eyes and saw her husband staring back at her with a pained look on his face.

"When are we going to have a serious conversation about saving our marriage? Do you know how hard this day has been for me?"

She slammed her hands on the counter. "And you think it was a cake walk for me? Just explain why."

"Explain what?"

"If this is a lie, why you?"

Logan dropped the knife. "I wish I knew. I've been going over all of this in my head for the last six months. Maybe this is a plot that's bigger than breaking up our marriage."

Robin rolled her eyes. "Here you go again. I'm supposed to believe a DNA test that says you are the father is a big scheme by big pharma because you don't want to allow patients to be used as test subjects? This isn't a

James Bond movie." Robin remembered reading that statement in the divorce papers. She had laughed then and she still thought it was a lie.

"That's the only thing that makes sense, because I never slept with that woman. Robin, you're all I need. All I've ever needed. Why is that so hard for you to believe?"

Tears welled up in her eyes and she finally said the one thing she'd never admitted out loud. "Because I can't give you a baby, Logan. And I know we . . . Family is important and if she can give you . . ."

Logan rounded the bar and pulled Robin off her stool and into his arms. "Do you think I'm that guy? That I would do the one thing to you that I know would tear you apart? You want honesty? Here it is: I wanted kids because you did. My family is in my arms right now. I don't know what I have to do to prove to you that you're enough, but I'll spend the rest of my life doing it."

Robin pounded her fist against his chest and burst into tears. She couldn't find the words to say to him. Her pain echoed in each sob. Logan held her against his chest and let her cry.

Logan had never felt so helpless in his life. Not even when he lost his first patient. Robin's pain broke his heart on levels he'd never thought humanly possible to understand. He had no words to comfort her. He couldn't understand what he needed to tell her to soothe the pain that a lie had caused.

She took a deep breath and pushed back from him. The tearstains on her face made him want to cry, want to fight all of the people trying to break them apart. But more than anything, he wanted his wife to know that she was the only thing that mattered to him. To hell with his position at the hospital, with the enemies he'd made trying to do the right thing. They could have whatever they wanted if he could stop Robin's tears.

"Baby," he murmured.

"Did you call her that, too?" she sniped.

"Damn it, Robin! I didn't call her shit, but nurse. I didn't sleep with that woman and Liam is going to get the proof that I need."

She tilted her head to the side. "Is he? You guys are working together to prove . . . what? How many times do we hear that DNA doesn't lie?"

"It did this time. Robin, why would I do this to you? You are and have always been the love of my life." He felt her heartbeat slow down and he wasn't sure if she was going to faint, or if she was sharing the same memory that he was thinking about.

Logan knew he'd messed up at the Alpha party. He'd been upset that Robin wanted to stay in and study while he was ready to turn up over the basketball team's bid to the Division II Sweet Sixteen. But he didn't kiss Kelsey. She kissed him. Just happened to be at the exact same time that Robin walked into the frat house.

Sure, he'd pushed Kelsey away and chased after Robin, but when he caught up with her, she punched him in the jaw. And that shit hurt.

"Robin, let me explain."

"You kissing another woman was explanation enough. I told you that I wasn't doing this with you, player. But you want to make a fool of me?"

"That's the last thing I'm trying to do. Robin, I love you."

"And you show it by kissing another woman? That isn't love, that's you being an asshole."

He took a step closer to her. "Robin, I'm not trying to . . . Woman, I love you and whatever I have to do to prove it, I'll do it."

"Leave me the hell alone."

"That's not an option for me."

She pushed against his chest. "It's the only option you have."

He watched her as she stormed away from him and Logan knew he had to fight to get her back.

Then came the pep rally before the tournament. Logan listened to the band play, ignored the coach's speech, and searched the crowd for Robin. She wasn't there. His heart lurched at the thought that he'd blown his chance with the woman he loved. Robin changed him, made him believe that he could be a better man. She was his future. And he needed her to know that. Crossing over to the coach, he reached for the coach's arm.

"I want to say something," he said as he took the microphone from the coach's hand. "Aye! Listen up!"

The cheering crowd quieted. Logan looked around at the crowd again, trying to see if Robin had been there hiding behind someone else. He still didn't see her. Sighing, he brought the microphone to his lips. "We're going to win this game, because that's what we do. But every point I score is for one reason—I'm playing for Robin Richardson's heart. She's the woman I love. No one will ever be as important to me as Double R. So, Robin, if you

are here, know that I love you more than ball. More than
life. More than anything."

The crowd roared and Robin seemed to appear out of
nowhere. Logan dropped the mic and crossed over to her.
Pulling his woman into his arms, he kissed her and spun
her around.

Robin sighed as she walked away from him. "How did
we get here?"

"Because someone lied. Robin, ask yourself one thing,
why would I do this when I made all the mistakes in the
world when we were dating? I told you I wasn't going to
hurt you and I meant it." He placed a pan on the stove
and turned the eye on.

"Maybe you haven't changed. Maybe I've changed
too much."

Logan turned back to the stove and checked the heat
on the pan for the grilled cheese. "We're going to get to
the bottom of all of this. But I have to wonder when you
lost all of your faith in me."

Robin furrowed her eyebrows. He buttered four slices
of bread and dropped them on the pan. "Are you going
to answer the question?" he asked as he turned the heat
down.

"I hate to beat a dead horse, but the DNA test. All the
time you and this woman and how she disrespected me
in my house."

"And I checked her on that. I don't play those work
wife and husband games."

"What kind of games were you playing for that bitch
to come in here and feel that comfortable?"

Logan shook his head. "Not because something was going on with us," he said. "Believe me, I'm just as confused about this as you are."

Robin sucked her teeth. She found that hard to believe. "Why you, Logan?"

He dropped his head, then turned back to the pan on the stove. "Robin, I don't know any more than I knew when you walked out the door six months ago."

"Then how are we supposed to fix this?" She folded her arms across her chest. "All you're saying is you don't know. There has to be something."

"Liam is looking into this for me, because I'm not going to lose you over this lie."

Robin blinked, then pointed to the smoke coming from the pan. "But you're going to lose me over those burnt sandwiches."

"Oh shit." Logan grabbed the pan and removed it from the stove.

She shook her head and laughed. "I guess we're going to add grilled cheese to the list of foods you have burned for me."

"You distracted me, as you always do." Logan dropped the pan in the sink, then walked over to the freezer. "But look what I've got." He pulled out a frozen cheese pizza. "Technically, it is a grilled cheese sandwich."

"Only going to accept that because I'm hungry and I'm pretty sure everything is closed. And that salad is going to go great with pizza."

Logan crossed over to her and stroked her cheek. "I miss this."

She wanted to turn her head away, didn't want to feel her heartbeat speed up as his fingers danced across her skin. And she really didn't want to kiss him. She really didn't want to lean in to him and brush her lips against his. But she did. And she liked it. She missed it. Needed to have this kiss, fall into his touch and lose herself in her husband's arms. Her man. The man she loved and needed as much as she needed to breathe. Logan lifted her into his arms and sat her on the edge of the counter.

"Are you sure this is what you want?" he asked as he pulled his mouth away from hers.

"More than anything," she moaned as he stroked her back. "I need you."

"Not as much as I need you." Logan captured her mouth again, this time his kiss hotter, deeper and filled with need. She matched his intensity, because she really needed to be in his arms and know that he wanted her and no one else.

He slipped his hand between her thighs, stroking her until she was wet. Robin wouldn't have been surprised if she'd been dripping through her leggings. Obviously, Logan wanted to find out as he pulled them down to her ankles and buried his face between her legs. She quivered as his tongue danced across her inner thigh. His kisses and licks were soft, light, and smooth. But when he buried his tongue inside her, Robin screamed in delight. He knew all of her spots, knew how to make her moan, and knew what she needed. Robin needed every orgasm that his tongue brought her. And Logan continued to suck, to lick her as if she were a lollipop with a creamy center. And she was wet and creamy as she pressed her hips into his lips. Suck. Lick. Suck. Swallow. Robin screamed as he flicked his tongue across her throbbing bud. She grabbed his shoulders and tried to pull away from him. Logan held her closer, letting his tongue make her come again and again.

Robin closed her eyes and just allowed the peace of pleasure to wash over her. She couldn't remember the last time she'd felt so good. Logan tore his mouth away from her body and smiled.

"That was amazing," he moaned. "You taste even better than I remember."

"I can't even," she replied.

Logan grinned. "But we're just taking a dinner break right now. You're going to need your strength."

She dropped to her feet, feeling unsteady and satisfied. "I'm going into the den so you don't burn the pizza."

"That's what oven timers are for. I'll bring you a glass of wine."

Robin sauntered into the den and Logan couldn't tear his eyes away from her. Yeah, she needed to take all of that out of the kitchen if he was going to get the pizza cooked.

Robin reached for the TV remote when she sat on the sofa. Looking around the den, part of her wondered if anyone else had sat on the sofa snuggling up to her husband while watching home improvement shows. "Stop it," she muttered as she mindlessly flipped the channels.

"Talking to yourself?" Logan asked, seeming to appear out of nowhere. He handed her a glass of merlot. Robin took it from his hand and he closed his fingers around hers.

"I'm glad you're here."

"Me too," she admitted. Logan dropped his hand.

"Going to check on the pizza. Have you seen that new house-flipping show?"

Robin shook her head. "Guess we'll check it out."

A few moments later, Logan returned to the den carrying a tray of salads, pizza, and more wine. Robin cleared the medical journals from the ottoman in front of the sofa. "Light reading, huh?" she quipped.

"More like research. There's some shit going on at the hospital and I believe . . . We don't have to talk about that. Not tonight. I just want this to be about us."

If only it was that simple, she thought as she sipped her wine. "Looks good," she forced herself to say as he handed her a plate of salad.

"Not your traditional Christmas dinner."

She dug into her salad and smiled. "When have we ever done traditional?"

Logan picked up a slice of pizza and took a big bite. "The day we said 'I do.' "

Her white gown flashed in her mind. Their wedding had been traditional, on the shores of Folly Beach with her family and friends looking on.

"That was a beautiful day," she whispered. He placed his hand on top of hers.

"I need that back. I need your beauty in my life."

Robin closed her eyes. "Then you'd better be ready to do something," she snapped.

"You think I'm not? That's why Liam is looking into this and helping me find the truth."

Robin dropped her head. "If you're lying to me and just using your friend to help you cover your tracks, I'm leaving for good because I'm not going to keep living like this. I signed up for forever and you're ruining that." Her voice was a low and painful whisper.

He nodded; his eyes projected his pain. Robin shoved

a forkful of salad in her mouth and decided she wasn't hungry anymore. She pushed her plate aside and turned to her husband.

"When did you lose your trust in me?" he asked when their eyes met.

"What if you wake up one day and want a child. A family that I can't help you create."

Logan dropped his head in his hands. "How many times do I have to say this? You're all the family I need. As much as you wanted children, I could take it or leave it. But if I was going to have a child, it was going to be with you and no one else."

"Yet there is a little boy out there . . . ."

"He isn't my son. Hell, I don't even remember seeing her pregnant."

Robin snorted. "You didn't notice your number one nurse with a baby bump? What about the maternity leave?"

Logan shrugged. "I thought she was on vacation, so when she came back talking about a kid, I was as surprised as everyone else."

Robin grabbed her wine glass. "When did she tell you he was yours?"

He threw his head back and released a frustrated sigh. "A couple of weeks before those papers arrived."

She furrowed her brows as a deluge of questions popped into her head. He knew before those papers came that . . . Robin leapt to her feet, nearly knocking over the tray of food. "So, you knew she was claiming that you were the father of her child and you didn't tell me?!"

"Why would I bring that to you when there was no chance that I was the father? Look at you now, can you imagine what you would've been like then? Right when we were looking to adopt a child?"

She shook her head. "You took that choice away from me. You let me be blindsided. Thanks."

Logan stood up and tried to draw her into his arms, but Robin snatched away. "No," she snapped. "No."

"How are we going to work through this if you shut down and throw up this wall every time you think you're hearing something you don't want to believe?"

"Can we stop acting like you never cheated before!" There, she'd finally said it.

Logan blinked. "That was over fifteen years ago and . . ."

"But it fucking happened."

"And you said you forgave me, that we'd moved past it, and you accepted my ring. So, you've just been holding on to that all this time?" He stroked his forehead. "Waiting for me to make a mistake?"

"Cheating is a choice, not a mistake."

"And it's a *choice* that I made once. When I said I'd never do it again, I meant it."

"Yet, there's a baby and the papers say you are the father. That didn't just happen by accident."

"For the last time. That is not my child. I never slept with that woman."

"Have you seen the little boy?"

"No. I want to take another DNA test, to get the truth. But that means I'm going to have to contact Kamrie."

"Then we have to do it," Robin said. "If we're going to fight for the truth, then we're going to have to do it together."

This time, she allowed him to draw her into his arms.

Feeling his heart beat against hers, Robin melted in his arms. She tried to pack her doubts away, but she couldn't. She couldn't push away the images of Logan and another woman together. His lips touching hers, his fingers running up and down the small of her back.

Every time he did that to her, Robin's body tingled as if Logan had magic in his fingers. She closed her eyes as he made that move on her right then.

"Robin," he moaned. "I'm sorry this is happening to us."

"Not as sorry as I am. I hurt so much." Her tears poured from her eyes as if a dam had burst.

"Rob, you don't have to hurt. I didn't do anything."

"Maybe not this time, but you're going to want a legacy, you're going to want a child and then what?"

He took her face into his hands and wiped her tears away with his thumbs. "My legacy will be helping find a way to end heart disease, discovering a way to help our people live healthier lives. Or maybe even coming up with a less invasive way to perform a heart transplant. Or our legacy will be the babies we adopt and raise to be good people. But one thing my legacy will always include is you and how much I love you."

Chapter 9

She brushed her lips against his. Logan captured her pillow soft lips in a hot kiss that made Robin's knees quake. She didn't think of him and that woman now. She just wanted to make love to her husband. Wanted him to give her the pleasure she'd been missing for the last six months.

Before either of them could change their minds about taking that next step, Logan scooped Robin in his arms and bounded for the stairs. When he walked into their bedroom, Robin was wetter than the James River. He laid her on the bed and stared at her for a moment.

"You know this is where you belong," he expelled.

"And you're doing too much talking right now." She reached up for him and pulled him down on top of her.

Logan kissed her hard and deep and Robin sucked his tongue as if it were giving her life. He moaned as he palmed her breasts. Robin turned on her side and they wound themselves around each other, seemingly becoming one.

She broke the kiss and looked into her husband's eyes. Logan stroked her cheek.

"Bella," he whispered. "I love you so much."

Robin's lips quivered—she wanted to say she loved him, but she couldn't let those words escape her mouth, even if they were tattooed across her heart. She slid her index finger across his lips. "Make love to me."

"Gladly." He captured her lips and kissed her senseless. She pulled him closer and pressed her body against his. Logan's erection grew against her thighs and she moaned as he slipped his hand between her thighs.

"You're so wet for me." His warm breath heated her body as if she'd been struck by lightning.

"Inside."

Logan spread her legs, using his left hand to stroke her wetness. Robin moaned and arched into his touch. He pressed his index finger inside her; Robin nearly came instantly.

"Logan!"

He pressed deeper and she screamed. It was as if her soul were opening, ready to be loved again. Why couldn't everything flow like this? Why did the world have to be waiting outside when they stopped making love?

She bit her bottom lip as he moved his hand away from her wetness. "Please," she moaned. "Please."

"I want you on top of me. Need to look at you." He wrapped his arms around her and rolled over so that she was on top of him. Logan stroked her lower back as she straddled his awaiting body. This sex game was their favorite, making love with their eyes wide open. Robin used to believe that she saw into his soul as those warm brown eyes stared at her. Stripped naked, she and Logan always poured into each other. Always melted as one.

Robin gasped as he entered her. He pulled her closer as she ground against him. "Robin!"

"Yes, baby." Her words escaped her lips like a guttural moan. She gripped his dick with her sugar walls and bucked harder. Logan's body went limp as she drained him and he exploded inside her. Robin leaned forward and brushed her lips against his.

"Divine," she whispered before rolling off him.

Logan gripped her shoulder. "Look at me for a second," he whispered.

Robin locked eyes with him and fought back her tears. Her mind was filled with the image of him being with *that woman*. Why couldn't she just live in the moment? Just bask in the afterglow of his love?

You can. Stop being this way and believe in his love. Robin sighed and leaned into her husband's embrace.

"I've missed this so much," she said. "Missed you."

"Missed you more. Missed everything about you, Rob."

She kissed him slow, and as their tongues danced against each other, Logan's erection grew and all he wanted was to be inside his wife. As if she needed more, Robin threw her thigh over his.

He dove into her wetness, groaning with pleasure and thrusting deeper and deeper. Robin clutched his back, digging her nails into his tender skin.

"Yes! Yes! Oh my God," she cried.

Logan thrust harder as she rotated her hips to match his rhythm. Falling in sync, they matched each other stroke for stroke, moan for moan. Sweat dripped from their bodies as they reached their climax. Robin closed her eyes and snuggled up to her man. She couldn't move, her bones feeling like jelly. She welcomed the sleep that took over her body.

Logan watched Robin as she slept. Just holding her in his arms gave him a feeling of peace. He knew this was how his life was supposed to be. He loved Robin with his entire soul, and no matter what it took, he was going to get her back in his life forever. Brushing his lips across her forehead, he watched her eyes flutter open.

"How long have I been sleeping?" she asked.

"Not long. I just wanted to make sure that I wasn't dreaming."

Robin stroked his cheek. "That was kind of magical, huh?"

"Understatement of the century." He took her hand in his and kissed it. "I wanted to do that since you walked in the door."

She grinned. "Somehow, Christmas just isn't Christmas if we don't end up naked."

"Funny, but true." He nestled closer to her. "Does your family know you're here?"

"My dad does. I'm sure he told my sisters, and if I hadn't left my phone in the car, they would be blowing me up right now. Everyone except for Nina." Robin smiled, then looked up at Logan. "She was a beautiful bride."

"Did she wear sneakers?"

"No, Yolanda would've killed her. We had to fight her about the boots."

"Nina always had her own style. Clinton must be a really special guy."

"He better be," Robin muttered. Logan felt the subliminal jab but didn't say anything.

"So, what are we going to do now?"

"Clearly not sleep," Robin quipped.

Logan was about to reply when his phone rang. As much as he wanted to ignore it, when he saw the hospital's number on the screen, he figured it must have been an emergency.

"Dr. Baptiste."

"We need to talk, Logan," Kamrie said.

"This isn't a good time and why are you calling me from the hospital?"

"Our son is sick."

Logan ended the call and turned to Robin. Her face filled with suspicion and concern.

"Everything all right?" she asked.

Sighing, he thought about making up a story about the hospital checking on him, but he'd been screaming about telling her the truth and he couldn't start lying now.

"No. That was Kamrie."

Robin sucked her teeth and covered herself with the sheet. "Why is she calling you?"

Logan shrugged. "Said something about her son being sick. This is just a ploy. Just like the Christmas gift."

"The what? Why are you just telling me about this?" She sat up and threw her legs over the side of the bed.

"Because I was trying to avoid this," Logan groaned. "I'm not falling for her shit."

"Again, you mean?" Robin rose to her feet, silently second guessing everything that she'd been feeling moments ago.

"I never fell for anything to begin with. You know what, Robin, we can't move forward if we're going to fight about things I have no control over."

"Like you had no control over what she was trying to do or your wayward dick? I want to believe that you didn't sleep with her, that the little boy isn't yours, but you're not fighting like a man who's innocent!"

"And how am I supposed to fight, Robin?"

She got up in his face and glared at him. "Loud. You should be screaming from the freaking rooftops about this. You've done it before. You were loud about loving me, why aren't you loud about this?"

Logan dropped his head, hating to admit that his wife was right. He'd sat back and allowed this to snowball into a situation that would make him look guilty no matter what he did.

Had he played into the hands of those who wanted to take him down professionally while sacrificing his marriage? His silence seemed to set Robin off as she stalked to the bathroom and slammed the door. She turned the shower on and ignored Logan's knocks at the door.

Robin sat on the toilet as she ran the shower and cried. What if she had been wrong about everything and Logan was the father of that child? She dropped her head in her hands and groaned. Family was so important to her and she knew Logan wanted to build a legacy. She couldn't give that to him and it wasn't fair that he was denying his son.

But what if it isn't his son? Why don't you listen to your husband and move forward?

"Robin, open the door," Logan said.

"I can't look at you right now. Just give me a few moments to . . ."

"Open the door."

She stood up and opened the door. "Coming back here was a mistake."

He shook his head and pulled her into his arms. "You said we were going to fight for our marriage and I'm holding you to that."

"You said you didn't have anything to do with that woman, but y'all are exchanging Christmas gifts and talking on the phone. Are you claiming the child when I'm not around? What the fuck is really going on?"

"I don't know what's going on and I've been just as confused about this whole situation. Kamrie is trying to ruin my life and I don't know why."

"Maybe because you slept with her and lied about it?" Robin folded her arms across her chest and glared at him. She was tired of having the same conversation over and over again. Tired of allowing the same thoughts to creep into her mind and believing that the man she loved could destroy her like this. Logan slipped inside the bathroom and shut the shower off.

"What are we going to do to get past this?" Logan turned to his wife. But she wouldn't look at him.

"I need to know the truth and I can't depend on waiting for a report from Liam. I want to talk to Kamrie."

"You think she's going to tell you the truth?"

"I don't even know what the truth is anymore, but I want answers."

"And you think that you're going to get them from her?"

Robin groaned and gripped her hair. "Logan. I'm tired of this back and forth. I'm tired of loving you one minute and hating you the next. Do you know how hard this has been for me?"

As much as she didn't want to cry, tears dripped from her eyes and she wanted to crawl into bed and bawl. Logan sensed her discomfort and drew her into his arms. "Baby."

"Let me go," she gritted. "I'm going to see her. What hospital is she in with that little boy?"

"Robin, this isn't a good idea."

"I don't care what you think. If we are going to fight for our marriage then I need to hear from her. Find out why she's hell bent on destroying us."

Logan ran his hand across his face. "Fine, let's go."

"I need to talk to her alone. You going to the hospital with me is going to cause a scene—well, an even bigger scene."

"Why not go tomorrow? You had a long drive here and it's late."

"I'm going to sleep downstairs," Robin said as she brushed past him.

"Wait, don't do this." Logan reached out and touched her elbow. "Robin, we keep saying we're going to work this out, but . . ."

"But what, Logan? She's calling you, sending you Christmas gifts. What the hell am I supposed to think?"

"I don't know. But neither of us needs to talk to her right now."

She raised her right eyebrow at him. "Fine, but here's the last thing I'm saying about this tonight: If you have any contact with her, I need to be there. Don't hide anything from me about this. We fight together or there is no need to fight at all."

"You're right."

"And I'm not sleeping downstairs because I picked out this bed and I had a long drive to get here . . . ."

"Robin, you're going to have to sleep with me tonight, because I'm not passing up the chance to have you next to me."

She smirked at him. "So, you're going to force me to do something I don't want to do?"

"Nah, I'm going to bribe you with more food because I just heard your stomach growl and there is a good chance that I might make a jambalaya tomorrow."

She shimmied her shoulders. "I see you're not going to play fair."

"Nope."

Chapter 10

It was well after three a.m. before Logan and Robin actually went to sleep. The tension in the house had subsided some as they polished off the salads, pizza, and wine. They'd even shared a few laughs over the new HGTV show that they had watched. But Robin couldn't get comfortable in her own space with her husband. It came to a head when he'd reached for her foot while they lounged on the sofa and she recoiled at his touch.

"Sorry," she said. "It's getting late. My God, is it really this time of morning?"

Logan nodded, but didn't reveal his pain at his wife's rejection. "I'm going to clean up these dishes and meet you upstairs."

Robin yawned as she nodded. Rising to her feet, she reached for Logan. "Good night and thanks for the pizza."

"Anything for you, Double R." Logan hesitated to kiss her cheek, because he wasn't sure how much more rejection he could take from her. It was all or nothing with her. Despite the amazing lovemaking they'd just shared, Robin still didn't seem like her old self. She didn't trust him and it showed. He hated that feeling. Hated that he and his wife weren't in sync like they used to be.

Heading for the kitchen, Logan sighed. But took a vow to fight loudly to clear his name.

Kamrie hated playing this game with her little boy's well-being, but she had to do something to get Logan's attention. Nothing was working and it was time to kick things up a few thousand notches. The doctor in Logan was going to ignore a sick child for only so long. Maybe if she told him Jean had heart issues he'd rush to her side. Glancing at her watch, she wondered how long it would be before a doctor discharged the little boy from the children's hospital. Jean was fine. A slight fever from a common cold, but she'd made a big deal about it to get Logan's attention.

And. It. Didn't. Work!

I know his wife wasn't stupid enough to come back. Where is her pride? Kamrie stalked the waiting area in the emergency room. This wasn't how she'd envisioned spending Christmas. It should've been her, Jean, and Logan enjoying a holiday meal and opening presents. Why was he avoiding the inevitable? Kamrie knew he'd avoid a public case; she knew he wanted to keep things quiet at the hospital and she held the reins on blowing everything up in his face. He just kept pushing her and she was going to have to play her ace.

The difference between Logan and Thomas Lacy, the Atlanta doctor who forced her out of her hometown, was that Logan had a stellar reputation that he'd been intent on keeping. Lacy just did what his highfalutin wife told him to do.

Including breaking up with Kamrie and getting her fired from Emory University Hospital. Her family had money and pull with the board, so Lacy had carte blanche to do what he wanted, except when it came to his dick.

Kamrie knew she couldn't fight Dr. Lacy and his wife, but she also knew she wasn't going to walk away empty-handed. She'd gotten a glowing recommendation from her former lover and a job in Richmond.

At first, the plan was to work hard and mind her business. But Logan Baptiste made that so hard. Why did he have to be so nice? So handsome? And so married?

He was a skilled surgeon and working with him on several surgeries had given her so much insight on the type of man he was. The type of man she deserved in her life. He didn't use people, he saved people. Maybe he was the lifeline God had tossed her way after what happened in Atlanta. Didn't she deserve to be happy?

"Kamrie," the charge nurse said as she crossed over to her. "Great news, we don't have to admit little Jean."

Kamrie clasped her hands together and pretended to be happy. "That's great to know."

The nurse raised her right eyebrow at her. "I'm surprised you even brought him in for such a low-grade temperature."

"Better to be safe than sorry, right?" She folded her arms across her chest. "I know some people wait until there is a crisis before they get a child to the doctor and disasters happen."

The nurse smiled. "First child?"

"Yes, and he was a preemie. So, I'm a little extra careful when it comes to his health."

"Now it makes sense. But he seems really big for a preemie. And in great health. Someone is doing a great job."

"Jean means everything to me."

"Well, come on back with me so you can take your baby home and salvage what's left of Christmas."

She was going to have to figure out what it was going to take to make Logan accept her and his son. She didn't want to have to worry about money ever again. Logan could make that happen for her, and he was going to do it one way or another.

Robin woke up to the smell of cinnamon. It took her a minute to realize where she was. She was at home. With Logan. Glancing over at the digital clock on the nightstand, she saw it was nearly one in the afternoon. When was the last time she'd slept this long or this good? *Over six months ago.* Robin sat up in the bed and decided today she was going to do the work she needed to start to get her marriage back on track. Today would be a "no question" day. They were going to just be. Be together, be Robin and Logan like back in the day.

She pulled herself out of bed and grabbed one of his T-shirts and pulled it on. Then she headed down to the kitchen. "Something smells great," she said when she spotted him at the stove.

"Figured we needed to brunch, because it's too late to call it breakfast." He nodded toward the French toast and grits on the counter. "There's no butter in those grits, but plenty of cheese."

"Oh, you are winning this afternoon, Logan." Robin grabbed a spoon and dipped into the bowl of grits. They were delicious. "So good!"

"Wait until you taste that toast. Do you want syrup or powdered sugar?"

Robin raised her eyebrow and shot him a cool smirk. "You know I want both."

"Just checking." He opened the cabinet and pulled out a bottle of maple syrup. He poured the sticky sweetness in a pot to warm it up just the way she liked it. Robin grabbed two plates and loaded them with grits and French toast.

"I'm having bacon, too," Logan said. "Because it just seems right."

"I understand. The vegetarian food is for me. You don't have to partake." She winked at him, then reached for the warm syrup.

"Hold on," he said as he blocked her reach. "It's not warm enough and I haven't put the powdered sugar on yet."

"But I'm hungry now," she said with a pout of her full lips. Logan dipped his finger in the syrup and brushed it against her mouth. Robin licked the sweet stickiness from her bottom lip and rolled her eyes at him. "That's not enough."

"You know what they say, good things come to those who wait," he said as he reached for the powdered sugar and sprinkled the toast.

"Better not let that syrup burn," she said as they locked eyes.

"Right." Logan turned back to the stove and turned

the heat down on the pot. Then he drizzled the heated syrup over the French toast. "Now you can eat."

She smiled and took her plate to the breakfast nook. "I'll wait for you."

"Great," he said as he reached into the oven and pulled out a pan of bacon strips. "Looks like it's time to eat."

"I know it's midday, but where is the coffee?"

Logan snapped his fingers. "I have iced coffee with almond milk and monk fruit sweetener."

"So, I did switch you to almond milk?"

"Kind of. The health benefits got me more than your lectures," he said with a grin.

Robin stood up and headed for the fridge. "Whatever, man."

Logan wasn't sure what had changed overnight, but he liked this vibe between him and Robin. Maybe she was making the effort to work on their marriage. And damn, she looked good in that T-shirt. She returned to the table with two mugs of coffee. "Here you go."

"Thanks." He brushed his fingertips against her hand. "This feels good."

She blushed as she took her seat across from him. "Let's make today about us and this amazing food. And I'm not going to stop you if you want to make jamba-laya."

Logan laughed. "I'm going to have to hit the grocery store if we're going to do that."

"Since it's the day after Christmas, I don't think I'm going to put you through that hell. But we can't live on French toast and grits for the rest of the day."

He snapped his fingers. "I have shrimp and tomatoes."

Robin smiled. "Sounds like we're having a great dinner with shrimp and grits."

"And roasted tomatoes with mozzarella."

"Any wine?" she asked.

"Then I guess I'm going to the store after all," he said.

"Maybe we can go together, but first we're eating this amazing brunch."

Logan wanted to kiss his wife, wanted to ask her what had changed. But he didn't want to kill the vibe. Didn't want to start another argument that he couldn't win or hear her spit out questions he couldn't answer.

They ate in a comfortable silence and Robin even shared her grits with Logan after he'd eaten all of his. Grits weren't normally something she shared. Logan almost thought something was wrong with them until she started eating off his plate.

"So, do we be mature and wash dishes or get dressed and go get wine?" Robin asked as she scraped their dishes and set them in the sink.

Logan wrapped his arms around Robin's waist. "Why don't we just take a break and relax. We've got a DVR full of DIY shows to watch."

Robin nodded. "Logan," she whispered. "I love you."

"I love you too."

"And I missed this. Missed us." She wrapped her arms around his neck. "So, I want today to be . . . I want us to . . . I want my marriage back."

"So do I. But . . ."

She brought her finger to his lips. "What we need to do today is look at us. Maybe you were right when you asked me when I stopped believing in you and we should talk about it."

He looked around the kitchen. "You want to do this now?"

She shook her head. "Not right now. But we're going to have to look into it."

"I agree."

"But right now, let's watch these shows."

"Before we do that, I just want one thing," he said.

"What's that?"

"I want to kiss my wife so badly."

She shrugged her shoulders. "Then I don't know what's stopping you."

Logan leaned in and captured her lips in a sweet and tender kiss. He savored her taste and the softness of her lips. Pulling back from her, he smiled. "Why don't I wash the dishes and you warm up the TV. Did I tell you how amazing you look in my shirt?"

Robin smiled. "Nope, but I already knew. You couldn't keep your eyes on your plate while we ate."

He almost told her that he wanted to put her on his plate, but he wasn't trying to press his luck. *One step at a time*, he admonished himself.

As Robin sauntered out of the kitchen, Logan told himself that he was going to do what it took to make this feeling last. He pulled his phone out of his back pocket and sent Liam a text.

Please tell me you're making some headway on your investigation.

He put his phone away and cleaned up the kitchen. "Logan, I'm going to get my phone," Robin called out.

"Okay. Want some more coffee when you come back?"

"Sure."

As he heard the front door close, Logan grabbed the coffee and a couple of mugs, then headed for the living room. Setting the coffee on the table next to the sofa, he was ready to relax and watch six months' worth of home improvement shows. Looking at the door, he wondered what was taking Robin so long to get her phone from the car.

Robin wanted to scream when she saw that bitch walking toward her. Why was she at her house?

"Robin? Robin, are you there?" the voice from the other end of the phone called out. Robin was so damned pissed that she'd forgotten which one of her sisters she'd been talking to.

"I'm going to call you back, sis," she said, then ended the call. Crossing over to the end of the driveway, Robin cocked her head to the side. "What in the hell are you doing here?"

"Hey, Robin. I guess you're the reason why I haven't been able to get in touch with my child's father," Kamrie said. "Is Logan inside?"

"This is what you do now? You just come to my house and pretend it's yours?"

Kamrie sucked her teeth and flung her hair to the side. "Didn't you file for divorce? Why does it even matter what Logan and I do concerning our son? I get that you may have been feeling some kind of way and . . ."

Robin couldn't control her feelings or listen to another word coming out of Kamrie's mouth. She hauled off and slapped her with six months of fury bubbling over. "Get off my property!"

"You bitch. I should call the police."

"You're trespassing, so please call the police."

Kamrie pulled out her phone and held it up. "Sure, this is what you want? Police show up and they're going to want to know what happened, then there's going to be questions about what started the fight and everyone will know that the great Dr. Baptiste is a deadbeat. And then what? But it's your choice. After all, you're the one outside in a T-shirt. Looking like last night's trash."

"Why are you doing this?"

"Asking my son's father to be a part of his life?" Kamrie shrugged. "What mother wouldn't want this for her child? I guess you'll never know since you can't have a child of your own. But I guess you're still making your broken body useful."

Everything inside Robin seemed to freeze. How did she know? Logan had to have told her. Blinking, she refused to let this sorry excuse of a woman see a tear drop from her eyes. Maybe coming back home had been a nostalgic mistake.

"You should fucking leave!" Logan boomed from behind Robin.

"No," Robin said, turning around and spearing him with a cold look. "You two should talk. Seems like you do a lot of that with her." Logan reached for Robin, but she sidestepped him and he was confused as to what had happened out there.

He glared at Kamrie as she walked up the driveway. "Jean is sick and that woman hit me."

"Kamrie, you're going too far with this bullshit right now."

She took a step closer to him. "This can be really easy or really nasty. It's up to you, Logan."

"You're fucking insane, Kamrie. Nothing ever happened between us, and when I find out who put you up to this, all of you are going to pay."

"If anyone is going to pay, it's going to be you. Your wife can't give you . . ."

"Leave. Now!"

"This is going to come out, sooner or later. You can paint a pretty picture or you can watch everything that you worked so hard for go up in flames because you're a deadbeat father."

"That's where you're wrong. I'm nobody's father, and it doesn't matter how many times you say it or wish it to be true, that is not my little boy."

She raised her eyebrow and shook her head. "I guess you've made your choice."

Kamrie turned around and headed to her car. When he saw her drive away, Logan rushed inside to find Robin.

As soon as he opened the door and walked in, he was met with a smack to the face. "You son of a bitch!" Robin exclaimed. "How could you do this to me?"

Logan rubbed his cheek. "What are you talking about?"

"Nothing happened between you and Kamrie, but you decided to tell her about . . . everything?"

"What do you mean?"

"She taunted me about not being able to give you a

child. How would she know that if you didn't tell her? Was I the topic of your pillow talk?"

He reached out for her, but Robin jerked away so fast he almost fell to the floor. "Robin, please . . ."

"No!" She pushed against his chest. "This was a mistake. I don't know why I . . ." Robin's shoulders shook as she began to sob. "How could you share intimate details of our lives with your whore?"

"I didn't. Robin. I would never do anything like that to you or to us—especially since Kamrie and I didn't talk about you in or out of bed."

"I'm going back to my town house. I can't deal with you. Sign the divorce papers and let's stop playing this bullshit ass game." She rushed upstairs and slammed the bedroom door behind her.

Moments later, Robin, who was now dressed in the outfit she'd worn the night before, stormed out of the house, got into her car, and sped away.

Chapter 11

Robin was about ten miles from her town house when the tears stopped. In another five miles, she stopped calling herself an idiot. By the time she pulled into the parking lot of the complex, she decided that she wasn't the one who should be crying; she should've pounded Logan until he cried.

All he'd done was lie. How could she fight for their marriage when he'd violated her like her issues had been for the world to know. Not the world, but Kamrie. Of course, that woman would relish having something to hang over Robin's head. First her husband, then this child, and now her medical history.

Logan had to be the most inconsiderate asshole in the world to share that with her or anyone else who wasn't on Robin's medical team. If she didn't tell her family, why did he feel like he could tell his fucking mistress?

She took a deep breath, then opened her car door. She probably should've called her sister back, but she didn't want to talk to anyone right now. Robin wanted to smash something. Since Logan's head wasn't an option, she'd have to take everything out on her punching bag in the den.

Right after she unlocked the door, her phone began ringing. Knowing that it was either Logan or one of her sisters, Robin chose to ignore it. She reached for her pink boxing gloves and put them on. Then she attacked the bag, unleashing all of her anger, hurt, and disappointment. Her sweat replaced her tears and Robin punched until her arms felt like wet noodles.

She dropped down to the floor and released a howl. How was she supposed to move forward from this?

Logan crossed his fingers as he rummaged through his files, looking for the divorce papers. Robin's address had to be on them. Bingo! That last set of papers that he'd been sent had her Petersburg address right there. After typing it into his phone, Logan grabbed his shoes and headed for his car. He was willing to risk all the speeding tickets in the world to get to his wife and explain that he hadn't told Kamrie anything about their issues. He'd wondered how Kamrie had gotten hold of Robin's medical records, because that wasn't the first time she had thrown out that she knew Robin couldn't have children. That always gave him pause. Someone had given her too much information about his wife's life.

Just as he started the car, his phone chimed, indicating that he had a text message. Looking down at the phone, he saw it was from Liam, so he decided to respond. The message his friend left him made him shudder.

> That broad is crazy. I'm going to be back in town
> in the morning with a report. Hope you and
> Robin still have a chance.

"From your fingers to God's ears," Logan said as he sped down the highway. Normally, the trip to Petersburg would take over thirty minutes, but Logan was on a mission and he pulled up to Robin's town house complex twenty minutes after he'd left Richmond.

She didn't belong here. The townhomes could've been luxurious, but Robin had her dream house and he wanted her at home. No matter what. The last few hours with Robin at home reminded him of everything he could lose behind this lie and he wasn't about to let that happen. He scanned the numbers on the doors until he found Robin's address. Bounding up the steps, he heard a loud howl and his heart raced into overdrive. Logan banged on the door, screaming Robin's name.

He took a breath and decided he was going to kick the door in if she didn't open it in the next two seconds.

"Robin! Are you in there? Are you okay?" Logan readied himself to burst the door open as if he were the Kool-Aid man when he heard the lock twist.

A bleary-eyed Robin opened the door and glared at Logan. "Why are you here?" she gritted.

"Because I want you to come home. Why were you screaming? Is everything all right?"

She rolled her eyes. "No, everything is not all right, *Logan*! Just leave."

"I'm not going home without you, Robin. Not when I didn't do any of the things you believe I did."

"I'm not going through this with you again. I thought

we were on our way back to each other, back to the life we've always wanted, but clearly you've made a choice to tell that woman every little detail about our lives—my life! Fuck you, Logan."

"Please, hear me out, Robin."

She shot him an icy glare. "There is nothing left to say or do, other than you signing the divorce papers. I don't want anything else to do with you!"

"I'm not accepting that."

"Mother—Logan, you made your choice and I'm making mine."

"My choice has always been you, Robin, and I'll be damned if . . ."

She slammed the door in his face.

Logan banged on the door again. She could call the police, the National Guard, or the marines, but he wasn't going anywhere.

Minutes ticked away before she returned to the door and opened it. "I swear to . . . Logan, can you leave?"

"No, so you might as well invite me in." He offered her a limp smile and he could tell it wasn't working.

"What do you want to come in for? I'm sure Kamrie is at the house waiting for you to come back. Why did you follow me here?"

Now, he was getting tired of going back and forth with her. There was a big part of him that wanted to swing the door open, scoop Robin up in his arms, and take her back to Richmond. But he wasn't a caveman and the swinging curtains of her neighbors ensured that he would probably end up on the late newscast for kidnapping.

"Can I come inside and we'll talk about this?"

"What the fuck do we have to talk about?"

"Our marriage. Robin, we can't throw this away. I love you too much and I know you love me, too."

"What's love got to do with anything? Love should've kept you faithful, and if love couldn't do that, you could've kept my name out of your mouth while you were fucking your whore."

Logan placed his hand on her shoulder as he took a step inside the doorway. "I was not with Kamrie. I didn't tell her anything. Why do you think I would do something like that? I never told your family about the hell you went through and you think I would tell her? A nobody who never meant shit to me? Do you think that I'm that much of an asshole that I'd let your pain be fodder for someone to use as a weapon? I ached for you, I was there when you cried and battled cancer. That disease didn't take you away from me and I'm not letting anything else come between us."

Robin blinked back tears. "I'm sorry I trusted you with that. I should've turned to my family and I should've walked away from this marriage when I knew . . ."

"Walked away? Why would you ever do that?"

She turned her back to him and sighed. "I asked you to leave. Are you going to do that?"

"No. Not unless you're coming with me."

"Why would I do that?" She whirled around and faced him. The tears were gone and her face was contorted by anger. "She shows up at the house as if she's been invited. You keep playing the same song, but it's getting really tired. I'm tired. I should've stayed in Charleston and been with a man who wants only me."

Logan was sure if a piece of dust touched him, he would fall over. "What are you talking about?"

She pressed her index finger against her temple. "I'm talking about the real reason I drove half the night to get here. I know how to resist temptation; too bad you didn't."

Logan couldn't describe what he was feeling. Was it sadness, anger, disappointment, or a combination of them all? To think that Robin would consider breaking their vows out of a sense of revenge made his blood run cold.

"Who was it?"

"You have a nerve," she snapped. "Logan. It's time to end this. I'm tired. I can't fight anymore. I can't keep looking over my shoulder, waiting for the other shoe to drop."

"This is really what you want?"

She expelled a frustrated breath. "Yes."

Logan was just as tired as Robin was. "I can't give up on us. But if being my wife hurts you so much, then I'll let go."

Robin closed her eyes. "Thank you. You can leave now. I'll have my attorney reach out to you next week."

He turned toward the door and sighed. "Robin, I'm always going to love you."

She turned her back to him as he walked out the door.

When the door slammed behind Logan, Robin's soul shattered. What had she done? Was she really ready to end everything?

"Yes," she muttered as she locked the door. "It's time to move on." But how was she going to do that? What was life without Logan in it?

Despite feeling as if her muscles had been run through a blender, Robin climbed the stairs and went into her lonely bedroom. Unlike the king-sized bed she and Logan shared in Richmond, she would be crawling into a full-sized bed with a mattress that was a little too firm. Right now, she didn't care; she just wanted to go to sleep and wake up from this horrible nightmare.

As soon as she lay across the bed, her phone rang. Groaning, she reached for it. It was Yolanda, and Robin considered ignoring the call, but that would only lead to a call from Alex and maybe even her father. She wanted to say what she was going to say only once.

"What's up, sis?" she asked when Yolanda answered.

"You tell me. You're the one who hung up on me and never called back. Why did you go back to Virginia without telling anybody?"

Robin sighed. "I came home hoping to fight for my marriage, but that was a mistake."

"What do you mean? Do I need to come to Virginia and—"

"Bring it down. Logan and I have decided that we're going to go through with the divorce."

"Why? I thought . . . Are you okay?"

"I'm not *okay* and I don't want to talk about it or deal with it right now. I'm going to bed."

"I'm coming to Virginia."

"Really, Yolanda? What are you going to do other than make a mess? I'm fine. I'll be back at work next week and Logan agreed to finalize the divorce."

"And you're really fine with this?" Robin was touched by the concern in her sister's voice.

"I don't have a choice," she replied and tried to hide the fact that she was crying from Yolanda.

"Robin, please don't cry. I feel so bad for you and I

want . . . I'm coming to stay with you for a few days before I head to Charlotte."

"No, I don't want to put you out. I know you have to get ready for your boutique opening and . . . Why do you have a bodyguard?"

"Because your baby sister is a drama queen and so is Dad."

"That's not an answer."

"You spill your guts and I'll spill mine."

"Good night, Yolanda." Robin ended the call and turned her phone off. She didn't want to be bothered and she didn't want to face the fact that her marriage was over.

Logan decided that this would be the last time he drowned his sorrows in alcohol. But tonight, everything with alcohol in it was being downed like water. First, it was the leftover scotch. Then the bourbon, and finally, he found a bottle of red wine that had been Robin's favorite. He paused as he popped the cork and thought about the pain on his wife's face. How did Kamrie know about Robin's surgery? She shouldn't have had any access to Robin's records since she wasn't on her care team.

Either Kamrie was a cunning trick or she had someone higher up helping her. This shit had to stop. Logan didn't even bother pouring the wine in a glass. He just took the bottle to the head and gulped some down. Setting the bottle on the counter, he felt as if he was about to vomit. He tried to wrap his mind around the end of his marriage. But it didn't make sense. It wasn't the plan.

He wanted to celebrate a hundred years of being Robin's husband. He wanted to wake up holding her for the rest of his life, and now that had been taken from him.

Why? He went into the den and plopped down on the sofa. This wasn't going to be his future. A few minutes later, Logan was passed out on the sofa.

Morning slapped Logan in the face like an iron fist with brass knuckles on. His stomach lurched and he barely made it to the bathroom in time to vomit. He hadn't had a hangover like this since he was a freshman in college trying to prove he could hang with the big boys on the basketball team.

All he could do was thank God that he didn't have any surgeries scheduled for the foreseeable future. But he needed to go over to the hospital and find out several things. First, who did the DNA test, then how Kamrie got access to Robin's medical records.

Maybe finding out the truth and presenting it to his wife would stop the divorce from happening. And even though he had agreed to it yesterday, today he wasn't going to give up that damned easily. Nor was he going to let them—whoever the hell they were—win. And as much as he wanted to send Robin his customary good morning text message, Logan decided to give her twenty-four hours of breathing room.

His phone rang, smashing the silence in the house and making his head throb like a stubbed toe. "Yeah."

"Doctor Baptiste, this is Clorinda Kelly from human resources."

Logan hid his snort because he knew this call was coming eventually. "How can I help you?"

"It's come to our attention that there may have been

an improper relationship between you and a nurse on staff and we're launching an investigation."

"I figured this would be coming."

"We want you to come in and answer some questions tomorrow morning."

"What time?"

"Nine."

"Fine," he said, then ended the call. Logan rubbed his face with his hand and groaned. Now he was going to have to answer to these lies. How would he keep his reputation intact and did it even matter now since Robin wanted to make their divorce final?

Why in the hell did I agree to this bullshit? Logan headed downstairs to the kitchen and tried not to think about the good time he and Robin had there twenty-four hours ago. Her touch, her taste, and the hope that his marriage was going to get back on track.

Now, what did he have to lose? Logan planned to walk into that office and speak on everything that he'd felt about what was going on at the hospital, from the gossip to the influence of the pharma companies on the treatment of heart patients. Maybe this meeting would reveal more than his so-called scandal and give him a look into what was really going on. Logan headed for the kitchen and brewed a pot of strong coffee. He needed to clear his head and get ready for the meeting. But first, coffee. Once the pot was filled, Logan grabbed his favorite mug and smiled sardonically. It said, "I love my wife."

Logan filled the cup with java and downed it in a few gulps. Filled with caffeine, he decided that he was going to do some research on the pharma company the hospital seemed to be so tied to.

Cooper Drugs had been working with the current administration to test its heart medications on patients waiting for transplants. Seventy-five percent of the participants died in the experiments. The death rate had been why Logan wasn't interested in using the drugs with his patients.

He'd been pressured to use one of the experimental drugs on a patient who had been showing signs of rejecting his new heart. Logan had been sure that adjusting the antirejection medicine and adding light therapy would help his patient. But his superiors wanted Logan to use the Cooper Drug cocktail.

Logan had been suspicious of the cheaply made cocktail, which was supposed to shorten the need for antirejection medication and limit some of the side effects of current medication. But instead of taking the company's word for it, Logan began looking into some FDA tests and was alarmed by the results.

Then when he spoke to the administration, they told him that they wanted to help Cooper Drugs perfect the cocktail. But when Logan started asking questions about consent from the patients and where other tests were going on, things started to decline at the hospital. His surgery schedule was cut and then the drama with Kamrie started.

He hadn't put the two together until the allegations about Kamrie's son came to light. Were they trying to take him down with a personal scandal to stop him from asking questions about the experiments and the dying patients, not just at their hospital, but according to reports across the nation?

Was it someone in the upper echelons of the hospital

and the drug company looking to take Logan out of the game? Anyone who knew him knew there were three things that meant everything to Logan: his family, his patients, and his word. Now, it seemed that all three were under attack. This couldn't be a coincidence. But how was he going to prove it?

Maybe Liam had some answers that could fix things for him. He dialed his friend's number and hoped that he would tell him the keys he needed to get his life back.

"This is Liam."

"What's up?" Logan asked.

"You're dealing with a lunatic," Liam said. "Do you know why Kamrie left Atlanta?"

"To make my life a living hell?" he snipped.

"Seems as if she has a thing for married men. But she picked the wrong guy to have an affair with."

Logan snorted. "Did he really have an affair or was he another one of her victims?"

"Where are you right now? I have some actual proof that you can use for leverage and I'm starving."

"I've got ribs and mashed cauliflower."

"Shit, then I'd better stop at the liquor store so I can pretend you've got mashed potatoes and gravy. Is Robin there so we can go over everything together?"

Logan coughed. "Robin's not here."

"At Whole Foods trying to convince you that cauliflower and potatoes actually taste the same?" Liam laughed before Logan could respond.

"I wish. Kamrie showed up and all hell broke loose. She knew things about Robin and her situation that she shouldn't have known. Robin thinks it is another way that I've betrayed her."

"How does she seem to sniff out when you and Robin are together?"

"She's probably stalking me."

Liam snorted. "You wouldn't be the first doctor to fall under that trap."

"What do you mean?"

"You'll see. Make sure my ribs are fall off the bone tender."

Logan didn't know if that was going to happen because he had no idea how far Liam was from Richmond. But he could put together some decent ribs with his special sauce.

Cooking in the kitchen today wasn't the same as burning grilled cheese sandwiches with his wife. He missed her touch and her kiss. Missed her smell and her smart-ass mouth telling him that something was burning.

Despite missing her, Logan created his meaty magic and had a half rack of ribs and barbeque chicken wings ready by the time Liam arrived three hours later.

"Smells like a restaurant in here," Liam said as he crossed the threshold. He didn't bother heading toward the living room; he went straight for the kitchen. But Logan wished he'd showed him the evidence he'd found in Atlanta first.

Liam set a bottle of whiskey on the middle of the bar. "First things first. You're going to need a drink for this."

Logan grabbed two glasses and slid them over to Liam. Day drinking was allowed today. Even if it was early afternoon in Richmond, it was five o'clock somewhere.

"Start from the beginning."

The broad-shouldered man poured two full glasses of whiskey and pushed one to his friend. "As it turns out,

Kamrie is a social climber and doctors seem to be her favorite stepping-stone."

Logan snorted. "Not surprised."

"Well, you might be surprised to learn that she left Atlanta with a scandalous good-bye. Seems that she and one of the surgeons were having a hot and heavy affair."

"You told me this already. What's the point?"

Liam pulled out his phone and showed Logan screenshots of explicit text messages between Kamrie and the doctor. There were nude pictures from both sides and Logan almost threw up in his mouth as he read the messages.

"So, what happened when the wife found out?"

"Ever heard of Valerie Adams?"

Logan folded his arms across his chest. "You mean *the* Valerie Adams, one of the first black women to run a hospital in the south?"

Liam nodded. "From what I know she is not the one to play with. And Kamrie was playing with Valerie's husband, Dr. Lacy."

Logan's mouth dropped open. "You have got to be kidding me. I guess his smarts end in the operating room."

Liam shook his head. "She tried everything she's trying with you, but she seemed to forget that Valerie held her career in the palm of her hand. So, Kamrie was given a choice: Leave or kiss her medical career good-bye."

"But from what I understand, Kamrie came to Richmond Medical with glowing recommendations from her previous employer."

Liam took a sip of his whiskey. "That's because Valerie didn't want the affair to go public. Imagine the optics on this: administrator's husband sleeping with a nurse, sexual harassment lawsuit on deck."

"Kamrie sued them?" Now, Logan needed a sip of whiskey.

"That was the threat. She is not above using the courts to get what she wants."

"Or fake medical tests. How long ago was it that she and this man were together?"

"I was putting that together when Ms. Valerie found out and banned me from the hospital. She still doesn't want any of this to come out and she said that Kamrie is Virginia's problem."

"Wait, so all you know is that Kamrie fucked a doctor on her old job?" Frustration marred his handsome face as he swirled the brown liquid in his glass.

"Just because that woman kicked me out of her hospital doesn't mean that I didn't get what I was looking for."

Logan drained the rest of his drink and slammed the glass on the counter. "So, what do you have?"

"One of her nurse friends, who thinks I'm a handsome man and wanted my phone number, said Kamrie might have been pregnant when she left Atlanta."

"How are we going to find out?"

"That's where things get tricky. We're going to have to get an independent DNA test on the little boy and prove you're not the father."

"And how are we going to quietly do that?" Logan reached for the bottle of whiskey and poured himself another glassful. "Clearly, the boy's records have been falsified."

"There might not be a quiet way to do this. You're

probably going to have to go to court and get a judge to sign off on a DNA test to prove you aren't the father."

Logan rubbed his hand across his face. "I've been trying to keep this whole thing out of the public record. It's bad enough that the hospital knows about it now and wants me to come in for a meeting with HR in the morning. Going to court is going to have every newspaper and media organization in the area on this story like flies on shit."

Liam rocked back on his heels and folded his arms across his chest. "What do you really want to happen here? Shove some evidence in this woman's face and pay her off or do you want to save your marriage? Do you think if Kamrie goes away Robin is just going to come back and your life is going to be like it was before?"

Logan shook his head. He knew there would always be questions in Robin's mind if Kamrie and her son just disappeared. That woman had cut his wife to the bone and Logan wanted to return the favor.

"So, you think I need to take her to court?" Logan asked after downing his drink.

"That or break into her house and get a DNA sample."

"Well, that would be stupid. Maybe I can check with the hospital and—forget that. Someone on staff is working with her and I don't know who can and can't be trusted."

"That's definitely a problem but we have to do something to get that child's DNA legally. Otherwise, you're going to be her next victim."

"What about this surgeon in Atlanta? How is he going to react when we ask for his DNA?"

Liam smiled. "I already have it. We had coffee, and of

course when I started asking about Kamrie, he got pissed off and left—without his paper cup. It's in my lab now."

"Is that legal?"

Liam shrugged. "I haven't crossed the line, but it might be a gray area."

"How gray? Because when I present this information, I don't want there to be any questions as to what I can do to clear my name. And win my wife back."

Liam nodded and glanced around the kitchen. "So, where's the food?"

Logan laughed. "You earned it. I even have some coleslaw to go with the ribs." He crossed over to the cabinets and pulled out two plates. After filling them with ribs, chicken, and coleslaw, he slid one over to his friend.

"I guess this is enough for all the work that I've done," Liam said with a deep chuckle. "So, here's what we need to do: Find out what the HR department wants to say to you. Build up your evidence and then blow back at everybody who's been trying to ruin your life."

Logan lifted a chicken wing in salute. "And those bastards are going to pay."

Chapter 12

Robin woke up at four a.m. half expecting her pillow to be Logan, but it was her favorite body pillow. Soft. Damp from sweat and tears.

And she was so tired of crying. She made her decision and it was time to woman up and stick by it. Rolling over on her back, she stared up at the ceiling, deciding that she'd do some of that fancy painting she saw on HGTV and make her room a sanctuary. But who was she fooling, just like the day she moved into this town house, she missed her room, her bed, and her husband. What if he was telling the truth? Better still, what if she was going to wake up when the sun rose and the past six months had been a horrible nightmare.

There was no baby.

She hadn't served Logan with divorce papers.

They were just lying in bed holding each other.

Robin sighed and kicked out of the covers. That wasn't going to happen. Because everything that had destroyed her soul was real. After hopping out of bed, Robin dressed in her workout clothes and headed for her punching bag.

If she couldn't sleep, she might as well work out some aggression and stop crying. Robin punched until her arms once again felt like wet noodles. She knew she wasn't using proper form or anything as she boxed. She was just pushing through the anger and hoping that she wouldn't feel anything when she was done.

At least the tears stopped. Robin headed for the kitchen and started a pot of coffee; then it was time to do some work. She was still a lawyer with cases to defend. The time for feeling sorry for herself had ended. Waiting for the brew to complete, Robin headed to her small office and grabbed her files and laptop.

Part of her wondered how Nina and Clinton were enjoying their honeymoon. She hated that she couldn't celebrate with her sister the way she deserved. Just because her marriage had turned into a shit show, it didn't mean that her sister was going to have the same kind of bad juju. As a matter of fact, she was going to have a nice basket of wine, fruit, and some toys for couples waiting for them when they returned from their honeymoon.

She couldn't help but think of her own honeymoon. Logan had been on break from medical school and he'd walked into their apartment in New Orleans with two plane tickets in his hand.

They were going to Monaco. Robin had shared her love of Grace Kelly and her love affair with Prince Rainier with Nina back in the day. Robin had always been a sucker for a great love story. First her parents, then the romance novels she read by Beverly Jenkins, Brenda Jackson, and Deborah Fletcher Mello, and now she knew she was living one that would last forever.

What a fool she'd been thinking that she could make

her life read like her favorite books or be a carbon copy of her parents' marriage.

All Robin could hope for was that Clinton would take care of her baby sister like the heroes in her favorite books. Before Robin knew it, she was crying again. Now, she needed a shower before she could get to work. Heading to her bathroom, Robin turned her stereo on and pumped up her wake-up playlist, which was basically the entire *Jagged Little Pill* album by Alanis Morissette. The angst of the nineties record fit her mood as she turned her shower on and stepped underneath the spray. The water was cold at first, but as it heated up Robin decided to let go of the negativity and focus on her future.

What was a future without Logan in it going to look like? They had planned so many things together. Robin opening her own law office with regional offices in South Carolina and Louisiana, jet skiing on the French Riviera for their twentieth wedding anniversary and retirement. Then there was the scholarship fund they were going to create at Xavier University to give back to the place where their love began.

Damn me for wrapping my future in this man, she thought as she shut the shower off. Robin silently promised that moving forward she would depend on the one person who would never let her down: herself. No more seeking a happy ending with Logan, or any other man, for that matter.

She wasn't going to be disappointed again. After drying off and dressing in a tank top and yoga pants, Robin got to work on some of her cases that would easily be settled out of court. When her phone rang after several hours of working in silence, she nearly jumped out of her skin.

"This is Robin," she said when she answered without looking at the screen.

"You can stop pretending that you're working," Alex quipped.

"Actually, I am. What's going on? Let me guess, you talked to Yolanda."

Alex sighed. "She yelled, and threatened. Thank God she has this bodyguard around for whatever reason. I've never seen our sister put in her place with such ease before in my life."

"That almost makes me want to come back to Charleston and take a closer look at this phenomenon. And you don't know why she has a bodyguard either?"

"No need to do that, looks like the three of us are coming to see you tomorrow. So, are you in Richmond or Petersburg?"

"Why are you guys wasting your time driving all the way up here? I'm sure Dad would enjoy your company more than I will."

"You act like you have a choice in this. Is that woman really stalking you?" Robin could hear the concern in her sister's voice.

"That's Yolanda's overactive imagination. Alex, I really want to be left alone right now. I told Logan that he needs to go ahead and sign the divorce papers and he agreed."

"Does that mean we're celebrating or crying?"

"Like I said, that means I want to be left alone."

"And I think I told you we already have a plan to come there. Don't make me tell Daddy you have a stalker. He'll put a bodyguard on you, too. And for the record, no one will say anything about why Yolanda is under this man's protection. Not even Daddy, and he usually tells me everything."

Robin sighed, knowing her sister was right and the last thing she wanted was to make her father worry. "Fine, I'll text you my address and since you all are coming there'd better be some sweets from the bed-and-breakfast in a big basket for me."

"Is that your way of saying put Terell in the trunk and bring him with us?"

Robin rolled her eyes. Did she want to tell her sister—with her sometimes judgmental self—about what happened after Nina's wedding? Nope.

"I don't want to see Terell again. That is old news. Black history."

"Then why has he been here every other day since Nina's wedding acting like he's waiting for the cat to come back?"

"Bye, Alex. I've got work to do. And wait a minute, are you taking time off from work?"

"Two days to check on you isn't going to kill the business. And I'm just practicing for my vacation. In all seriousness, I'm worried about you."

Robin was worried as well and she wasn't sure if she wanted to share this with her sisters. It was easy to pretend when they were hundreds of miles away from each other. She could hide her tear tracks and her sadness with fake laughs on the phone. "I'm going to be all right, sis. I'm not the first woman who's been cheated on and I won't be the last."

"Robin, you've been through hell. You were a trooper for Nina, now it's time for us to step up for you. I know you like to pretend everything is perfect, but you can be as hurt as you want to be and lean on us."

Silent tears streamed down her face. Robin knew she was a lucky woman but hearing Alex on the other end of the line solidified that fact.

"I love you, sis," Robin said.

"I know you do. And I love you back. Are you really sure that it's over between you and Logan?"

"I'm not sure about anything right now except that I'm hurt to the bone."

"There will be a lot of chocolate chip cookies and wine in that basket, and tissues."

"You're the best, sis."

"I know," Alex said before saying good-bye.

Robin was all smiles when she returned to her work. After reading until her eyes nearly crossed, she decided that it was time to clean up her place for tomorrow's visit. She was actually looking forward to seeing her sisters and learning the ways of the bodyguard. Moving her punching bag into the corner and stuffing her boxing gloves in the coat closet, Robin was satisfied with the look of the place. But she needed food. So, she grabbed her sneakers and headed to Whole Foods to stock up.

She almost reached for her phone and called Logan to see what he needed. She hadn't done that in months, but today she felt compelled to do it.

I'm slowly losing my mind out here, she thought as she got into the car.

Logan wanted to see his wife. He wanted to hold her and tell her about everything Liam had discovered on his trip to Atlanta. But he was sitting at the kitchen table, sipping strong coffee, trying to figure out if he should sign the divorce papers Logan Jean Baptiste, Dr. Logan J. Baptiste, or if he should just mark a big *X*.

After twenty minutes, he decided he wasn't signing at all. Not when he had a chance to save his marriage. But how was he going to get Robin to listen? He knew that she was hurting and the last thing he wanted was to cause her pain. But he couldn't just allow her to believe the worst of him. Maybe this said something about his marriage that he hadn't wanted to admit.

Had he and Robin lost their connection and this was just a sign showing how much had changed between them?

She had been complaining about the long hours he'd put in at the hospital last spring, and if he had been smarter, Logan would've told her why.

The drug company had been digging its heels in to get the surgeons to use their new antirejection medication, but he wanted facts and research. So, he'd been digging into deaths at the hospital.

Then he stopped getting a lot of transplant surgeries. More deaths. His questions had been ignored and then the hurricane hit the city. Like all of the doctors and nurses who'd been on that shift, Logan worked for twenty-four hours straight. He'd been tired, and when there had been a lull in activity, he'd crept into his office for a nap. But first he'd texted Robin to make sure she was all right.

His wife had reminded him that she grew up in Charleston and made it through worse hurricanes than this one. She just wanted to make sure he got some sleep and didn't try to come home.

Logan had wanted to kiss her through the phone.

Now, he just wanted to hear her voice, wanted her to tell him she was coming home. But that wasn't going to happen anytime soon. She made it clear that their marriage was over and he didn't want her to hurt. The last thing he'd ever wanted was to make Robin sad, cry, or hurt. That's why it was important to get to the bottom of these lies and let his wife know that he was still the man she'd married and the man who would love her until he took his last breath.

Liam walked into the house without knocking, reminding Logan that he needed to take his key back from his friend. "Thought you were going to the hospital today," he said as he set a bag of food on the kitchen counter.

"That's tomorrow."

Liam tilted his head. "What are you studying?"

Logan pushed the papers away. "My divorce papers."

Liam sucked his teeth as he pulled the greasy food from the bag. "Throw that shit away. Remember the nurse who liked me?"

"What about her?"

"She called me today and said she had some things to share with me about her friend and she's coming to Richmond."

"That sounds like she's trying to lead you to a booty call."

Liam shrugged as he handed Logan a white Styrofoam to-go container. "Could be or she could be the link we need to get Kamrie to tell the truth about that kid."

"So, you think you've got the magic stick and you're

going to be able to get all of this information from a woman who claims to be Kamrie's friend?"

Liam dug into his fried rice. "That's why I'm the detective. A real friend wouldn't have opened up about her buddy like Ms. Nurse did."

Logan opened his package and saw Liam had saved the fried food for himself and he'd gotten a salad for him. "Good looking-out," he said as he passed him a bottle of water.

"Bought you that so I don't have to hear a lecture about this." Liam held up his food.

"I keep telling you, one day you're going to end up on my operating table if you keep eating like this."

"And you're going to keep me alive because I get you out of trouble. I'm going to tell the nurse that she should meet me at the Jefferson. Make her think she's about to get the five-star treatment, then shit will get real."

Logan stabbed at his spinach salad. "Hopefully she's going to be real with you."

The men finished their food in silence and Logan decided that he wasn't going to sit there and wonder how his wife was doing; he was going to call her. Rising from the table, he told Liam that he was going to make a call.

"Hopefully she'll answer," Liam replied in between sips of water.

Robin had grabbed the last bag of groceries and was trudging up the steps again. She'd actually overdone it at the market, but this was her first time having guests at her place and she wasn't about to have her sisters talk about her not having food available for them.

Her phone rang and she nearly dropped the bag of groceries. If it was Alex again, she was going to scream. She set the bag on the top step and pulled her phone from her pocket. Logan's face appeared on the screen and she thought about hitting ignore. But she answered.

"What?"

"Robin, I . . ."

"Do you need something?"

"Yes, I do. I need you."

"We're not doing this. Have you signed the papers?" She closed her eyes. Asking that question made her heart shudder. She didn't want him to sign those papers, but this was the right thing to do, right? He'd betrayed her. Shared too much with the woman he claimed he didn't sleep with. How else would that *woman* know about . . . everything?

"I'm not signing them," he said in a low tone. "I know you think I'm the scum of the earth, but I'm going to prove you wrong."

She sighed heavily into the phone and wished she could tell him the truth. She didn't think he was scum and she didn't want her husband to walk away from their marriage. But what choice did she have? The trust was gone, and without being able to believe in him, she knew she'd learn to hate him.

Robin never wanted to hate Logan. "Can we stop this?"

"No. And I'm only saying this because I know there is more to all of this than just making it seem as if I betrayed you."

"What else is there, Logan? Why would that woman know all about my medical issues if you didn't tell her? It's not as if I had the procedure done at Richmond Medical."

"Robin, I swear I don't know, but I didn't tell her. Do you really think that if I kept it from your family I would tell Kamrie?"

"How the hell do I know? DNA says you're the father of her child. I can't be sure what you did and didn't tell your work wife."

"Is this what . . . ? Robin, you know I was—I thought I was friends with Kamrie. I never needed another woman because I knew who was at home waiting for me. You have always been all the woman I've needed. When did you stop believing that?"

Robin closed her eyes and tried to remember when that moment happened. Was it when the doctor told her that she wouldn't be able to have kids? Was it when he held that little girl in Whole Foods and she knew that would never be their reality? Or was it the day when that woman walked into her house and told her how she took care of her husband at the hospital?

"I have to go. I have company coming tomorrow and I have to get ready."

"Robin, please! Can I come see you tonight and talk to you about some real facts?"

She hated herself when the word yes dripped from her lips.

"See you soon."

She wanted to tell him not to come, but he'd already hung up and she didn't have the heart to call him back.

Robin wanted to see him, wanted to see this evidence. What if he was telling the truth? Would that change everything? Would they pick up where they left off in their marriage or would they have to start over?

Logan would have questions about trust. Maybe she was on her way to pushing him into the arms of another woman. Would she have to explain that her lack of trust had more to do with her insecurities about her body and the inability to have his child? It may have been an old-fashioned way of thinking, but she wanted to be the wife and mother she'd grown up admiring.

Now, she couldn't be that icon. That hurt. Hurt her that one day someone else could give him the one thing that she couldn't. And no, she didn't believe Logan's reassurances that she was all he needed. How long would that last? People changed. And if it wasn't Kamrie, how long would it be before it was a real affair or real child?

And who's to say this isn't a real child already? That nagging voice seemed to be getting louder every day and Robin couldn't ignore it anymore. Tonight, she was going to have to make a hard decision and stick to it.

No matter what Logan showed her, their marriage was going to end. It wasn't just because she believed that he had cheated, but she loved him enough to let him go.

Robin quickly put her groceries away, then considered changing her clothes. She stopped short of pulling her yoga pants and tank top off. This wasn't a date. This was the end.

But being the true Southern belle that her parents raised, she cut up some of the fresh fruits and veggies she'd gotten from the market and placed them on the coffee table in the living room. Then she poured two glasses of merlot.

Next, she sprayed her favorite scent, honeysuckle cinnamon, throughout the house and lit two vanilla-scented candles. Then she reminded herself—again—that this wasn't a date. She blew the candles out.

Now, she was watching the clock.

Chapter 13

Logan hated visiting Robin. She should've been home. Should've been in his bed eating whatever vegan food she was into these days. Or was she vegetarian? Didn't matter. She needed to be home. In his arms. Looking up at her town house, he couldn't wait for the day that she would sell it. Whatever she wanted to do with the money, he'd be behind it. She could take a trip with her sisters or she could take that solo trip to Italy that she had been talking about since they met in college.

But he wanted this place gone. He wanted his wife home.

After putting his car in park, Logan walked toward the front door. He rang the doorbell and waited to be invited in, like a vampire from that HBO series they used to watch. The porch light flickered on and Robin opened the door.

She looked amazing with her clean face and her hair brushed back from her face. It was as if time had rolled backward and she was that fresh-faced freshman who had stolen his heart.

"Wow," he breathed.

"Come in," she said, then turned her back to him. He followed Robin into the living room and smiled at her snack offering. No meat. He probably needed it after the way he and Liam had been eating lately. "You can have a seat and a glass of wine."

Logan sat on the sofa and reached for the glass she'd nodded toward. "Thanks."

They sat in an uncomfortable silence as they munched on the fruit. Robin took a sip of her wine, then focused on him. "So, you said you have some facts?"

"Liam is working on proof that Kamrie's son isn't mine and this is a pattern for her."

"Having kids and blaming someone's husband of being the father?" Robin fingered her wine glass, her voice teeming with sarcasm.

"Actually, yes." Logan began telling her about Liam's investigation and the affair that brought Kamrie to Richmond Medical. "What happened with her and the surgeon in Atlanta didn't happen here, because I didn't sleep with that woman. Liam said we need to get an independent DNA test to prove I'm not the father. I know I've been trying to keep all of this quiet, but it's time to get from underneath this."

"Why now? You had months to deal with this. Months that you kept this hidden from me."

"If I'm honest, I thought this would blow over. I thought it was a stupid prank. But now I see it's more than that."

"So that means if you had taken this seriously then we wouldn't be here?"

He ran his hand across his face and sighed. "Robin . . ."

Robin gulped her wine, then turned away from him.

"What kind of life do you want? And are you sure it's going to always include me?"

Logan placed his hand on her shoulder. "What kind of question is that? You are one of the biggest parts of my life."

"And what happens when you want more out of life? The one thing I can't give you?"

He ran his hand across his face again. "Can you still love me? Because that's all I will ever need from you. Why don't you believe me?"

"People change. Life changes and things that didn't matter to you become the one thing you want."

"Let me be clear, I'm not going to change my mind about not having a child without you."

"You can see into the future now?" Robin reached for a slice of pineapple and Logan placed his hand on top of hers.

"I know I can't see a future without you in it."

She slipped her hand from underneath his. "We can't do this. I love myself enough to . . ."

Logan shook his head and brought his finger to her lips. "What we can't do is give up on us, on our love. Why do you want to end our marriage?"

She raised her right eyebrow at him. "Because you haven't given me a reason to believe you weren't unfaithful. I'm not going to play the fool for you because I love you."

"That's how you feel?"

Robin wiped her teary eyes and sighed. "Logan, I don't know what I feel. One minute I want to hate you, want to forget that I ever knew you. Then I think about how you . . . Logan, I'm all twisted up inside and I don't know how to fix this."

"Believe in me, in us. I'm going to prove that Kamrie is a damned liar."

Robin leaned into her husband and he wrapped his arms around her. Logan brushed his lips across her forehead. "I don't want to lose you. And I'm not going to divorce you."

"Logan, I don't want to hold you back from living your best life, with a woman who . . ."

"My best life is with you. Robin, when did you start doubting me so much?"

She pulled out of his embrace and looked him straight in the eye. Her silence gave him pause and he dropped his head.

"Did you ever believe that we were forever?"

Robin knew she should've been honest. She had her doubts about their marriage when he started putting in longer hours at the hospital but never talked about his surgeries as he had when he saved a life in the past.

She didn't tell him about the times she went to his office to bring him lunch and found Kamrie there. The first time, she'd written it off as Logan being busy. The second time, her ire had been raised. Why in the hell was that nurse always around? When she'd finally asked him about it and his relationship with her, Logan had blown it off. That never sat well with her.

Kam was his right hand, he'd say. They were just friends and she had nothing to worry about. She had believed him until she couldn't anymore.

Robin stroked her forehead. "You spent a lot of time

with her, said you were just coworkers. Then she became your friend."

"Because I thought she was my friend. I didn't want anything to do with that woman that wasn't work related."

"Then how did this happen?" Robin sighed and rubbed her hand across her cheek.

"Because she has an MO, according to Liam."

"What made her choose you?"

Logan shrugged. "Don't know and don't care. Just know that she was never an option for me. I have the woman I need and want right here."

Robin wanted to believe it. She wanted this to be the moment that she said she was going home. But there were still too many unanswered questions. The little boy. Kamrie knowing about her surgery. She needed answers before she could truly try to work on fixing her marriage.

"My sisters are coming tomorrow and I don't want to have puffy eyes because I'm crying all night," she said. "But it hurt me when Kamrie threw it in my face that I can't give you a child. And it hurts me to know that one day that's going to matter to you."

"How many times do I have to tell you that it will never matter to me? Rob, we were already looking at adoption. Remember that?"

She nodded as her tears flowed freely. "That's why I can't believe you would . . . I can't believe all of this happened when we were starting our life with our new normal."

Using his thumbs, Logan wiped her hot tears away. "There may be a few other reasons why this is happening. I hadn't been doing a lot of surgeries and transplants over the last ten months."

Robin furrowed her brows. "Why not? You're the best they have on staff."

Logan nodded. "Because I didn't like the new medicine the hospital had been using on transplant patients. Too many people were dying. I wanted to see results of clinical research. The more questions I asked, the less I was on the schedule. So, I was snooping around. Then all of this hell broke loose."

"Why didn't you tell me? You know your wife is a lawyer. Maybe I could've helped you."

He stroked her cheek. "I thought I could handle it and I didn't want you worrying about me."

She pushed his hand away. "See, see? I'm tired of you treating me like I'm a fragile piece of china! It's been that way since the surgery." Robin leapt to her feet and started pacing.

"What do you mean, Robin?"

Robin shot him a cold stare and threw her hands in the air. "What do I mean?" she mimicked. "Just what the hell I said. You think I'm glass and everything is going to break me. Is that when you turned to your *work wife* because you thought your real wife was too fragile to deal with real life?"

Logan stood up and crossed over to Robin. He tried to draw her into his arms, but she pushed him back. "Answer me, damn it," she demanded. "You know, I felt like you went from a protector to a helicopter mom after I was released from my doctor. I knew what I had to do to heal, but you acted like you couldn't touch me unless it was for a medical reason for three months, Logan. Three fucking months. Do you know what that made me feel like?"

"I–I . . ."

"I wasn't your goddamn patient. I was your wife. I wanted you. I needed you. And you were Dr. Baptiste. I needed my fucking husband. So, I believed that you cheated. You weren't the man who claimed he couldn't get enough of his Double R. You made me feel like I wasn't . . ."

"I'm sorry," he cried. "I never meant for you to feel that way. Robin, I was scared. I didn't want you to die. So, yeah, I was cautious. Overly cautious. But that didn't mean I was going to turn to some other woman."

Robin glared at him. "And it didn't occur to you to say these things to me? I wanted us to go to therapy and you kept saying no. We both suffered because of my cancer, but you made it seem as if I was just going through it alone and you were fucking Olivia Pope and had it handled. That's why it was easy for me to believe you and that woman . . ."

He pulled her into his arms and let her cry against his chest. Logan stroked her hair. "And my dumb ass thought I was being strong for you. Robin, I was scared. I thought I was going to lose you."

"But you didn't."

"I've lost so many people I've loved in my life, and if God was going to take you, I wouldn't have made it. I never wanted you to feel like I was weak and you couldn't have my shoulder when you needed it. Was I overprotective? Yes. And I don't regret it. I just wish I had talked to you about how I was feeling so we wouldn't be here now."

"Where do we go from here?" She pulled back from him.

"How can we fix this?" he asked.

"Have you figured out that I don't need to be wrapped in bubble wrap to live?" she asked.

Logan nodded. "But, do you understand that nothing can change how I feel about you? That my future is nothing without you in it?"

"Yes."

"How are we going to move forward?"

She locked eyes with him and expelled a sigh. "We're going to fight everybody. From the hospital to Kamrie and anyone else with a problem with us. And when we win, the world will know not to fuck with us ever again."

Logan smiled. "That's my Double R. Rough rider." He bent his head to kiss her, but she turned away.

"Our first fight starts in the morning because Alex and Yolanda are not feeling you at the moment. If I let you kiss me, we're going to have some amazing sex and you won't be able to drive home."

"So, what's the problem?"

"Alex and Yolanda are coming here in the morning. I'm going to have to ease them into this reconciliation."

"Well, if I'm here in the morning, we could put on a united front. Because I'm not against having amazing sex with you tonight."

Robin laughed. "Logan." Her voice was a deep purr. "It is a little late."

"And I did have a glass of wine. I'd hate to get a DUI."

"That was lame."

He nodded. "Any excuse will do. Robin, I want you."

"Maybe if you leave early?"

"Set the alarm. I actually have a meeting at the hospital in the morning. But that doesn't mean I can't spend the night." He winked at her and Robin's knees turned to jelly.

"Yes, it does." She smiled, knowing he was going to wake up with her in the morning.

"You could at least show me where you sleep. I just want to make sure you're comfortable."

"You're a hot mess, you know that?"

"And that's one of the reasons you love me," Logan said as he inched closer to her quivering lips. "You know what I was afraid of these last six months?"

She shook her head.

"You telling me that you didn't love me anymore."

Robin wrapped her hand around his neck and pulled his lips down on top of hers. She didn't know how not to love Logan. Even when she tried. His tongue brushed across hers as Robin pressed her body against his. She nearly gasped at how quickly he was aroused. Just like the old days.

He always said her lips were magical. Robin broke the kiss and smiled at her husband. "I guess I can show you my bedroom."

"And then you can show me where you put your clothes after you take them off before you go to bed."

"Maybe I sleep in my clothes."

He shook his head and laughed. "Whatever, woman."

Robin took his hand and led him toward her staircase. "Am I treating you like glass if I pick you up and walk up these stairs with you in my arms?" Logan asked.

"No."

He gathered her in his arms and Robin kissed him on

his neck, knowing he was ticklish in that very spot—two inches underneath his earlobe.

"Oh shit, Rob," he moaned.

"Just checking."

"Mess around and I'm going to drop you."

"The only place you'd better drop me is on the bed. Get moving, Baptiste," she quipped. Logan took the steps two at a time as Robin stroked his chest. She nodded toward the master bedroom.

As soon as he walked in, Logan eased his wife onto the bed. "Nice room."

She shrugged. "Great place to sleep."

He lifted her tank top up, revealing her flat stomach. Leaning forward, he ran his tongue across her belly button. Robin closed her eyes and moaned. Tonight felt different. Logan's touch made her tingle with desire, not hunger, like the other night.

She wasn't thinking about her unfaithful thoughts, she just wanted to love her husband. Wanted his touch more than she needed her next breath. And Logan wasn't about to disappoint. His fingers danced across her breasts, the tips teasing her nipples until she wanted to beg for his lips. And when he locked eyes with her, Logan knew what he needed to do next. His tongue lashed her diamond-hard nipples until Robin cried out his name.

His free hand slipped between her legs, stroking her through her pants. She was wet, her desire leaking from her panties. Robin didn't have to wonder if Logan felt her need.

"These have to go," he said as he pulled her yoga pants down in a swift motion. Next, her panties were around her ankles. Logan made quick work of taking them all the way off so he could spread her legs and dive face first into her wetness.

When his tongue touched her throbbing bud, Robin moaned. As he deepened his kiss and sucked her pearl, she screamed his name and clutched the back of his neck. "Yes, yes," she moaned as he licked and sucked her into submission. The orgasm attacked her senses and made her bones feel like gelatin.

Logan looked up at Robin's sated face. She purred and opened her arms to him. Logan eased into her embrace and she wrapped her legs around his waist. Robin brushed her lips against his and ground against his hardness.

"Make love to me," she moaned as she gripped his ass. Logan plunged inside her, thrusting deep and slow. Robin mirrored his movements, sucking him inside her valley while their satisfied groans filled the air.

Robin felt her connection with Logan return. Their hearts beat in sync, their heat burned with the same intensity. She hadn't felt like this with him for a long time. This sex wasn't just physical. There seemed to be a spiritual awakening, like back in the day. Before she second-guessed every touch. Before she wondered if he had been with another woman and made her scream.

This moment made her realize that this was her man, as he'd always promised he would be.

"My God, I love you," she cried as she reached her climax. Logan held her against his sweaty chest and kissed her cheek.

"I love you more," he said. "My candy girl."

Chapter 14

Logan took a deep breath as his phone blared his wake-up song. He could smell Robin's delicate lavender scent. He had to open his eyes to make sure he wasn't dreaming. Nope. His wife was in his arms and he didn't want to move. Didn't want to think of the real world of bullshit waiting outside the door.

He had that meeting with HR. He had to get a judge to prove that he wasn't a father and hope that the fallout from all of this wouldn't put his career in jeopardy. Things hadn't changed so much where Logan thought that the black surgeon wouldn't be dragged through the mud because of these lies.

What would this mean for his patients whom the hospital wanted to use those horrible drugs on? Yeah, staying in bed with Robin would be the best way to forget about everything that was waiting for him.

The song continued, getting louder, and Robin turned over to face him. "I know you're not sleeping," she said, her voice sounding like a warm drizzle of honey.

"Still trying to keep this same energy. If I move, then it means the real world is actually real."

"When have you ever hid from hard things, Logan?"

He tilted his head to the side and looked in her eyes. He saw something that he'd been missing. She believed in him. That gave him everything he needed to face what was on the other side of the door.

"What time is it?" Robin asked as she yawned.

"Five after six."

"When's your meeting?"

"Nine."

"Good. I've got time to feed you. How does oatmeal, eggs, and chicken sausage sound?"

"Where are the grits?"

"Oatmeal is healthier. But since you didn't balk at chicken sausage, I guess I can whip up some grits with no butter."

"That's just wrong."

She thumped his bare shoulder. "I have something better. A plant-based substitute. Tastes just like butter, and if it fools you, then I won't have to get compared to Nina when it comes to cooking."

"Y'all do her so wrong. Maybe if someone taught her how to make grits," he quipped.

"Sounds like you just volunteered. Good for you." Robin rolled out of his arms. "If you want to take a shower, there are fresh towels in the bathroom."

"I'll take a long shower, if you join me." He offered her a randy wink.

"Then I guess you don't want to eat. You have to drive back to Richmond and you know how rush-hour traffic can be."

"Can I see you tonight?" he asked as he rose from the bed. "At our place?"

"Um, I tell you what, if you have Liam come over with his information, I'll be there."

"I can do that. But let me go on the record and say that having that guy be the reason you're coming over has me feeling some kind of way," he said.

Robin got out of the bed and touched Logan on the shoulder. "We're not where that's even remotely funny."

"Sorry."

She pinched his shoulder. "And that's why you're showering alone. I'll get breakfast started." Robin glanced at the digital clock on her nightstand. "Knowing my sisters, they are going to be here sooner, rather than later. You need to get it together."

He nodded toward the bathroom. "This is me, getting it together."

Robin darted down the stairs and started cooking breakfast for Logan. As she boiled the water for grits and heated the pan for the chicken sausage, Robin couldn't help but smile. This used to be study time for the couple. When she was getting ready for the bar exam, Robin would cook and Logan had flash cards.

As they drank coffee and ate eggs, he made sure his wife was ready to pass her test. It worked: Robin had passed the Louisiana bar, the Virginia bar, and the South Carolina bar with her husband's tutoring and support.

Sighing, she thought about the drama she and Logan had to deal with now. Was she ready to believe that her husband hadn't betrayed her? Though last night had been magical, she couldn't help replaying that woman outside of her house saying those things about her not being able to give Logan a child. Hearing that coming out of Kamrie's mouth made her feel like she'd been telling the truth about her affair with Logan.

But he made it seem as if he hadn't been the one to share her deepest fears with that woman. Was it possible that this was some big conspiracy, as Logan said? But why would anyone be that cruel just to bring him down?

What if Logan was right and this was something deeper than ending his marriage?

Robin stopped in midstir of the grits. Why would anyone want to launch a personal attack on him like this?

And why did I fall for it? Robin thought. *We didn't come this far for him to do something like this. But what if it isn't a conspiracy?* She started stirring the grits with fury. She wanted to get rid of this feeling that Logan was still lying to her. That he was living a double life and deceiving her. Would he do that? Could he do that? Had she been wrong all of this time?

"Hey," Logan said as he walked into the kitchen, shirtless. "What did those grits do to you?"

Robin looked up at her man and smiled. Maybe that's why she'd passed the bar, because he had always been shirtless when he held up those flash cards. He always had a great chest.

"Was thinking about some stuff and got caught up. The grits are almost done," she said as she spooned some of the plant-based butter in the pot. "Why don't you have a shirt on?"

"Because I know how you like looking at my chest." Logan crossed over to her and brushed his lips against her neck.

"If you don't want a burnt breakfast, you're going to

have to keep those lips to yourself." Robin lowered the heat on the grits, then turned to face her husband.

"I'll risk it," he said, then kissed Robin slow and deep. She wrapped her arms around his neck and lost herself in the sweetness of his mouth.

Logan broke the kiss and stroked Robin's hair. "This kitchen is too small."

"Too small for what?"

"To put you up on the counter and have you for breakfast." He ran his index finger down the center of her chest.

Robin smacked his hand away. "One-track mind."

"Maybe we can cook something up together in our kitchen tonight."

"You do realize that my sisters are coming here and they're expecting me to be balled up in an emotional hole cursing your name?"

"So, what do you think the reaction is going to be?"

Robin shrugged. "They're going to have their thoughts, as they always do. But I have the final say. It's my life. Still, you might not want to be here when they arrive." She turned back to the grits.

"Good point. Since I keep a suit at the hospital, I'll go straight to the meeting, then reach out to Liam. Maybe he got some information from this nurse he met in Atlanta."

"Liam is a really good friend to do this research for you and help clear your name."

"According to Liam, I'd better make this work."

"He's always been smart. Glad you kept him as a friend."

Logan snorted. "He's lucky too. Had the nerve to have a crush on you."

Robin fixed his plate and grinned. "You're mad because the man has good taste?"

He took the plate from Robin's hand and nodded. "I had already put the word out that Robin Richardson was my woman. And I mean it, to this day." Just as Logan leaned in to kiss her, the doorbell chimed.

"Oh shit," Robin gritted. "I knew they were going to be early, but damn."

"Want me to go out the back door?" he asked as he looked longingly at his plate.

"No, let's do this now." Robin headed for the front door and, not surprisingly, saw her sisters and a gorgeous man with blue-green eyes standing there. He was big and looked like he'd kill anyone who laid a hand on Yolanda Richardson.

"Well, good morning," Robin said when she opened the door.

"Please tell me you have coffee," Yolanda groaned.

"Wait," Robin said. "Aren't you going to introduce me to your friend?"

Yolanda rolled her eyes and Alex stifled a laugh. The man extended his huge hand. "Charles, ma'am," he said.

Yolanda sucked her teeth. "She knows who you are. Are you going to invite us in or not?"

"I have company and I don't want to hear y'all's mouth. But I do have breakfast waiting."

"Who's here?" Alex asked as she brushed past her sister and started toward the kitchen. Robin grabbed her arm.

"Again, Alex, I don't want to hear a word!"

When the Richardson sisters entered the kitchen, Robin closed her eyes and waited for the explosion.

"Oh my fucking goodness," Yolanda exclaimed. "What are you doing here? And where is your shirt? Robin, are you sleeping with this guy?"

"You mean, my husband?" Robin said. "What kind of question is that?"

"One that needs answering, because I swear you were just crying about this asshole less than twenty-four hours ago," Alex said, then turned to Logan. "Can you put on a damned shirt?"

He spooned his grits into his mouth and shook his head. "Good morning, ladies," he said after swallowing.

Yolanda snapped her fingers. "Charles, why don't you kill him?"

"It doesn't work like that, Yolanda," Charles said. "Is he a threat to you?"

"Yes."

"Yolanda!" Robin exclaimed. "Stop it!"

Logan pointed to the stairs. "I'm going to grab my shirt."

Charles headed out of the kitchen and crossed into the living room.

"What the hell, sis?" Yolanda asked.

"My husband and I are going to work things out because there's a lot going on that . . ."

Alex waved her hands. "Nah, because you said he was sharing your personal business with that bitch who says he fathered her child. You keep going back and forth with that guy and you're the one who ends up suffering!"

Robin folded her arms across her chest. "I'm going to do what I think is right for me and my future."

"Really? That's what you're calling this thing?" Yolanda asked. "The DNA test says—"

"We don't know that the DNA test is real and we're . . . I'm not explaining myself to y'all because I love my husband and I believe . . ."

"What changed?" Alex asked calmly. "Why are you all of a sudden drinking the Logan Baptiste Kool-Aid?"

"Because I never did what I was accused of," he said as he returned to the kitchen with a shirt on.

Yolanda lunged toward him but held back. "I swear if I wouldn't get put out of my sister's house, I'd punch you in your face."

"Yolanda," Alex said with a sigh. "Stop acting like . . . yourself."

Logan crossed over to Robin. "I've got to go. Sorry to leave you alone with all of this."

"I've been handling these two all my life. I've got this." Robin leaned in and gave Logan a quick peck on the lips. Yolanda groaned.

"What in the Twilight Zone have we stepped into?" she asked.

"Are y'all hungry?" Robin asked.

"Is it vegan?" Alex asked.

"No."

"Then yes," she replied.

"And where the hell is the coffee?" Yolanda snapped.

Driving to the hospital, Logan wondered what was going on at Robin's place. She was right about her sisters' anger, but he hoped that he'd done the right thing by leaving her alone to explain everything. The truth behind everything that had happened in the last six months sounded like a plot from a poorly written thriller novel.

And Alex was already suspicious of anyone who wasn't born a Richardson. Yolanda was just mad and who knows what Nina thought. Hopefully, she wasn't spending her honeymoon thinking about what was going on with her sister.

But he didn't need to think about that. He had to focus on the meeting with HR at the hospital. Maybe someone would drop a hint as to why he was being systematically destroyed. For a change, traffic on the interstate wasn't bumper to bumper and there were no accidents. Logan arrived for his meeting about thirty minutes early.

He dashed into his office and grabbed that suit he kept in the closet. While he was changing, Logan looked around his office and noticed that things looked as if they had been rifled through. Granted, he had taken some time off, but why would anyone need to go through his office when his patient files were all digital? After tying his necktie, he sat down at his computer and looked through his patients' files. Two of his heart transplant recipients had been switched to the Cooper Drug cocktail since he'd been gone. Logan banged his hand against his desk, then changed the orders in the system to what he had originally prescribed.

Then he looked around to see what if anything had been taken from his office. The Cooper Drug files were the only thing he had in his office that would be valuable. But who had access to his office while he was on leave? Looking at his watch, he realized that he needed to head to the human resources department and do his investigation later.

Heading down the hall to the human resources office, he noticed the sideways glances from his coworkers and wondered what rumors were floating around the hospital about him. Had they been discussing Kamrie's lie, forgetting all of the good that he'd done for the hospital, for his coworkers and patients? Was this what things had come to now? Dirty looks and hushed conversations when he passed by?

If he was discredited, did this mean he could be replaced by a doctor who would use the dangerous drugs and cost patients their lives?

How the hell am I going to stop this? Logan walked into the HR office and smiled at the receptionist.

"I'm here for a meeting with Clorinda Kelly."

"Dr. Baptiste, right?" the woman asked.

Logan nodded. The woman rose to her feet and told him to have a seat. "Just got to make sure they're ready for you."

Logan sat down on one of the plush chairs in the corner of the office. He wondered who *they* were.

Before he could get somewhat comfortable, he was called into Kelly's office. "Good morning, Dr. Baptiste," she said. "Please have a seat."

Logan looked around the room and saw the head of the cardiology department, the medical director, and a man who looked as if he was a lawyer. All Logan knew was that this wasn't going to be an informal meeting. But he wasn't going to show an ounce of intimidation.

Clorinda cleared her throat as she sat behind her desk. "Dr. Baptiste, we're here because of allegations made against you by a female staffer and to inform you that we're launching an investigation into the allegations."

"Do I have a right to know who my accuser is?" Logan asked.

Clorinda looked toward the man who Logan had assumed was the lawyer and he nodded. "Nurse Kamrie Bazal. She told us that you made unwanted sexual advances toward her, and during the hurricane when the hospital was on the lockdown, you, um, sexually assaulted her. That resulted in a pregnancy. And you have denied that you are the father."

Logan chuckled. "Because I'm not and everything you just described is a lie."

"But in today's climate, we have to take these allegations seriously and investigate it thoroughly."

"So, what does this mean for me?" Logan asked.

Dr. Ryder Carter, the head of cardiology, cleared his throat. "Well, we can't have you on staff right now. So, we're going to have to suspend you during the investigation."

Logan folded his arms across his chest. "And this is just about the accusation from Kamrie?"

"Wh-what do you mean? Isn't that enough?" Carter stammered.

"Huh. This has nothing to do with the drugs you're pumping into patients that's killing them?" Logan fought the urge to grab his boss and shake some sense into him. But he had to play it cool.

"So," Clorinda said. "Are you looking to file a complaint as well?"

"I just want answers," Logan said quietly.

"About?" Carter asked.

"Maybe I need to get my attorney involved because there's a lot of slander going on right now. And while you're here, Dr. Carter, why don't you explain why I've been removed from the surgical schedule for so long? Like right after I refused to use medications from Cooper Drugs on my patients. Do you want to explain what that was all about?"

"That is unrelated to the reason why we're here. And it has nothing to do with the allegations you're facing. Which had been floating around the hospital for a while. We didn't want you to put our patients at risk by having you in the operating room with Nurse Bazal."

"But giving them untested drugs that put their lives at risk was all right?" Logan rolled his eyes. "And if these rumors have been swirling for so long, why did it take this long for you all to decide to address it?"

The other men looked at Clorinda as if she held the answers. "That's not important," she finally said after a pregnant pause. "We're going to place you on administrative leave with pay while the investigation is ongoing."

"Or," Dr. Carter said after he cleared his throat, "you can resign, take a severance package, and start over at a new hospital."

Logan tilted his head to the side and gave the offer a split second of consideration. Wouldn't this make it easier for him and Robin to reconnect? Maybe they could move to Charleston and he could take a position at the Medical University of South Carolina. But could he—in good conscience—leave his patients and so many others at the mercy of Cooper Drugs?

"How badly does Cooper Drugs want me gone for you to make this offer? Are the lives of our transplant patients just a dollar figure for you guys?"

Carter slammed his fist on the edge of Clorinda's desk. "I'm one step from just firing you outright and no one would even think I was wrong. What Cooper Drugs is trying to do is help people and you won't even try."

"Because people are dying and this is unethical!" Logan exclaimed and leapt from his seat.

"All right, gentlemen!" Clorinda said. "It's best that we end this meeting before things get too far out of hand."

Logan nodded and stormed out of the office. Now, he was really wondering if the whole Kamrie lie was a part of the conspiracy. He was 100 percent sure that this meeting had nothing to do with the alleged sexual harassment complaint. He decided to skip going back to his office and head home. As he got on the elevator, Kamrie hopped on behind him.

"Surprised to see you here," she said with a smile.

"Don't talk to me. Save all of your correspondence for Clorinda."

Kamrie pressed the emergency stop on the elevator. "I told you there was an easy way to handle this."

Logan sidestepped her and pressed the button to restart the elevator. "And just so you know, there are cameras in here. So, if you decide to say something happened, this time there will be proof."

Kamrie got off on the next stop. "This isn't over. You're going to take care of our son, one way or another."

"Then I guess I'll see you in court," Logan said as the doors closed. By the time Logan made it to his car, he was seething with anger. Too many people wanted his head on a platter. Too many people were playing with his life and he was going to put a stop to it.

Chapter 15

Robin was two seconds from telling her sisters to get out. They'd spent the whole morning tag teaming her as to why she shouldn't give Logan a second chance. Even when they ate her amazing breakfast, drank her coffee, and ate the last of her melons, Alex and Yolanda railed on.

"How about this," Robin said. "Y'all wash my dishes and I'm going to go into my office so you two can talk about me in private, okay?"

Alex shot her sister a cold look. "Don't act like that. And I'm not washing your dishes." She tossed a rag at Yolanda. "Let Yo-Yo do it since she has so much pent-up angst these days."

Robin glanced at her younger sister. "Why do you have a bodyguard?"

"Why are you trying to change the subject?" Yolanda shot back.

"Because I'd like to know why that super attractive man is in my living room and you—Miss Flirty McFlirt-Flirt—have ignored him."

Alex burst out laughing. Now, Robin knew there was a hell of a story waiting to be told. Yolanda tossed the dishrag back at Alex. "I don't like that man. Okay. That's it. The end. And if Nina wasn't on her honeymoon, she'd still be digging my foot out of her . . . This is nosey Nina's fault."

"Tell the truth," Alex said, her voice taking a serious tone.

Yolanda rubbed her forehead. "Maybe I saw something I shouldn't have and there have been threats. But I'm sure once I move to Charlotte, I'll be safe and he can go back to where he came from."

Robin waved her hands. "What kind of threats?"

Yolanda shrugged, then reached for the dish soap. "Death threats."

"Someone is threatening your life and you didn't tell anyone?" Robin exclaimed. "Something happened here in Richmond?"

Yolanda raised her right eyebrow. "You want to go there, sis?"

Alex shrugged her shoulders. "She does have you there."

"Can you at least tell us what happened?" Robin asked.

"I don't want to talk about it. Other than to say, Daddy overreacted."

Alex rolled her eyes. "You know if Daddy ever has a heart attack, the blame will lie with Nina, Yolanda, and Robin. I'm just putting it out there."

"I'm sorry we can't be boring and robotic like you, Alexandria the Great," Yolanda quipped, then dropped the soap on the counter. "I'm going to take a walk." She stormed out of the kitchen. Even though Robin and Alex didn't see Charles follow her out the door, Yolanda's groan let them know he was on his job.

"Guess this means you're on dish duty," Robin said as she patted Alex on her shoulder.

"Can we talk about your sudden change of heart?"

"No. You and Yolanda have done enough talking."

"Okay, so how about I listen?"

Robin raised her right eyebrow. "With your mouth shut?"

Alex pouted. "Yes. Is there another way to listen?"

"I don't know, have you ever done that?"

"Whatever."

Robin threw her hands up. "All right. I was ready for him to sign the divorce papers. I wanted him to and I had decided that I couldn't be with a man who could betray me the way he had. If he was cold enough to tell this woman that I couldn't have children after they had one together, I couldn't forgive that. But that man didn't line up with the man who nursed me back to health after my surgery. The man who tried to go vegan with me when I knew how much he loved steak. And I realized, a lot of this was about my insecurity and losing trust in my husband because . . ."

"Well, a DNA test saying he's the father does kind of erode trust."

"See," Robin said. "I knew you couldn't keep your mouth closed."

"Sorry, sorry. Continue."

"Last night we faced some hard truths. Even before the so-called affair, I was pushing Logan away. But I love my husband and I don't care what any of you think. I'm going to fight for my marriage. There's a lot more going on at the hospital and we're going to get to the bottom of it."

"So, now you're his ride-or-die wife?"

"Yes, I am. We've been together too long to let outside forces pull us apart."

"And if you find out that there was some truth to any of this?"

"Then you'll be my alibi witness," Robin said with a wink.

"Don't even joke like that!" Alex said as she walked over to the sink.

Robin crossed over to the coffee machine. "I'm not joking."

"You can't even kill a spider."

"Facts. And I'd never kill my husband."

"And clearly you won't leave him either. For his sake, I hope he didn't cheat on you," Alex said as she began to wash the dishes.

Me too, Robin thought as she made two cups of coffee for her and Alex.

Logan drove from the hospital to Liam's office in Glen Allen. The town on the outskirts of Richmond gave Liam enough anonymity to spy on anyone. And those whom he crushed with his investigations never thought to look for him in the rural enclave. And Liam had taken down some powerful people, including a racist governor who had been keeping undocumented workers as domestic slaves while lobbying against immigration.

Then there was the senator who had written the heartbeat bill but paid for his mistress to have an abortion in

DC. People in Richmond knew that Liam got results. Logan prayed that his friend would get these kinds of results for him with this investigation.

Pulling into the parking lot of Liam's office, Logan was disappointed not to see his friend's car there. "Should've called first," he muttered as he pulled out his phone and sent him the recording of the meeting.

Liam texted him back immediately:

At the hotel with the nurse. Will listen to this and call you back.

Thanks.

Now Logan had to figure out what to do with his nervous energy. He definitely wasn't going to Robin's because there was no telling how her sisters would react to seeing him again. Well, if she was going to visit him later tonight, he might as well head to the grocery store and stock up on her favorites. Logan cranked up his car and headed back to Richmond.

His first stop was Whole Foods to get radicchio and vegan cheese to make a salad with bite. He also grabbed a bag of Kicking Horse Coffee. He laughed at the fact that one of Robin's favorite coffees was called Smart Ass. Then he chose the wine: merlot and pinot noir. Since he knew he wasn't going to get full off a salad, Logan grabbed two steaks and a couple of potatoes. Glancing at his watch, he wondered when Liam would be done at the hotel. And he really didn't want all of the details as to what he was doing. All he could hope for was that she would give Liam the ammo he needed to bring

Kamrie down; then he could get to the bottom of the administration's relationship with Cooper Drugs. But more than anything, he'd finally get to clear his name with his wife. And that was the most important thing.

When Logan arrived home, Liam's car was parked in the driveway. "That was quick," Logan said as he emerged from the car and popped the trunk.

"You talk about a person who knows what the word *vomit* is, that was Miss Lady. If those are the friends that Kamrie has, she doesn't need enemies."

"Did you listen to my recording?"

Liam nodded. "Whose corn flakes did you piss in? Someone really wants to get you. So, I've been looking into Cooper Drugs. They have a number of drugs that are being recalled by the FDA and a lawsuit ongoing to keep a black box warning off their antirejection medication."

"I knew it!" Logan exclaimed. "Why in the hell would the hospital want to use these drugs if all of this is going on?"

"Money, money, money," Liam sang off-key.

"How do we prove it?"

Liam stroked his forehead as he watched his friend grab the grocery bags. "We're going to have to discuss that and everything else over dinner. What's in the bags?"

"Food. And Robin is coming over and she's on board with helping us."

"And with sticking with this whole marriage thing?"

"She was this morning, but her sisters are here, so . . ."

"You still might be on her shit list?"

"I don't think so," he said as memories of the night before flashed in his mind. "But I know we have to show Robin that I didn't betray her."

"That's going to be a lot easier now. I'm glad to know that you didn't screw around on Robin. Because I'd have to kick your ass."

Logan rolled his eyes as they walked into the house. "I need to file a claim against Kamrie. She cornered me in the elevator after the meeting."

"She's bold. And stupid. I don't think she's involved with the drug company. You just happen to be the next rich doctor she wants to sink her hooks in."

Logan walked into the kitchen and set the bags on the counter. "Why me?"

Liam shrugged. "Maybe it was just because you were there and she saw you a lot? According to her so-called friend, Kamrie wants the easy life she thinks doctors provide for their wives. She grew up poor and doesn't want the cycle to continue."

"Clearly she's not poor. Do you know how much nurses make? Is she a gambler or something?"

"How deep do you want me to look into her past? Because I thought the purpose of all this was to expose her lies. It doesn't matter what her backstory is. Let her find a therapist and deal with her shit on her own."

"You're right, I guess. It's just part of my nature to want to know what makes people tick and . . ."

"She isn't a patient and I don't think you can give her a transplant that would remove crazy."

Logan nodded as he started unpacking the groceries. Liam smiled when he saw the steaks. "You got the good meat today. You sure Robin isn't going to run out of here when she sees this?"

Logan laughed. "My wife and I have an understanding about food."

"Must be nice. At least your nightmare is coming to an end and you can expose that woman Kamrie for the liar that she is. Maybe she'll go back to Atlanta and seek support from that child's real father."

"Let's hope we can prove that and get her off my back." Logan opened the steaks and then his phone rang. When he saw it was Robin, he smiled. "Hey, babe."

"Your in-laws are driving me crazy," Robin said. "And they want to come to Richmond for dinner with us. Alex said she has questions."

Logan looked at the food he had purchased and wondered if he had some other meat he could cook. Then he remembered the chicken in the freezer; he could make it work. "Tell Alex she should've been nicer this morning and I would've made jambalaya."

"She doesn't deserve it. And Yolanda has a bodyguard who's going to be there. But I don't know if this guy eats. He only moves when Yolanda does."

"Why does she have a bodyguard?"

"I don't know the full story, but she must be in serious danger. It's kind of scary."

"Maybe y'all should stay here. I got suspended today, so I'm going to be home."

"What?" Robin exclaimed. "Why?"

"We'll talk about it when you get here. I can tell you this, they showed some of their cards today."

"We should be there in an hour." Logan heard Robin tell someone that he didn't cook jambalaya.

When they hung up, Logan shook his head.

"Sounds like you're having a lot more company than this food is going to feed. Better call Uber eats for backup," Liam joked. "'Cause I'm not sharing my steak."

"Don't worry, I've got this," Logan said as he crossed over to the freezer.

Robin didn't consider that she was eavesdropping since Yolanda and Charles were having a disagreement in her home. But she didn't want them to see her as she tried to decipher what they were talking about.

"How smart is it for you to go to Richmond when that's where you're being hunted?" Charles asked. His voice was deep and angry.

"I'm going to my sister's house, which is in a totally different neighborhood. And I'm not in my vehicle. Why are you being like this?"

"Because I was hired to keep you alive. Yolanda, this isn't a game. You keep trying to do things your way, take risks, and put yourself in danger. I'm not going to let that happen."

She sucked her teeth and took a step closer to him. "You know, if you'd take that stick out of your ass, your life would be so much better."

He smiled and shook his head. "You have a mouth on you."

Yolanda offered him a smirk. "You'd be amazed as to what this mouth can do, Chuck."

Chuck? Robin thought. *That's a little familiar.* She leaned in closer to see what was going on and almost gasped when she saw Yolanda in that man's arms, kissing him as if they had done this many times before.

What. The? One thing Robin knew for sure was that she wasn't going to tell Alex what she saw. Robin started coughing as she walked into the living room, giving

Yolanda and Charles a heads-up that she was walking into the room.

They stepped back from each other and turned toward Robin. "Hey, so, Alex and I are ready if you two are."

Yolanda rolled her eyes. "He doesn't think I should go."

Robin looked over at Charles. "Why shouldn't she go? What's really going on here?"

"I'm here to protect your sister, and if she wants to give you more details, then that's up to her."

"I can tell you this, nothing is going to happen to my sister at my house, but if you feel like it's safer for her to stay here then . . ."

"Hello!" Yolanda snapped. "I'm standing right here and I can make my own decisions. I'm going to Richmond and you will deal with it."

Charles shook his head. "Fine, but you're going to stay inside and keep your head down. And this is the last time that you ignore my orders."

"How about I fire you?"

"I don't work for you, so you can't."

Robin fought the urge to laugh. Charles was totally in control here and Yolanda was not pleased. But if this was what it took to keep her sister safe, then she was going to cheer for it. And somehow, she was going to have to get Yolanda to tell her the whole truth about what was going on.

"We're ready," Yolanda snapped.

"Alex," Robin called out. "Let's go."

Alex bounded down the stairs with her phone pressed to her ear. "Yes, that's fine. We can open the honeymoon hideaway for them. Great." She turned to her sisters and held up a finger. "No. That won't be necessary. I'll be back tomorrow."

Yolanda elbowed Robin in the side. "And this is supposed to be a calmer, more serene Alex."

"I heard that," Alex said. "I thought we were ready to go."

"We are. Is everything all right at the bed-and-breakfast?"

Alex fanned her hand. "A good problem to have. We're overbooked for the New Year's Day breakfast. You should come, Robin."

"Um, I don't know if I'm going to be able to make it. I have to go back to work and then I have this stuff to work on with my husband."

Alex rolled her eyes and headed for the door. "Who's driving?"

"You are," Yolanda and Robin said.

As they climbed into Alex's car, Robin couldn't help but notice that Charles was holding Yolanda's hand. Okay, just how was he guarding her body?

"Um, have you noticed those two?" Robin whispered to Alex.

"Yep. And they think they're hiding it," Alex replied in the same whisper. "Anyway, Nina sent me a text and said she doesn't want to come back from her honeymoon. I told her if she didn't bring Clinton home, I was going to come get them."

Robin laughed. "Of course you did. I kind of feel like I put a dark cloud over Nina's wedding. I wanted to be there for her and be happy, but . . ."

"Honey, Nina and Clinton had a wonderful wedding."

"Yeah," Yolanda said from the backseat. "And honestly, Alex was the only one who noticed that you'd left the reception early. Nina and Clinton were so caught up in dancing and kissing each other I think they felt as if they were the only ones in the room."

"That's so sweet," Robin said with a smile. "Can we make a quick stop at Whole Foods? I know Logan probably has no dessert."

"Where is Whole Foods?" Alex asked. "I have a straight route to your old house and . . ."

"Just take the next exit. I live here, remember?" Robin quipped. She directed her sister to the grocery store and hopped out of the car. Alex followed her inside but Yolanda and Charles remained in the car.

"I bet the windows will be fogged up when we get back," Alex quipped and Robin's knees buckled.

"Okay, you're making sexy time jokes?"

"Listen, watching those two is a romantic comedy from hell. What did you come in here to get? You know I left all of those cookies at your other house. We could've had those for dessert."

"Those are my cookies. I'm not sharing. Besides, there is this vegan chocolate cake that Logan and I like."

Alex scrunched her face up. "Vegan what? I thought you gave that up."

"I'm not a total vegan; there are some foods that I still enjoy."

"So, that's where all your weight went? Girl, you'd better eat a chicken leg quarter and some grits with real butter."

"Real butter? What are you talking about?"

"Those grits you made this morning with that fake butter. I don't know who you thought you were fooling."

Robin sucked her teeth and playfully swatted her sister's arm. "Didn't stop you from eating them."

"Okay, I was hungry."

Robin laughed as they walked over to the bakery and she grabbed the lush chocolate cake. "This is going to be the best cake you've ever eaten."

"I'm going to tell Roberta you said that mess."

"You'd better not." Robin laughed, thinking about how the family's long time cook would feel about her statement.

After paying for the cake, they headed back to the car. And the windows were not steamy. "I should've bet you," Robin said as they got into the vehicle. The drive to her Richmond home was uneventful and Robin tried to hide her excitement about seeing Logan. After all, they'd spent the night together. But the fire for her husband had been reignited and she loved the feeling. She had real hope that she and Logan would be able to withstand this storm. That they would be happy again.

When Alex parked the car, Robin leapt out of it as if she were a kid heading for a toy store with money in her pocket.

Yolanda sucked her teeth. "This asshole better be a changed man or—"

"Let her have this," Alex said. "If Logan didn't cheat on her and they can fix their marriage, we should support them."

"Well, I hope we don't have to kick his ass."

"I can hear you, Yolanda," Robin said as she unlocked the door. When they walked in, the scent of roasted chicken and spices greeted them. The sound of Liam and

Logan's laughter filled the house. "Looks like the party already got started."

Logan peeked around the corner and smiled at Robin. She crossed over to him and hugged him tightly. "Your in-laws are still in fight mode," she whispered. "Be careful."

Liam cleared his throat. "Can I get one of those?"

"Hell no," Logan snapped. Robin thumped him on the shoulder, then crossed over to Liam and gave him a sisterly hug.

"It's good to see you," he said. "Back where you belong."

"You mean here at the house and not in your arms, right?" she quipped.

"This isn't funny at all," Logan said. "What's in the bag?"

Robin placed the cake on the counter. "Cake."

"The one from Whole Foods?" Logan asked with a smile on his face.

She winked at him.

"Look," Yolanda said from the entrance of the kitchen. "Sorry to bust up this reunion. But where is the food?"

Alex glanced around the kitchen before walking in and looking at the food on the stove. "You were serious about no jambalaya?"

Liam glanced at Alex and smiled. "I can make jambalaya."

Alex gave him a sideways glance. "So."

"Ouch," he said as he turned to Robin.

"Introduction time," Robin said. "Liam Jones, this is my older sister, Alexandria Richardson, and younger sister Yolanda. And Charles. He will probably break your arm if you touch her."

"All right then," Liam said. "I see that sarcasm is a family trait."

"And how do you know Robin and this guy?" Yolanda asked. Charles placed his hand on her shoulder and she shrugged it off.

"We went to Xavier together," Liam said. "In another universe, Robin would be Mrs. Jones."

Logan groaned. "Like hell."

Yolanda laughed. "Well, I would say something, but I'm hungry and I don't have time to be snarky. Can you cook, Liam?"

"No, he can eat," Logan quipped.

Yolanda rolled her eyes. "Nobody is talking to you."

Logan walked over to the cabinets and pulled out some plates. Robin crossed over to him and helped him with the plates. "What did you make?" she asked.

"Um, we got chicken and steak for the meat eaters. I got a special salad for you and some jasmine rice with scallions."

"Wow. You really pulled this together."

"Well, the original plan was to pack Liam a to-go plate and take you upstairs to work up an appetite."

"That was so not the plan. We're supposed to go over the evidence that Liam has proving that you didn't father a baby with that woman."

"Yeah, that part," he said with a wink. Logan nodded to her sisters, who were staring at them with frowns on their comely faces. "Guess they still don't believe me?"

"Not at all, and they think I'm out of my mind to be here."

"Well, we're going to have to change that," he said as he handed Robin her plate of salad. "Okay, guys, let's eat."

Logan and Robin handed everyone a plate of food. Yolanda and Charles headed for the living room while

Liam and Alex joined Robin and Logan in the dining room. Before Robin could take a bite of her salad, Alex lit into Logan.

"How in the hell did this woman have the audacity to say you were the father of her child if you didn't sleep with her? What kind of person does something that can be refuted with a fucking DNA test?"

"Damn," Liam mumbled. Alex shot him a cold look.

"Alex, I didn't sleep with her and, unfortunately, this is a pattern with her."

Alex cut into her chicken, then pointed her knife at Logan. "And you know this how?"

Robin shook her head. "Bring it down, Alex," she said.

Dropping her knife on the table, Alex shook her head. "I'm not going to bring it down, because Logan made a promise to me when he married you. And it seems like he broke it. Also, when my sister was sick, you should've told me."

Robin brought her hand to her face. "Alex."

"No. She went through a lot without the support she needed. Then this. What if she had relapsed because of the stress you caused?!"

"Alexandria!" Robin shouted. "I get it. But . . ."

Alex dropped her fork. "But nothing. I almost lost two of my sisters in the last eighteen months—I'm pissed. I tried to hold it in but sitting here and watching you forgive without a second thought has me puzzled."

Logan patted the back of Robin's hand. "Let me say something. I'm not going to apologize for doing what my wife asked me to do. Robin didn't want to worry you guys because we knew what she was facing could be fixed. There were times when I wanted to call you, Alex, because I didn't think I was enough for my wife. But I made a promise to her and kept it."

"Too bad you didn't keep your wedding vows," Alex muttered.

"And this is why no one wanted you to know anything. Stop being so damn judgmental. And for the last time, this is my life."

"And you're just going to let him ruin it?"

Robin leapt to her feet. "You know you can leave now."

"Ladies, ladies," Liam said. "I know I'm not family here, but let's take a breath. Kamrie Bazal is a liar and was probably pregnant when she took the job at the hospital."

"What?" Alex and Robin said.

Chapter 16

Logan had never seen Alex get that quiet that fast—especially when she thought she was right about something. Liam glanced at Robin as she returned to her seat. "Do we want to do this now?" he asked.

"Yes," Robin said.

"I went to Atlanta to see what this woman's deal was. There are plenty of rumors about her being one of those women who wants to be a doctor's wife and she thought she'd found her mark. But the problem was she picked the wrong doctor."

"What do you mean?" Robin asked.

"She slept with the hospital administrator's husband," Liam said.

Alex shook her head. "She sounds like she needs help and Jesus."

"Shh," Robin admonished her sister. "I guess sleeping around wouldn't stop her from getting another job, but why would she try to pass off that man's baby on my husband?"

Liam took a quick bite of his food, then looked up at Robin. "Because he's a doctor. And her goal, according to the nurse who was her best friend, is to be a doctor's wife. Get his money and benefits."

"Then the bitch should've gone to medical school," Robin snapped. "Why Logan? He's not . . ."

"She might have been pushed in Logan's direction for another reason, as you already know," Liam said.

Robin rolled her eyes. This situation made her blood boil. Knowing the kind of doctor Logan was and had always wanted to be, it hurt her to see his career being reduced to this because of a scandal and greed.

Logan nodded. "Over the last few months, nearly a year actually, I've been fighting with the administration about a drug company and using their drugs on our patients. I was taken off the surgery schedule and I started nosing around. It didn't go unnoticed."

"Was that what your meeting was about today?" Robin asked.

"Something like that. They wrapped it in a sexual misconduct allegation. But my boss offered me a severance package and recommendation for a new job."

"What?" Alex exclaimed. "That's illegal—isn't it? And if you were guilty of being a sexual predator, why would they just ship you off to another hospital? Don't y'all take an oath to do no harm?"

Logan nodded. "And that's what I'm trying to uphold."

"Can you prove any of this?" Robin asked. Logan could see that she was putting her lawyer hat on. "Do you have any proof that these drugs are harmful to your patients?"

"I have some unscientific data. But I know that this company isn't FDA approved and there have been a few deaths of transplant patients who have been taking the antirejection medication from Cooper Drugs. Two years ago, our hospital had a 10 percent mortality rate when it came to transplants. This year, 30 percent of our transplant patients haven't made it."

"That's a lot," Liam said as he stroked his chin. "Have any of the families come to you with questions?"

Logan shook his head. "I wouldn't use the drugs with my patients, so my surgeries are still in the 10 percent range. I just feel like people have died for money."

"You need to get a family to file a lawsuit," Robin said. "Then the hospital would have to go public with what's going on."

"I can start digging and keep your hands clean," Liam said.

Logan nodded. "All right. Let's do it."

"I'm sorry," Alex began. "At the risk of being accused of sticking my nose where it doesn't belong, what about this woman and the child she says is yours?"

Logan cleared his throat. "We're going to have to fight her in court. And I get the feeling that it will be a big deal. The hospital will probably use the suit against me to get what they want."

"Have you thought about leaving Richmond Medical?" Robin asked. "Maybe go into private practice or work at another hospital?"

Alex nodded in agreement. "Because if the administration is coming for you, you should take your expertise elsewhere."

"But I don't want patients to suffer," Logan said.

"So, it's your job to suffer?" Alex asked. "And take my sister down that road with you? You're not Jesus on the cross."

Logan bristled at her statement. But she did have a point and it stung. Robin had suffered a lot because of this lie. How much did he want his wife to endure?

"What if we offer Kamrie a payoff?" Liam asked.

"Absolutely not," Robin snapped. "I'm not going to watch her profit from a lie. We're going to fight her, the hospital, and anyone else who plans to stand in our way."

"Well, damn," Logan muttered as he stroked his wife's thigh.

"All right," Liam said. "I'll get to work in the morning."

Robin sighed. "And I'll file papers with the court to get a DNA test on the little boy."

Logan was about to say something when Yolanda walked into the dining room. "Y'all done with all the screaming and whatnot? 'Cause, I was told there was dessert."

Everyone broke into laughter. Robin stood up. "I'll get the cake, and if you and Charles want to stop being antisocial, y'all can join us in here."

"Maybe we were just trying to avoid the conflict," Yolanda said with a grin. "Although we heard everything."

Yolanda and Charles joined the rest of the crew at the table as Robin doled out slices of chocolate cake and poured glasses of merlot. Charles opted for water. Logan watched Robin playing hostess and felt so much peace, even if he knew a huge battle was looming. But he had his wife back and he couldn't have been happier. When she crossed over to him with his cake and wine, Logan pulled her on his lap and brought his lips to her ear. "I love you so much."

"Love you more."

"Oh my goodness, get a room!" Yolanda joked.

Robin sucked her teeth. "You know this is my house and I can do what I want in every room in it."

"Can we eat without having to see y'all kissing every five minutes?" Yolanda said.

Robin leaned down and gave Logan a quick peck on the lips. "Nope."

"This is usually when I leave," Liam said. "They get like this all the time. But I'm going to eat my cake first."

After dessert was finished, Alex led everyone out of the kitchen and told Logan and Robin they could do their own damned dishes.

"I like and fear her," Liam said as Logan walked them out the door.

"Lean more toward fear. Alexandria's bark is as tough as her bite."

"I can hear you," Alex said. "Logan, you'd better take care of my sister and don't make me have to come back here over some bullshit." He crossed over to his sister-in-law and gave her a tight hug.

"You remember that promise I made you—I haven't let you down."

"And you'd better not."

Logan turned around and saw Robin standing at the door with a sly smile on her lips. He couldn't wait to close the door and be alone with her.

Robin waved to her sisters, happy that she'd told Alex where her spare house key was and she didn't have to drive back to Petersburg to let them in. Tonight, she was going to sleep in her own bed with her husband's arms around her. Logan walked up the steps and pulled Robin into his arms. "Now that we're alone, what are we going to do?" he whispered as he brushed his lips against her neck.

"Clean up the kitchen."

"You're no fun."

"And nobody told you to be Emeril tonight."

Logan ran his hands down her body and Robin trembled in delight. "Well, as it turns out, I don't have to go to work in the morning. So, I can take you upstairs, tuck you into bed, make love to you, and clean up the kitchen in the morning."

Robin ran her hand across his chest, admiring how his cotton T-shirt showed off his sculpted chest. She'd tried but failed to focus on her dessert while they were at the table and not what was underneath that white shirt. That's probably why Yolanda had started yawning and reminded Alex that she was needed in Charleston in the morning. Her sister had been clutch.

"You're right," she said. "You can clean up in the morning and we can go straight to bed."

"How about a bath first? I've got that lavender bath oil that you like so much."

"Mr. Baptiste, are you trying to seduce me?"

"With all my might."

"I'm going to make it easy for you," she said as she pulled out of his embrace and stripped down to her lace demi bra and matching black boy shorts.

"Damn," Logan muttered. "You wore those for me, didn't you?"

She looked over her shoulder and winked at him. "Sure did." Logan met her on the stairs, then scooped her up in his arms.

"I can't wait to take them off."

Robin leaned in and kissed him with a slow, burning passion. Logan nearly stumbled as he carried her to their bedroom. Robin laughed when she saw the bed hadn't been made. She always made up the bed before leaving the house. But when Logan slipped his hand between her thighs, the unmade bed didn't matter and the quip she'd planned to say was replaced by a moan as he stroked her wetness.

"Lo . . . logan," she moaned.

"Say it again."

"Logan." Her voice was dripping with need.

He laid her on the bed and made short work of removing her bra and panties. Slipping his finger inside her wetness, Logan stroked her clitoris with the pad of his index finger. Robin screamed in delight. Seconds later, his tongue replaced his finger and Robin felt as if she was on the edge of an explosion. Suck. Lick. Suck. Robin's thighs trembled as the waves of her orgasm washed over her.

Logan knew how to play her body until she purred and that was just what she was doing as his tongue circled inside her. "Oh, baby," she breathed. "Oh, yess." And with one last lick, he took her to the brink of pleasure.

"That's the meal I've been waiting all night for," he said as he eased up her body and wrapped his arms around her.

"Was it worth the wait?"

"Oh yeah," he said as he pulled her on top of him. Robin straddled him and pulled his pants down. Logan's erection sprang forward, rubbing against her thighs.

"Looks like you're ready for some action," she said as she leaned against him and kissed his neck.

"Always ready for you," he said as he dove inside her. Robin rode him slow, arching her back as he stroked her breasts.

"Oh, Logan! Oh my!" She bucked harder and Logan dove deeper. Robin tightened her grip on his cock as she leaned back and gave him a slow grind. Logan moaned with delight as he and Robin reached their climax together. She collapsed against his chest and Logan held her tightly.

"I could hold you forever and that wouldn't be enough time," he breathed against her ear.

"I'd let you hold me forever." Robin stroked his cheek. "So, the real work starts tomorrow."

Logan shook his head. "We're not talking about that in this bed," he said. "This is the no drama zone. Just you and me."

"I like that. Because we've got some reconnecting to do. I'm sorry that . . ."

"You don't have to apologize. I was so concerned with your physical health that I didn't think about how you were feeling emotionally and I should've known better."

She offered him a half smile. "There was just so much going on inside me and I didn't know how to deal with it all. I just had these dreams of having a perfect family and when . . ." Tears streamed down her face. "I thought I'd failed us. Because of all the dreams we'd talked about, all the things we had achieved, we didn't have our baby."

Logan wiped her tears away and kissed her forehead. Robin cried silently against his chest. And for a change, her tears weren't about pain, hurt, and disappointment.

This was the kind of conversation she and Logan should've had months ago. But she was afraid and didn't know where to start.

"Rob, there's nothing about you staying alive that is a failure. And maybe I pushed too hard to tell you that we had other ways to make a family when I should've listened to what you needed and not try to fix you. You were never broken."

Robin exhaled and melted against her husband. "Thank you."

"I love you."

"Love you more."

Moments later, the couple drifted off to sleep, not letting each other go.

Logan woke up when he heard the shower going. That's right, Robin was back. She had to go to work and he didn't. Reality was really biting now that he knew he wasn't going to be able to save his patients from dangerous drugs. He had to make sure that he got things rolling on the lawsuit against the hospital so that he could expose what was going on with Cooper Drugs and the transplant patients. His career was probably over there. But having a private practice might be a good move for him. Then he and Robin wouldn't have to leave Richmond. She had her career and she was doing just fine. He couldn't, in good conscience, ask her to leave everything she'd built behind.

Besides, Logan knew if he had to start over, he could do anything with Robin by his side. Logan climbed out of bed and grabbed his boxers and slippers. He decided he'd get the kitchen cleaned up and make his wife break-fast before she headed to work. Before he made it down-stairs, he heard Robin swearing.

Turning around, he headed into the master bedroom. "What's wrong, babe?"

Robin wrapped a towel around her body and shook her head. "Um, I just realized that I don't have any clothes here, nor do I have a car to drive back to my place and get some."

"That's pretty bad. Well, we should talk about your other place."

"Yeah." She crinkled her nose as she ran her fingers through her hair. "We can rent it out for a little while or check the market value and sell it."

"You're cool with that?"

"Are you saying you don't want me to come home?"

Logan pursed his lips. "Hell no. I want you to pack up your stuff and move in now. I just want to make sure we're making decisions together."

She leaned forward and kissed him. "I get it. And I appreciate you. And you know what would make me ap-preciate the hell out of you?"

"What's that?" Logan smiled and tugged at her towel.

Robin swatted his hand away. "If you would go to Pe-tersburg and grab me some clothes. Actually, my black suit that's hanging on the closet door and my laptop."

"I feel like I was set up."

"I'll make it worth your while when you get back."

"Now, that is an offer I can't refuse. Where are your keys?"

"Downstairs in my purse," she said. "I'm even going to clean up the kitchen for you."

"You're so sweet," he said as he headed downstairs and grabbed her purse. When he opened it, her phone fell out on the table. Logan wasn't suspicious, but when he noticed an unread message on her home screen, he couldn't help but read it.

I've been thinking about you a lot. Hope to hear from you again soon.

He shoved the phone back in her purse and headed out the door. Had Robin been seeing someone else during their separation?

Chapter 17

Robin loaded the last of the dishes into the dishwasher, then wiped down the counters before starting the machine. She was going to cook breakfast, but since Logan was going to be passing one of their favorite restaurants—with vegan breakfast options—she decided to send him a text and ask him to pick up one of her favorite specials. She tightened the sash on his robe and inhaled the woodsy scent of his body wash that lingered on the material. Robin felt so good being home again—this was the right place to be. When she picked up her phone, she groaned at the message from Terell. He needed to leave the past in the past. Besides, there was no chance that they would be more than friends from high school.

Robin felt a little guilty that she had been ready to use him to make herself feel better over her husband's perceived infidelity. Terell knew she was married and had to know that a bridge to them being more than friends burned years ago. Did she really have to tell him? Robin ignored his text and asked Logan to grab breakfast once he got her clothes. She bounced into the living room and curled up on the sofa. The DVR was still filled with unwatched DIY shows from HGTV. Glancing at the clock on the mantel, she realized that she didn't have to be in the office for another three hours, since she didn't plan to go in until one. She clicked on one of the shows and closed her eyes.

What felt like seconds later, but was really an hour and fifteen minutes later, lips brushed across her forehead, waking her up.

"Um, Logan," she said when she locked eyes with her husband.

"Got the food and some clothes. But you look super comfortable in my robe."

"It feels good too. But let's eat." She wiggled her eyebrows at him. Logan set the food on the coffee table and then handed her a mug of coffee.

"How did I miss you making coffee?" she asked as she accepted the mug.

"All that snoring you were doing made it easy for me to walk in, hang up your clothes, put your laptop on the dining room table, and take a bite of your frittata. Also, make this coffee."

"You're so dirty."

"If that's your way of saying hungry, then I'll be that."

Robin grabbed his hand and brought it to her lips. "You know I love you, right?"

"I know. And I love you too."

They sat and ate breakfast in silence. Robin glanced at Logan and realized how much she had missed times like this with him. "What's wrong?" she asked when she noticed the pensive look on his face.

"Nothing, just trying to wrap my mind around what I

need to do today. Going to court to file these papers
and . . . I saw your phone this morning when I grabbed
your keys."

"Oh. That was . . ."

"So, do you have something you need to tell me?"

"There's nothing to tell," she said. "Terell is an old
friend from high school and I saw him at Nina's wedding."

"You just saw him?"

"I wasn't unfaithful to you. But it did cross my mind."

Logan folded his arms across his chest. "Did it?"

"Can you understand what had been going on with
us when he approached me? How confused and upset I
was about me thinking that you had a baby with that
woman?"

"So, if you saw him at Nina's wedding, then that was
after you sent me back to Richmond."

"Didn't I come home to you?" she snapped.

"You did, but what did you do before you got here?"

Robin stood up and turned toward the stairs. "I'm
going to get dressed and go to work. I have nothing to
hide from you and I'm not trying to keep anything quiet.
If you want to look at my phone again, you'll see that I
never replied to him. There isn't anything between us
except high school memories."

Logan followed her into their bedroom and called her
name. "What?" she asked when she turned around.

"You left me over a lie. You filed for divorce because
you thought I cheated on you and I'm just supposed to
be okay with this?"

"Did I say that? But you begged me to trust you and I
don't get the same consideration?"

"But you didn't trust me," he exclaimed. "And I don't want to play tit for tat with you. . . ."

"Then what the hell do you want, Logan?"

"Nothing," he said with a sarcastic laugh. "Because obviously the only person in the marriage who can make a mistake and get forgiveness for it is my perfect wife. I'm just guilty for breathing."

"Then what are we fighting for?" she asked in a quiet voice. "What was last night all about?"

"I thought it was about us finding our way back to each other, but you've been sitting on this secret and making me feel like an ass all of these months."

"You had that woman in our house, you ignored all of the signs that she was problematic."

"And you snuck around with your old high school fling?"

"I didn't." Robin snatched his robe off and pulled her underwear on. "I can't do this when I have to get to work and file papers for you to prove that you didn't fuck around on me."

"At least you're going to have proof." Logan stormed out of the room and Robin collapsed on the bed.

Logan didn't see things turning out this way. In his head, he wasn't even going to say anything about the text message. He was just going to have breakfast with his wife, go over the forms they needed to file to get the paternity test on Kamrie's son, and clean up the kitchen. He didn't want to think about Robin being with another man. Or even considering it an option. But had she? Did she really think she needed to take things that far? Logan had been nothing but honest with her about Kamrie. He never slept with her. But Robin had some dude telling her he couldn't stop thinking about her. What the fuck was he thinking about? How her thighs felt wrapped around him? How her lips felt pressed against his?

Logan slammed out of the house and got into his car. He needed to try to clear his head, but his mind was filled with Robin and this mystery man. Did she feel like the only way she could come back to him was to have an affair of her own? Even if he hadn't? Logan pulled into the parking lot of a coffee shop near the hospital and sat there for a few moments.

He needed to focus on the fight that he had to be ready for. The fight for his career and his reputation. Logan couldn't help but wonder if he still wanted the fight for his marriage to be on this list.

Logan walked into the shop and noticed Dr. Carter having an intense conversation with a woman dressed in a business suit. He inched toward a table not too far from the duo but out of their eyesight to see if he could hear what the discussion was about.

"This is unacceptable, Ryder," the woman said. "Your hospital is supposed to be using the Cooper Drug cocktail for the transplant patients so that we can show the FDA the drugs are safe and we can get our approval."

"The drugs aren't safe. Patients are dying at a rate that my doctors are starting to notice."

The woman sighed and rubbed her forehead. "Then get rid of those doctors. You're at a teaching hospital and you can blame the deaths on the students. There are ways to make this work. Or do we need to cut our funding to you and the hospital?"

"Now, Veronica, you're being ridiculous. I'm taking all the risks here."

"You said that you suspended the main problem since taking him off the surgery schedule didn't work. What else do you need me to do for you so that we can continue our lucrative partnership?"

I knew it, Logan thought. He wished that he had been recording the conversation, but with the background noise, it probably wouldn't have been helpful. He slowly rose from the table and exited out of a side door. Once he was in the car, he called Liam.

"What's up, Baptiste? You're going to live a long time. I'm on my way to your house."

"Good, because I just heard some information that's going to blow the lid off why the hospital has been shitting on me."

"Where are you?"

"Heading back to the house. I went to the coffee shop near the hospital and Dr. Carter was in there talking to a woman named Veronica. I think she's from Cooper Drugs. She said that they had a lucrative partnership."

"I'm going to do some research as soon as I get to your place. Are we going to bring Robin in on this? Maybe it's time for you to file that lawsuit."

Logan expelled a deep breath. "I'm not sure if Robin is . . . Let's see what we can find out first."

"I'm not even going to ask. I'm pulling up in your driveway."

"I'll be there in ten minutes."

* * *

Liam was about to sit on the porch when Robin opened the door. "Liam, what are you doing here? I thought you were my driver."

"Logan didn't call you? Looks like he might have some evidence against his bosses at the hospital."

"We had an argument and I haven't talked to him since he left."

Liam looked down at his watch. "He should be here shortly. What's going on with you two? I know y'all have been under pressure with all of this stuff going on. But, Robin, I've never known two people who belong together like you and Logan."

She closed her eyes. "Maybe we don't belong together," she said so low that Liam didn't hear her.

"Cancel your driver and help us save some lives today," Liam said with his signature smile.

Robin pulled her phone from her purse and canceled her ride share service. "Fine. You want some coffee or some juice while you wait?"

"Thought you'd never ask. Oh, I have donuts in the car. Can you eat those?"

"Already had breakfast, so I'm good," she said with a grin. Liam followed Robin inside and she started a pot of coffee. As Liam pulled out his laptop, he told Robin about the conversation he had with Logan and how they could leverage this information to get Logan his job back.

Robin tried to pay attention, but she couldn't help but think about how angry Logan was over that text message.

Over nothing. Was that how she made him feel? But it wasn't as if he had gotten a DNA test saying she was Terell's kid's mom. He wanted her trust, but where was his trust in her?

"Robin?" Liam said, breaking into her thoughts. "You all right?"

"Yeah. I need to call my office and let them know I'm going to work from home today." She headed for the living room and heard the door open in the foyer. Logan was home.

"You're back," she said.

"Yeah, there was no need for me to move to Petersburg."

"So, you want to be petty now?"

"No, Robin, I don't. Liam and I are trying to get to the bottom of what's going on at the hospital. If you want to help, please do. But if we're going to argue about your . . . Let's get to work."

"I need to call my office and let them know I won't be in. Then I'll meet you guys in the dining room."

Logan gave her a curt nod and walked away. Robin closed her eyes and took a deep breath before making her call.

Logan nodded at Liam before taking a seat across from him. "Do I even want to know what's going on with you and Double R?" Liam asked.

"Let's just focus on what I heard."

"Did you get a look at Veronica?" Liam asked as he turned his computer around so Logan could see the screen.

The screen showed the drug company's website and a picture of the woman he'd seen in the coffee shop. She looked a lot different with a smile on her face rather than the scowl that she had been offering Dr. Carter.

"That's her."

Robin walked into the room. "What y'all got in here?"

"A drug executive who just had a public argument about her killer drugs," Logan said with a broad smile. "When people used to say everything happens for a reason, I thought it was some bullshit. Today, I see what that actually means."

"O-kay," Liam said. "What are our next steps?"

Robin cleared her throat. "I think you should let him know you have an intent to file a suit to stop the use of Cooper Drugs at the hospital."

Liam nodded and pointed at Robin. "That's a good idea. What you heard sounds like Carter might be on the take alone."

"Yeah," Logan said as he stood up and started pacing back and forth. "But what's worse is they want to pin these deaths on the medical students and that could be devastating to an intern."

"That's pretty low," Robin said. "I can draw up some papers, and if you want, I can go to the meeting with you. As your attorney."

Logan raised his right eyebrow but didn't say anything for a beat. "All right, I'll take the papers to Carter, and not that you aren't a brilliant attorney, maybe another lawyer from your firm should go."

"Really?" she snapped.

"Yeah," Logan said. "I mean, how serious am I going to look walking in his office with my wife?"

Robin dropped her head. "You do have a point. I'm going to grab some coffee." She dashed into the kitchen and Liam kicked Logan underneath the table.

"Go talk to her."

Logan stood up and followed his wife to the coffee maker. "Robin."

"What?" She didn't turn around and face him.

"Can you look at me?" A beat passed and she did turn around. Her eyes shone with unshed tears. "I'm sorry. Oh God, this is uncharted territory."

"Are we actually going to be able to make this work? It seems like . . ."

"I didn't want to lose you when you left me in June, and I don't want to lose you now. So, you and that guy . . ."

"Nothing happened."

"But you said you were tempted."

"Because I was hurting. But there was no way that I was going to do what I'd thought you had done to me."

Logan closed the space between them and took her empty mug from her hand. "We've both made mistakes and we're probably going to make some more, but I love you so much and I can't go through this life without you in it."

"Logan," she breathed. "I think about the future and there isn't one where you aren't in it."

He brought his forehead against hers. "All right, so we're making today day one of our future."

She stroked his cheek. "Yes."

Logan captured her lips, kissing her slow and deep.

When they broke the kiss, Logan stared into Robin's eyes. "I love you."

"I love you too."

Robin fixed coffee for her and a mug for Logan. "Thank you," he said when he took it from her hand.

"All right, let's get to work."

Chapter 18

Robin, Logan, and Liam sat at the table for about two hours, crafting documents, making phone calls, and getting work done on sending the papers to the court to get the paternity test ordered.

"I'll be happy to serve this to that bitch," Robin said as she pressed the send button to the court.

"And that's a cat fight that will make the news for sure," Liam quipped. He looked down at his watch. "I don't know about y'all but I'm hungry."

"When are you not hungry?" Logan asked with a head shake. "And I don't have any leftover steak, so don't ask."

"Damn. Well, I hope you've got something more than vegetables. No offense, Robin," Liam said.

"All taken. But lunch is on me and I'll get some healthy stuff for me and whatever greasy, heart-clogging mess y'all want."

"Ouch," Liam said.

Robin pointed at Logan. "And you should totally know better."

"I do. Normally, but these were some tough times and Liam is a bad influence."

"Y'all just going to act like I'm not here?" Liam quipped.

"We've been doing it all of these years, why stop now?" Logan said with a laugh.

Robin shrugged and pulled out her phone to order food for them. After they decided on what they were going to have, Robin got to work on her overdue cases. As she typed, she felt Logan watching her and it felt like they were at Xavier all over again. She realized that she owed her husband an apology. Not just for believing the worst in him, but for her own transgressions. Though she didn't cheat on him, the fact that she gave it such consideration because of a lie made her understand why he was hurt. She couldn't ignore that.

"Logan," she said when they locked eyes. "We need to talk, in private."

He nodded and stood up. The couple headed into the living room. Robin sat on the edge of the sofa and Logan took the arm beside her. On a normal day, she'd say something about his sitting on the arm of the furniture. Today, she just placed her hand on his thigh. "These last six months have been something that I can't find words for."

"I know. And it seems as if every time we're close to making it back to where we belong, something else pops up to keep us apart."

"And this time it's all on me." She looked up at Logan and sighed. "That text message this morning meant nothing, in my mind. But we went months without talking. I made you out to be the bad guy and pretended that I was going to walk away from this marriage."

"Rob, you had every right to feel like that when those papers came."

"And I can't take your feelings for granted and expect you not to feel some kind of way about that text. Everything I felt and had six months to process, I can't expect you to be over it in a matter of hours."

"But I'm over it. You've never lied to me, Robin. And if you say nothing happened with you and that guy, I can believe it."

"And I should've believed you. Logan, I'm sorry."

"There's enough blame to go around for what happened between us. When you said you had a bad vibe about her, I should've listened."

"We could go on and on with the shoulda, woulda, coulda dance, but it isn't going to change anything."

"So, we're just going to burn this all down and start over—again."

"For the last time."

"Damn straight." Logan leaned down and pulled Robin into his arms. "And I'm going to seal this with a kiss."

Robin melted in his arms as he kissed her with a smoldering passion. She reluctantly pulled back from him. "We do have company in the dining room."

"Hey, Liam," Logan called out. "Go home."

"Negro, please. The food ain't here yet," Liam responded.

Kamrie snuck into Logan's office wondering if he was going to come back to the hospital anytime soon. He wasn't taking her seriously, and somehow, she had to make him take responsibility for her son.

"Nurse Bazal, what are you doing in here?" Dr. Carter asked from the doorway.

"Um, I was just checking to see if Dr. Baptiste left any orders for his patients before he left the other day."

"So, you saw him the other day? What did he say to you?"

"Nothing really," she said.

"How far are you willing to take this sexual harassment claim?" Carter asked.

"It's not just a claim."

"Well, you know that he's currently suspended, and if we want to keep that kind of doctor off the staff, then maybe you need to go public with what happened to you. With the hashtag Me Too, you could collect some real money from what you suffered."

"How much money are we talking?" Kamrie's eyes glistened with greed.

"More than enough to take care of your child for the rest of his life."

"I'm listening."

Dr. Carter glanced around the hallway to make sure no one passed by and caught any part of their conversation. "Maybe we should go into my office, where we can talk candidly and in private."

Kamrie followed the portly doctor to the elevator. Once they reached it, she wondered why Carter was so interested in getting rid of Logan all of a sudden. But if it meant that she was going to get a hefty payday, then she would consider it. They rode the elevator in silence. She wondered if a marriage to Logan was still the endgame. He hadn't fallen for the lie; his wife had come back and maybe this was the way for her to secure her future.

There was no way she could go back to Atlanta; that bitch had made it clear that if she came back to Georgia she'd never work again.

But if she had enough money, she could go back to Atlanta and rub her child and everything else in Valerie's face. She didn't deserve Thomas. She had everything and didn't know how to share at all. Okay, so she'd been out of line when she'd gone after the administrator's husband.

But she didn't do it alone. Thomas had a role in making Jean. If only he would've accepted his responsibility, then she wouldn't be in this situation.

They got off the elevator and Dr. Carter opened the door to his office, then ushered Kamrie inside. "Have a seat," he said as he turned the overhead lights on. She sat down and faced him.

"What are we really doing here?" she asked. "I've complained about Dr. Baptiste before and you didn't do anything."

"Let's cut the bullshit," he said. "If there was anything going on with you and Dr. Baptiste, I'm sure it was a willing exchange. You guys had a lot of chemistry and the rumor mill was working overtime talking about your closeness. But I'm not stupid, Nurse Bazal. Premature babies don't weigh seven pounds."

"Your point?"

"That's not Logan's baby. That was a full-term baby and you know it."

"The DNA test says differently." Kamrie rolled her eyes. "And I'd like to see anyone prove a DNA test wrong."

"This is why you should go public with your story of this so-called upstanding doctor being a deadbeat father and a sexual predator."

"That's going to ruin that man's career."

"So, were you just out to ruin his marriage?" Dr. Carter asked.

Kamrie folded her arms across her chest. "And your point?"

"Think bigger, Nurse Bazal. It's pretty obvious that all of your little schemes didn't work to get you what you wanted. If you want to continue to play the victim, work here and have people talk about you behind your back until you quit, then fine. Continue to do whatever you've been doing. But I'm talking about getting you money."

"Fine," she said. "What's the plan?"

Logan and Liam cleared the dishes and Robin e-mailed her assistant to see if all of the filings had been taken to the court. When she got her answer, she went into the kitchen to help wash the dishes.

She was surprised to see that the kitchen was spotless when she walked in, despite the fact that Logan and Liam had eaten a lot of barbeque ribs and coleslaw. "Look at this!" she said. "Teamwork does make the dream work."

"And before you find some more work for us to do, I'm out of here," Liam said.

"Just when I was about to ask you guys to clean the garage," she joked.

"Well, now that you mention the garage, we need to get your car," Logan said as he glanced at his watch. "And before rush hour traffic would be nice."

"We've got a few hours or we can spend the night there?" Robin said with a wink.

Liam threw up a peace sign and headed out the door.

Logan pulled Robin into his arms. "You know that bed in Petersburg is too small."

"You're right. But it was perfect for me. However, if we stay tonight and pack everything up, I can start looking for a property management company to put the town house on the market."

"What do you think about selling it?"

Robin shrugged. "At some point that might be a good idea, but one thing I learned from Sheldon Richardson is that you should always have property in your portfolio."

"Pops and Alex would be so proud of you right now."

Robin thrust her hip into his. "Don't you dare tell them I said that. Next thing you know, Alex is going to offer me a job at the bed-and-breakfast."

"Would it be that bad?"

Robin furrowed her eyebrows. "You met my sister, right?"

"Point taken. Well, I'm going to pack up some food so we can have a farewell meal at your place."

"Jambalaya?"

"You know it."

Robin clasped her hands together. "Great. I'm going to secure some boxes so we can get packed."

As she started to leave the room, Logan called her name. Robin turned around with a smile on her face. "I love you," he said.

She blew him a kiss. "Love you back."

Chapter 19

On the drive to Petersburg, Logan didn't stop singing off-key from the moment they left the driveway to the highway.

Robin joined him as a bad background singer when the R&B station played New Edition's "Candy Girl." But when they hit the interstate, Robin flipped the radio to NPR.

"Thanks for the concert," she quipped.

"That was just the opening act, but I see you're out here hating the player and not the game."

"I think the nineties are calling—they want their lingo back."

"Good thing you're a great lawyer, because you aren't funny."

"Better than your singing. It was never good, just thought it was cute that one of the most popular guys on campus didn't mind embarrassing himself to get the girl."

"But it worked, so I'm going to say I'm the winner!"

"Yes, you won, but I keep winning." She leaned in and kissed Logan's cheek.

"Hey, woman, don't get me distracted. You know those

lips are my weakness. That's the only reason I suffer through listening to NPR when we're in the car together."

"Good to know."

When they arrived at Robin's town house, she was happy to see that the moving company had dropped off boxes and a garbage container. "They work fast," she said as Logan parked the car.

"They must know how much I need you at home," he said as he got out of the car. "But you know we don't have to pack this place in one night."

"I know that, and trust me, I didn't think we would." Robin walked to the back door of the car and grabbed the grocery bags Logan had packed.

"Good. What are you going to do about the furniture? It still looks pretty new."

"Fully furnished town house for rent, imagine the people who will be willing to move here."

Logan crossed over to her and took the bags from her hands, giving her a chance to unlock the door. After unloading the groceries, Robin and Logan started putting the boxes together. She looked at him as he taped the bottom of the larger boxes. "You know what this reminds me of?" she said.

"What?"

"When we moved into our first apartment together in New Orleans."

Logan chuckled. "The one you didn't tell your father about."

"Explain how I was going to tell my dad that we were moving in together before we got married? You've met him."

"Yes, I have. And I'm not saying you were wrong. But

you came up with all the creative excuses as to why he shouldn't come visit."

Robin laughed. "Alex knew you were my roommate. And she never told."

"That's a shock."

She tossed a sheet of bubble wrap at him. "Y'all give my big sister a hard time for no reason. To know her is to love her. Alex took on a lot of responsibilities after our mother died and she forgot to have her own life."

"But you two have always been close."

"Because I don't take her shit and I'm not that much younger than her. You would've thought Nina was her baby. Sometimes I felt sorry for her. And Yolanda was just a little bully." Robin laughed. "I don't know where we would be without each other."

"I'm not going to lie, when I met Pops and Alex, I think she scared me more."

Robin crossed over to him and took the tape from his hand. "You had it right. Dad wants us to be happy. Alex, well . . . Alex wants to be right."

"I hate it for the guy who falls for her."

"Somehow, I don't think she's going to ever let that happen. Being in love means letting go of control. That's not my sister's style."

"Stranger things have happened."

"Well, if Alex ever lets go and falls in love, he's going to catch hell from Yolanda and Nina."

"And you're just going to sit on the sidelines and watch? Right."

"What are you trying to say?"

"You Richardson sisters stick together and I'm lucky I made the cut."

Robin leaned in and kissed him on the cheek. "Yes, you are."

"Then you all should give the new guy a chance," he said. "What new guy?"

"Yolanda's man. When they were over for dinner, y'all barely said two words to the man."

Robin shook her head. "That's not her man. That's her bodyguard."

"I'm sure he is guarding a lot more than just her body. I don't think I've ever seen chemistry like that. Not since you tried to play with me in the study group."

"I wasn't playing with you. I mean, who comes to a study group meeting shirtless?"

"Someone who had just left practice," Logan quipped. "And it was hot."

"Bullshit," Robin whispered, then kissed him on the cheek. "I tell you what, I'll put these boxes together if you want to go work your magic in the kitchen."

"Wow. You just want me in the kitchen chained to a stove?"

"Not chained—that's for the bed," she said with a wink. Logan rose to his feet and wiped his hands on his pant legs.

"Don't promise me a good time." Logan headed for the kitchen and Robin turned the local news on.

"This is a CBS 6 news exclusive. A local nurse speaks out about a culture of sexual harassment and assault at the hospital where she works."

Kamrie's face popped up on the TV. "What the hell?" Robin grabbed the remote and turned the volume up. As the blond news anchor gave the background on the exclusive, Robin called Logan into the living room.

"What's going on?" he asked, then looked at the screen. "Ah, shit. Why is she on TV?"

"Shh," Robin said as the interview began.

"Kamrie Bazal is a surgical nurse at Richmond Medical Center and she said she moved here from Atlanta because of the hospital's stellar reputation. But what she found when she arrived was something totally different."

The camera cut to a crying Kamrie. "This has turned out to be the worst decision of my life," she said, then wiped her eyes.

"Crocodile tears," Robin muttered.

"She's a good actress."

They focused in on her interview. "There is one doctor on staff who thought he was untouchable. He would flirt with me and I ignored it. We were oftentimes partnered on serious surgeries together. But when the hurricane hit the city last year and we all had to stay at the hospital for a twenty-four-hour shift, he took things to another level."

The reporter's voice-over began. "Bazal said that she was sexually assaulted that night in the doctor's office. Because there haven't been any charges, we aren't naming the surgeon. But according to Bazal, he has been suspended from the hospital while her allegations are investigated."

"I'm going to sue them for this slander!" Robin shouted.

"Calm down, babe," Logan said as he stroked her arm.

"Bazal said she was sexually assaulted by the surgeon during last year's hurricane that shut down the city and that assault led to pregnancy."

The camera cut back to Kamrie and her son, whose face was hidden. "My son is the best thing that has come out of this situation. I love him so much."

"Has the doctor taken responsibility for his son?" the reporter asked.

"No. He denies this is his son. Despite what the DNA test says."

Robin grabbed the remote and turned the TV off. "I can't wait to take her down. Why would she do this now?"

Logan shook his head. "It doesn't make much sense, but nothing about this whole situation has made sense."

"Logan, have you thought about accepting the offer from the hospital and walking away from all of this?"

"If I knew I wouldn't be putting patients' lives in danger, I'd do it. If I knew for sure that she was going to disappear and stop trying to ruin my reputation, I would. But this is not something I can come back from. They've checked every box."

"But there is one thing they forgot: You have people who love you, who will work for you to get the truth out there. What she's saying right now is full of lies and we have to make her stop."

"Thank you for being here for me."

Robin stroked his cheek. "I wish I had been there from the start. I feel like I'm one of those people who let you down."

"I was hurt more than anything, Rob. But I understand where you were coming from and how thinking I had an affair and a child was a knife that cut deep."

"But had she told this story from the beginning, there is no way I would've believed it. What's made her switch things up now?"

Logan rose from the sofa and shrugged. "I'm going to cook. You put these boxes together."

Robin blew him a kiss as he headed for the kitchen.

But inside she was seething with anger. Now it's one thing to try to destroy a marriage, but to try to ruin everything that Logan had built and label him a rapist?

It was taking everything in her not to get in her car and drive to that witch's house. She wished she had Yolanda's moxie and Nina's spunk. If she did, she would be at Kamrie's house with that woman in a headlock.

She couldn't do that, though. There were legal actions pending, and going after her would allow people to figure out the doctor she was talking about. Besides, Kamrie would get served with those papers tomorrow and have to come to court.

Once the real DNA test results came out, she was going to have to come up with a new story. And Logan would be able to clear his name before more dirt was thrown on it. Robin finished taping the boxes together and started wrapping up her books on the bookshelves. Then she decided to dust the shelves she had cleared and try not to think about the lies that the city of Richmond just heard about her man.

And this story was going to go viral. As soon as it did, people would start digging and this was going to hurt Logan.

Robin shook her head and reached for another box. How many books had she brought here?

She was about to reach for some books on the top shelf and her foot slipped from the stool underneath her. Before she could hit the floor, Logan was there to break her fall. "I knew you were doing too much," he said as they leaned against the sofa.

"I had all this angry energy. Guess it got the best of me."

Logan ran his fingers through her hair. "Yeah, you always clean angry."

Robin turned to face him. "Maybe I was daydreaming about knocking her out and my almost fall was the universe telling me to chill out."

"Or you're clumsy."

"Ha," she said, then kissed the end of his nose.

"I could tell stories about all the falls I've saved you from, but I won't."

She wrapped her arms around his neck. "And I appreciate that. Keep in mind, you aren't always the star athlete."

"Nah, you just made me nervous and I'd trip over myself."

Robin brushed her lips against his. "I made you nervous? I find that hard to believe."

Logan rubbed her back. "I know I wouldn't have made it this far without you, and when I thought I'd lost you, I didn't know how I was going to go forward."

"Thank God you won't have to find out. I'm never going to let you go—ever again."

Logan nibbled on her bottom lip. "You know what, we've got quite a bit of time before the jambalaya is ready. How do you want to kill the time, without falling down and hitting your head?"

"Um, you can take the books off the top shelves and I will make us some of that famous Richardson Bed and Breakfast iced tea. Alex brought me a care basket."

"With cookies?"

Robin shrugged. "That may be a good possibility, but I haven't decided if I'm sharing yet."

Logan crossed over to the bookshelf and started removing the books. "You're going to give me some cookies," he said.

"Aren't you just being a little presumptuous? Do you know how hard it is for me to get those cookies?"

"All you have to do is call Alex."

"And that's the hard part."

Logan shook his head as Robin walked into the kitchen.

Logan had gotten all of the books off the top shelves of the floor-to-ceiling bookshelves. How did this woman have the time to buy all of these books and the shelves in the time they were apart? Fun fact, he was going to donate half of these boxes to a woman's shelter.

By the time he got to the third bookshelf, he decided that more than half of these books had to go. And he'd let Robin know that this was the right thing to do.

"Wow," Robin said when she walked into the living room with a tray holding a pitcher of iced tea and cookies.

"Oh, you do love me," he said as he crossed over to her, then took the tray from her hands and set it on one of the empty shelves. "Can we talk about these books?"

"I needed something to do to occupy my time this summer," she said with a shrug.

"You read all of these books?" He pointed to the three full boxes.

"Most of them. I started with self-help and moved down to women's fiction. Then I was depressed and needed to read romance to get happy and stop thinking about shooting you every other day."

"Well, at least you're honest. How about we keep the books that brought you joy and donate the others."

She nodded in agreement, then reached for a cookie and handed it to him. Logan broke the cookie in half and took a bite. "These are amazing."

"I know," Robin said as she munched on her half of the cookie. "When we were little, Dad would bring twelve cookies home and tell us we could only have a cookie if we were really good. Of course, Mom would give us the cookies anyway. Alex and I learned that telling Mom we had a bad day at school meant we would get cookies. And whatever sweet talk she gave Dad at the end of the day must have worked because we never ran out of cookies."

"You have a lot of your mom in you, don't you?"

"That's what Dad says, but Nina is more like our mother than any of us. And she never got a chance to know her."

Logan stroked her cheek. "At least you had a chance to know your parents when you were younger. That's important."

She took his hand in hers. "Are we going to start crying now?"

"No. We're going to drink that amazing tea." He gave her a quick peck on the cheek. "Then I'm going to make dinner."

Robin handed him a glass of tea. "It's really good." She winked at him as she took a sip. Logan took a sip and nodded in agreement.

"Delicious."

"Almost as good as that jambalaya," she said with a smile.

"It's not ready and I knew you were in the kitchen too long."

She took his glass from his hand and set it on the empty shelf. Then she grabbed the remote for the stereo and turned it on. The smooth sounds of Marvin Gaye filled the town house and the couple swayed together. Robin leaned her head against his chest and Logan almost forgot that there was a world outside of this living room or that there was going to be hell to pay real soon. Did he really want Robin to be in the center of it?

Damn, she smelled so good.

"Logan," she moaned.

"Yes, baby?"

"Um, I think you need to go into the kitchen."

"Shit," he said as he let her go. He ran into the kitchen to check on their dinner. It was only a little scorched, which was a good thing. After moving the pot from the heat, he stirred it and added a few splashes of hot sauce to finish the meal off. Moments later, Robin skipped into the kitchen and wrapped her arms around Logan's waist.

"Can we eat now?"

"A little bit longer, babe, got to get all of the flavors to come together."

She kissed him on the back of his neck. "Okay then. I'll get the tea and set the table."

Before Logan could respond, his phone rang. Robin reached into his back pocket and handed it to him. He glanced at the screen and didn't know who the caller was. He hit ignore and handed the phone back to Robin.

"Who was that?"

"I don't know, that's why I didn't answer. Shit, no cornbread."

"Well, you made enough for us to have some tomorrow. And I'll make the cornbread."

"Cornbread or that cakey cornbread?"

"Here we go. You know you love my cornbread."

"All that's missing from your cornbread is buttercream icing and candles. It's a cake."

"And that crispy flat thing you make with the tang is not cornbread. It's almost a potato chip with too much pepper."

"You should be used to it by now and you love it more than you want to admit."

"Okay, then. Looks like you're going to be making the cornbread tomorrow."

"I knew this was a setup." Logan dipped a spoon into the pot and took a taste. Before he could tell Robin it was time to eat, his phone rang again. She pulled it from his pocket and handed it to him again. Logan shook his head when he looked at the screen. "Same strange number."

"Maybe you should answer it."

He hit the ignore button. "We're going to eat a peaceful dinner first."

Robin crossed over to the cabinet, where he assumed she kept the bowls. "Let's eat." She passed the bowls over to Logan.

After he filled them with the jambalaya, Logan headed into the dining room and set the bowls on the table. Then he reached his hand out to Robin so that they could say a prayer before eating. Once they said, "Amen," Logan kissed the back of Robin's hand.

"What if we move to Florida when all of this is over?" Logan asked.

"That was the retirement plan."

"True, but we could always retire early, become beach bums, and do charity work."

"Yeah, I'm not ready to slide into retirement life right now. Don't you have a friend who owns a business in Miami?"

"Man, I haven't talked to Jon in years. He is the gaming master these days."

"Maybe he has a campus like Google and needs a doctor on staff. Because I know you and that whole retired mentality is going to last a good week."

Logan laughed. "They say you're supposed to marry someone smarter than you and clearly I did that."

Chapter 20

Robin was stuffed and wanted nothing more than to leave the dishes for later. But her inner child, who had to wash dishes after dinner every night, wouldn't let her. Logan followed her into the kitchen to help with the dishes, since he'd messed up the kitchen anyway. She couldn't help but think back to the early days of their marriage. Robin expected some hard days, but the hell of the last six months was never supposed to be a part of the plan.

It was all right, though. They were going to fight together and anyone who stood in their way was going to catch hell.

"What are you thinking over there, Double R?"

She smiled at her husband. "I was just thinking about us and everything we've gone through these last six months. I mean, we had a lifetime of bullshit dumped on us and I don't want to deal with that again."

"Me neither. Because this ain't what I promised you when we took our vows."

Robin dried her hands and crossed over to Logan. "You know what you did promise me, though?"

"What's that?" He drew her into his arms and brushed his lips against her cheek.

"That you're going to hold me until I go to sleep," she said.

"It's a little early for bed, isn't it?"

"Depends on what you want to do in the bed."

"Well, you know what's up." They headed for the bedroom. Logan laughed as he looked at the bed. "This is staying here, right?"

"Yes, and you can stop clowning my bed."

"It's the right size, for you."

Robin hopped on the bed and slowly stripped out of her clothes. "At least I'm willing to share my space with you," she said with a wink.

"And thank you for sharing it with me." Logan eased onto the bed and dove between her thighs. He stroked her wetness until she moaned. As she purred, Logan replaced his fingers with his tongue and Robin arched into his kiss. He made her feel so good as his tongue lashed her throbbing bud. She held on to the back of his neck as he licked and sucked her into submission.

"Yes, yes, yes," she cried as her thighs trembled. The heat of her orgasm washed over her body and she melted into the sheets.

"Best dessert ever," he said as he pulled his clothes off.

"Glad you enjoyed it. Because I know I did." Robin ran her hand across his chest as he snuggled up in the bed beside her.

"You know that was just the beginning," he said as he brought his lips down on top of hers. Robin wrapped her leg around his hip as they kissed. She needed him inside her. Wanted to feel every inch of his hardness deep inside.

She reached down and rubbed his hardness until he was wet with drops of precum. "Damn, baby," he moaned as her hand moved up and down.

Robin rolled over and straddled her husband. Locking eyes, Logan gripped her hips and Robin ground against him. They fell into a rhythmic dance. Robin held on to his shoulders and met her husband stroke for stroke.

Their moans filled the air like jazz music. Covered in sweat, they collapsed against each other and closed their eyes. "This is why I married you," she quipped.

"I feel so used," he joked.

"You have not been used at all. A fair exchange is not a robbery."

"Good, that means we . . ." Logan's phone rang again.

"You're just going to have to answer it," Robin said as she inched to the edge of the bed and grabbed his pants. After taking his phone out, she handed it to him. "Please just answer it."

"Dr. Baptiste," he said as he answered. "Um, I have no comment on that. How did you get this number?" Logan ended the call and tossed his phone on the nightstand.

"Who was that?"

"The media. They put two and two together."

"Probably because we filed the papers in family court," Robin said as she shook her head. "If I had known she was going to go on TV and tell these lies, I would've never suggested that you make this move."

"Come here," he said as he tugged at her waist. "We

knew this was a possibility before Kamrie got on TV with her lies. We just have to swerve and regroup."

"Do we need to call Liam in on this?" Robin asked.

Logan stroked her thigh. "At this moment, nope. I just want to lie here with my wife—not my lawyer." He looked up at the wall in front of the bed. "No TV?"

She rolled her eyes. "You know I hate having a TV in the bedroom."

"I understand why now. I think I had a fight with the one in our bedroom after someone sent me some divorce papers."

Robin sighed and stroked his cheek. "I'm sorry I did that."

"Me too. That hurt a lot, Robin. You know I can't live without you."

She closed her eyes and pulled him closer. "Logan . . ."

He brought his finger to her lips. "I just want you to know that I would never choose another woman over you."

"I know that and I should've believed it from the start. But, well, you know what set me off."

"Yeah. But let's go back to May, when we were look- ing to adopt a child. Do you still want to do that?"

Robin sighed. "Bringing a child into all of this wouldn't be fair to him or her right now. Or all three of them."

"Three of them?"

"You know I wanted three babies. But definitely not spaced as far apart as me and my sisters. It always felt like it was me and Alex versus Yolanda and Nina. You know, with stuff around the house, but out in those streets, you messed with one of us, you had it with all of us."

"You and your sisters were a gang."

She smacked him on the shoulder. "We were not a gang."

"Keep telling yourself that, it doesn't make it true."

"Whatever, Dr. Baptiste." Robin glanced at the digital display on her bedside clock. "It's really too early to call it a night."

"That's where the TV would come in handy."

"Or we—and by we, I mean you—could finish cleaning the kitchen and I'll draw us a bath. I have an amazing bath bomb that's good for stress."

"You had me at bath." Logan leaned in and kissed Robin slow and deep. Breaking the kiss, he winked at her, then said, "Don't have the water boiling, please."

"Oh, stop! Why don't you bring up some tea when you're done. The pitcher in the refrigerator has bourbon in it."

"Gotcha," he said, then slipped his boxers on and headed downstairs. Robin dashed into the bathroom and started filling the garden tub with water. She couldn't help but wonder if that call had really been the media or something else.

It's time for you to trust your husband. Just stop it. Robin went into the linen closet and grabbed her mango bath bomb. She dropped it in the water, then grabbed two shower sheets for her and Logan.

Moments later, he was walking into the bathroom with two full glasses of the spiked tea.

"That was a quick cleanup."

"You have a dishwasher. I'm using it," he said as he gave her a slow once-over. "I was about to hand-wash those dishes but I knew you were up here naked and wet."

"I haven't gotten in the bathtub yet."

Logan set the glasses on the counter and pulled Robin into his arms. "I know there's one spot that gets wet without the use of the tub."

"You are something else." She tugged at his boxers. "Get naked and get in the tub."

"Yes, ma'am." But before he did step into the water, Logan slipped his hand between Robin's thighs. And he was right. She was dripping wet with desire. "Told you so." He stepped out of his boxers and into the tub. Logan sat down and then Robin joined him, sitting with her back against his chest. The soothing scent of the mango and jasmine oil enveloped them, giving the couple a feeling of peace and stillness.

Logan massaged Robin's shoulders and rubbed bath oil across her back. "Mmm," she moaned sweetly. "I was supposed to be helping you relax."

"You are. I've always liked touching your body. Now I see how you stay so soft."

"You mean to tell me after all these years, you just figured this out?"

Logan shrugged as he stroked the small of her back. "I thought it was cocoa butter and black girl magic."

"You get an A for effort, doc."

"You should've been a professor at Xavier," he quipped.

"And your grades would've been better in undergrad if you had focused more. You killed it in med school."

"Yeah, I did. That's why all of this bullshit going on right now is . . ."

"No. This bath is supposed to remove stress, not reset it."

Logan kissed her neck and then leaned against the

wall of the tub. "Lean back," he said. She did and he put his arms around her waist. They sat in silence until the water went cold. Now it was the perfect time to go to bed. The couple rose from the tub and dried each other off. Logan cupped Robin's cheek. "I've missed this."

"Me too."

"Let's go to sleep, okay?"

"We will as long as you keep your hands to yourself."

"Don't throw your leg around my waist and we're going to have a good night's sleep," he said with a wink. "Because I have to sleep naked."

"Then no spooning, all right?"

Logan dropped his towel. "I make no promises."

"Then you must not want to sleep. But to help you out, I'm going to put on my flannel PJs."

"That's cruel." He followed her into the bedroom, and true to her word, Robin put on a pair of black and red flannel pajamas with the feet sewn in.

"Why in the hell did you get those?" Logan asked.

"I get cold at night and you weren't here."

"Not because I didn't want to be."

She crossed over to him and wrapped her arms around him. "I don't know how I'm going to ever make this up to you."

"Here's a hint: After tonight, burn these." Logan ran his hand down the shapeless garment.

"Got it." She leaned in and gave him a slow kiss. "But FYI, the zipper is in the front."

"Good night, Robin."

* * *

The one thing Kamrie didn't expect after going on TV with her story was a call from him.

"I thought your wife said we could never speak again. Why are you calling me now, Thomas?"

"Kamrie, what's going on with you right now?"

"I'm getting what's mine."

"By ruining another doctor's reputation?" Thomas asked.

"You seem to be doing fine. What the hell do you want?"

He sighed into the phone and then his voice got really low. "There was a man here asking a lot of questions about you and us."

"Do you know who the man was?"

"Some detective, I think. Kam, what have you done to cause people to look into your past?"

"Is it my past that you're concerned about or your own?"

"That's not fair and you know if things were . . ."

"Save the bullshit for the next nurse," Kamrie snapped. "You still let her lead you around by your little balls and you just do what she says."

"I have a career and you know I . . ."

"I know you're a coward and I'm doing what I have to do to take care of me and mine. If you're still happy riding your wife's coattails in Atlanta, leave me alone."

He chuckled and Kamrie hung up the phone. How dare he laugh at her. All of this was his damned fault. Why couldn't he have just kept his promises?

If only Logan was really Jean's father. He would make sure that she and her son would be good. And since he didn't want to make a life with her, she'd just dent his wallet. Why wouldn't he want to have a family with her? He couldn't get that with his wife. What had changed?

Granted, Logan wasn't walking around the hospital crying about what was going on after his wife's surgery. But when she'd overheard the story of Logan and Robin, she figured he'd be easy pickings.

Much easier than her situation in Atlanta. Logan's career didn't depend on his wife and Kamrie loved that. But it hadn't mattered in the end. If Dr. Carter's plan didn't work, then she was going to have to go back to Atlanta and drop the bomb on Dr. Thomas Lacy and his bitch of a wife, Valerie. Like, surprise, Thomas is a father.

It would serve Valerie's obnoxious ass right. She was old enough to be that man's mother. Did she really think she could satisfy him beyond her funding his dreams?

Kamrie wasn't in love with Thomas, but she did enjoy the scandalous nights at the hospital, in five-star hotels, and even in the basement of Thomas and Valerie's house.

She looked at the phone, ready to save the number that he'd called from, but she realized he had called from an unknown number. At least he was better at covering his tracks now.

Chapter 21

Robin and Logan woke up before her five a.m. alarm went off. "Morning," he said, then pulled her into his arms.

"It still looks like night to me."

"Yeah. We've got a big day."

She nodded and kissed him on the chin. "I'm going to make sure we have someone to serve Kamrie this morning. I'm thinking we should make sure she gets served at home. The folks at the hospital don't really need to know what's going on right now."

"Agreed. Might get another false DNA test."

Robin rolled her eyes, her mind flashing back to the day she got that DNA test at their front door. "And we should probably get moving so that you can get some clothes."

"Actually, I have a bag in the trunk. No need to fight rush hour traffic before we have to."

"Wish you had told me that before I set this alarm," she said as the phone began to chime. A few seconds later, Logan's alarm went off as well.

"Was going to surprise you with breakfast," he said with a wink.

"I'll still pretend I'm surprised. But I'll make the coffee." The couple rose from the bed and Logan grabbed his discarded pants and pulled them on.

They headed down to the kitchen and Robin pulled out two avocados from the refrigerator. "You know what I want," she said with a smile.

"Avocado toast and eggs. So predictable," he quipped, then got to work making the food.

Robin started the coffee and opened the fridge to grab the orange juice. She poured Logan a glass and set it next to him.

"You're too sweet," he said, then sipped the juice. Logan made the toast sort of like French toast. Robin could never make her mashed avocados taste like his. And Logan never shared his secrets.

After making the toast, he fried a couple of eggs for them and Robin poured them full mugs of coffee. Logan took his coffee black in the morning. Robin needed cream and sugar this morning. She didn't want to admit it, but she was nervous about what was going to happen when Kamrie got her papers. Was she going to go back on TV and name Logan? What would her family think about all of this? She needed her father's strength today, but she didn't want to involve him in all of this.

He said he was going to support her no matter what. Looking at the clock on the stove, she knew it was too early to call him.

"All right," Logan said. "Breakfast is ready."

"Great."

Logan took her hand in his as they bowed their heads in prayer. Robin asked God to let this day prove that she and Logan were doing the right thing. That their marriage was going to survive and they could go back to their happily ever after.

A feeling of peace washed over her and she knew that everything was going to be fine.

"Amen," Logan said.

"Amen," she replied, then kissed him on the cheek. "One day, you're going to have to give me the secret to your avocado toast."

"Nah, knowing how much you love it, I'm playing that close to the chest so you can never let me go."

"Oh, you are so dirty."

He shrugged and grabbed his coffee. "Whatever it takes to keep you in my life, I'm going to do it."

"You know I'm not going anywhere, ever again."

"Holding you to that."

After eating breakfast, they each took a shower, then dressed and headed for the office together. "Do you think I should make a statement to the media?" he asked as he drove.

"No. We're going to try to keep your name out of this for as long as we can."

"Right. But I just don't want other people to control the narrative."

"At this point, if anyone says your name, we're in position for a huge lawsuit. Nothing that witch has said can be proven. You haven't been charged with assaulting her and that little boy isn't your son. And when we find out who faked those DNA results, we're suing them, too."

"Remind me to stay on your good side."

"I thought you already knew that." She squeezed his thigh.

Logan grabbed her hand and kissed it. "Yolanda is

the one I really should be worried about. She's the real gangster."

"Obviously not. I'd love to know what's really going on with her and why she's in need of a bodyguard. Alex doesn't even know; she would've told me already."

"As if you need another thing on your plate. I'm sure Pops is taking care of her. Sheldon wouldn't let anything happen to his girls."

"I know, but I'd still like to know what's going on with my sister. It was bad enough when we almost lost Nina." Robin still felt sick when she thought about her sister's near fatal accident in Charlotte. Nina had pulled out in front of an eighteen-wheeler, and for a few days, it looked as if she wasn't going to make it.

Thank God she had pulled through.

"But you didn't. Remember that. She's on an island somewhere being a newlywed."

Robin snapped her fingers. "That reminds me, I have to send them a basket. I really feel like I put a cloud over her wedding."

"I'm sure you didn't."

When they arrived at the office, a couple of Robin's colleagues had shock etched on their faces. Everyone at the office knew Robin was getting a divorce. She made it clear that she wanted nothing to do with Dr. Logan Baptiste, yet here they were.

"Sheila," Robin said to the receptionist. "Is Clark in his office?"

"Yes," she replied. "And I'm super happy to see you guys."

Logan smiled as Robin led him to the huge corner office. "Guess everyone knew we were over."

"Clark was handling my divorce."

"Then this isn't going to be awkward at all," he said as he opened the door to the office.

Clark looked up from his computer as they walked in. "Well, well, look what the cat drug in."

"Good to see you, too. How were your holidays?" Robin asked as she and Logan sat down.

"The holidays were amazing. But I have to say seeing you two together leaves me happy and confused right now," he said as he looked from Robin to Logan. "I'm no longer filing these divorce papers, right?"

"That's correct," Logan said.

"So, what's going on now?" Clark asked.

"I'm taking Logan on as a client in the phony fatherhood scam with Kamrie," Robin said. "I wanted to let you know and make sure you're okay with it."

"Yeah, that's just fine and it's good to see that you all are trying to get to the bottom of this."

"Great, because she should be getting served today."

Clark nodded. "Good. Cases like this make a mockery of the family court system. Frauds like this make it harder for real parents who need assistance."

Robin sucked her teeth and nodded. "I wish there was some way for this to stay private, but since she took her lies to the media, some reporter is going to put two and five together and think they have a story."

"And we'll have a libel or slander suit." Clark turned to Logan. "But I have to ask, are these allegations true?"

"Hell no." Logan's face burned with anger.

Robin placed her hand on his thigh. "Calm down, we have to ask these questions."

"Sorry, Clark," Logan said. "But I've been fighting against lies for too long."

The attorney nodded. "I get it. But when we sue everybody, I want to make sure we got the whole truth on our side."

"We absolutely do have the truth on our side."

"Great, because you two are one of my favorite couples and I don't like people fucking with my friends." Clark shook his head. "Let's make this a happy New Year for everybody but that nurse."

For the next three hours, Clark and Robin laid out everything that could happen after the summons was delivered to Kamrie. The court date was probably going to be two weeks out because of the holiday. But afterward, things were going to start moving fast. Robin told Logan she was going to make sure the DNA test was handled by a separate lab that wasn't related to the hospital.

"Good idea," he muttered.

"And here's the hard part," Clark interjected. "Do you still want to work at Richmond Medical?"

Robin wanted to know the answer to this question as well. She had her opinions, but she wasn't ready to tell him what she thought—yet.

Logan squeezed the bridge of his nose. "I want to stay and see if I can get Cooper Drugs out of the hospital. I made some enemies in that fight. I feel like a lot of what's going on right now is because of that. But I gave so much of myself to this hospital."

"And what are you getting in return?" Robin asked in a low voice.

"What do you think we should do?" Logan asked.

Robin waved her hand. "Nope. Not going to make that

decision for you. Remember, you wanted to keep your reputation intact when this all started and that's why you didn't fight this whole thing head-on before it got out of hand." Robin's voice had a little more fury than she meant for it to have.

"Do I need to step out for a minute?" Clark asked.

"Yes," Logan said.

"No."

"Yes," Clark said. "This has moved from an attorney-client conversation to a husband and wife one. I'm going to grab some coffee."

Once they were alone, Logan turned his chair to face Robin. "All right, let's get this out," he said.

Robin wiped her face and stared into his eyes. "I don't want you working there anymore."

"I know."

"And it has nothing to do with Kamrie, but it's about how they're treating you and you're trying to do the right thing. If they are willing to do all of this to you, why do you owe them anything?"

"It's not about them, it's the patients."

"And you think that the hospital is the only place where you can help people?"

"Maybe the hospital is my safety net."

She took his hand in hers. "But why? You're a brilliant doctor, and right now the hospital is holding you back. Maybe it's time to expose the truth and move on. Are you ready to do that?"

Logan tilted his head to the side. "I'm not sure."

"This has to be your decision. If you asked me to walk away from this firm, I'd have to be ready for it."

"You're right and it's pretty clear that the longer I stick around trying to make changes from the inside, the more I'm going to be hurt by it."

"So, what's our next move?" she asked, then squeezed his hand.

"We're going to fight and expose them. I'm going to call Liam and make sure his Cooper Drugs information has been vetted and then we're going for their necks."

Robin smiled. "I'm here for it."

"Then let's do it." Logan leaned forward and kissed Robin's cheek. "I love you for having my back like this."

"We're a team. And a pretty unbeatable one, at that."

A few minutes later, Clark returned to the office with his coffee. "Everything all good in here?"

"Perfect," Robin said. "We need to meet with our investigator before we move forward with any litigation against the hospital."

Clark nodded and clasped his hands together. "All right, I'm ready."

Robin and Logan stood up, then shook hands with Clark. "Do you think you can schedule us for tomorrow morning?" Logan asked.

He pulled his calendar up on his computer screen. "Ten-thirty works for me."

"We'll see you then," Robin said as Logan pulled out his phone and called Liam.

"Liam," Logan said when his friend answered the phone. "What's going on?"

"Are you in your office? Robin and I need to talk to you about your investigation into Cooper Drugs."

"Actually, just left the office. I'm heading for downtown to check out a few things."

"Cool. Can you meet us at the house?"

"Yeah. I'll be there about one-thirty. I think I found proof that your Dr. Carter is on the take and a paper trail."

"That's exactly what we need. I might even have time to grab some jambalaya from Robin's place."

"Oh no. If you made it over there, then it is missing all the good stuff." Liam laughed.

"All right then, but ribs are out."

"Damn. I guess I'll bring my own food and y'all can eat the rabbit food."

"See you soon." After hanging up with Liam, Logan turned to Robin.

"Let me guess, he wants some greasy meat for lunch?" she asked.

"He's bringing his own."

She smiled. "Good, now I don't have to worry about the house smelling like meat all night." She leaned in and kissed Logan on the cheek. "Let's go kick some ass."

Chapter 22

When Robin and Logan arrived at their house, they headed for the dining room. It didn't take long for Robin to turn it into a war room. She had three whiteboards with photographs of the people who needed to be taken down affixed to them. First was Kamrie.

Robin had written everything that she'd done underneath her picture: *Fake DNA. Sexual harassment allegation, previous allegations against another doctor.*

The next board had Dr. Carter's picture on it. *Payoff from the drug company. Risking patients' lives for money. Trying to play my husband like he's stupid*, her notes read. Logan had to laugh at that last remark.

The final board had the hospital building on it, but no notes. "What's up with this board?"

Robin pulled her reading glasses off and looked up from her laptop. "Not sure yet. If Dr. Carter is acting alone, we may not have a case against the hospital. But I'm thinking they may be liable for the fake DNA test. That took some inside planning. Did Kamrie pay someone in the lab and has this happened before?"

Logan held up his hands. "Hold on, Olivia Pope," he said. "We don't have to take the whole world down."

"They almost brought our world down. Do you think I care about these . . ." Robin closed her laptop. "I'm just looking at every option. They owe us a lot more than whatever we can get from any lawsuit."

He crossed over to her and wrapped his arms around her shoulders. "Baby, we're going to get this right, but we don't have to be on attack mode with the world."

She patted his hand and sighed. "I'm just so angry. And I want a pound of flesh for all of the time that we spent apart and wasted when we could've been getting our life where we wanted it to be."

"We're going to get back on track and be even better." He turned her chair around and knelt in front of her. "I know how painful all of this bullshit has been; I've gone through it with you. Hell, I've felt it more than you could ever know."

"Then why aren't you angry? Why aren't you ready to make these bastards pay?"

Logan stroked her cheek. "Oh, I'm very angry. I'm angry as hell. But there's nothing we can do about the past and the last thing I want to do is hurt the hospital."

"The safety net that is weighing you down?"

"A lot of people get saved there. I want the right people to pay and we're going to make that happen."

Robin took his face in her hands. "So, I'm going too far?"

"Just a little bit. But I love you, though. Let's take a break." Logan stood up and held his hand out to Robin. "I've still got some fresh tomatoes and mozzarella."

"Mmm," she said with a smile, "any bread?"

He nodded. "And spinach."

"You really knew I was coming home, didn't you?"

"My faith has always been strong." Logan kissed her on the forehead and headed for the kitchen. Robin followed him and took her regular seat at the breakfast nook. Logan gathered the ingredients for the grilled tomato and cheese sandwiches.

"You got some noodles?" she asked.

"I do, and some marinara sauce. Sounds like we're having a side of spaghetti with these sandwiches. One day, we're going to stop eating like college students."

Robin shrugged. "It keeps us young." She was about to hop off the stool and kiss her husband when the doorbell rang. "That must be Liam."

"Of course, because he knows how to interrupt a good thing."

"Um, you know we need him." Robin winked at him, then bounded to the door.

While Logan chopped cheese, tomatoes, and onions, he listened to Liam and Robin banter about Liam's low-key crush on Alex and how he hated all vegetables. "Damn, woman. You've been doing some work. I guess that's why you've got the doctor in the kitchen."

"I can hear you," Logan called out.

"Good." Liam walked into the kitchen and set his food on the edge of the counter. "Aww, the famous spaghetti and grilled cheese. If I had known you were making a classic, I would've skipped the ribs."

"Yeah right," Robin said. "I bet you got coleslaw and fries."

"You think you know me, Double R. I got potato salad

and fries," Liam said as he opened his container. "And I have good news."

"What's that?" Logan asked as he filled a pot with water.

"I got a look at Dr. Carter's financials and unless they are handing out bonuses at the hospital or Uber is a hell of a side gig . . ."

"What do you mean?" Robin asked as she swiped one of Liam's fries.

"He's been getting forty thousand dollars a month and he's been getting it for the last two years, like clockwork."

Logan let out a low whistle. "That's damn near a million dollars."

"Enough of a motive to keep that killer drug circulating through the hospital," Robin said. "And you said you heard him talking with a woman from Cooper Drugs, right?"

Logan nodded. "Liam, you sure that money has come from Cooper Drugs?"

Liam nodded. "It's been funneled through an offshore account that leads back to—wait for it—Veronica O'Malley."

Robin's mouth dropped open. "The vice president at Cooper Drugs?" Liam shot her an appreciative look. Robin shrugged.

"I Googled her," she said.

"And," Logan said as he pulled his phone out of his pocket, "I've got a picture of them together."

"Let's eat," Liam said. "Because we have this in the bag."

After Logan fixed plates for him and Robin, the trio sat at the bar and ate in a comfortable silence. Robin stroked Logan's thigh. "This nightmare is about to be over," she said.

"Let's hope so," Logan said.

"Got a question," Liam asked. "Your sister, the bossy one, is she single?"

Robin shook her head. "Liam, you are not ready for that kind of smoke. Alex isn't the one or the two."

"But she is gorgeous. Your father has some beautiful kids."

"Don't get put out," Logan said.

After lunch, Liam left his files with Robin, then headed back to his office. Once the couple was alone, they decided to catch up on their HGTV shows. While they snuggled up on the sofa, Logan wished that he didn't have to move an inch for the rest of his life. Robin felt so good against his thighs. He ran his fingers through her hair and smiled. "I've missed this," she whispered.

"Me too. And I'm not talking Chip and Joanna here," he said, nodding toward the TV.

"When all of this is over, maybe we should actually do one of these projects." Robin looked up at Logan with a smile on her full lips. She could've asked him to walk naked down the middle of Interstate 95 south and he would've said yes.

"There's something else I wanted to talk to you about when this is over," he said quietly.

Robin closed her eyes. "What's that?"

"Do you still want to look into adoption?"

Logan felt her stiffen. Maybe he should've kept his mouth closed. But he knew how important it was for her to have a child and if that's what she needed and wanted . . .

"I don't know, Logan. After all of this and . . . I don't know if I want to bring a child into this craziness. Every time you're Googled in the future, this is going to be one of the first things that shows up. Kamrie isn't going to go away easily."

"You can see into the future now?"

"No, but that crazy bitch doesn't just disappear."

"You have a point there. Maybe we can help her disappear."

Robin pointed to the screen, where the renovation crew was laying a concrete slab for a patio expansion. "Like that?"

"No, because that would be a crime."

"Wishful thinking."

"What if we offered her a settlement to disappear?"

"Hell no. Pay her off for lying? Fu—"

Logan patted her thigh. "Got it, but I was just putting an idea out there."

"We're not doing that. Consider that a bad idea."

He kissed her on the forehead. "Got it. But this is going to get uglier before it clears up."

"How much more are we going to face?" Robin exhaled in frustration. "We're done for the day. All we have to do now is wait for her to answer the summons."

"Yep. Got an idea."

"Hope it's better than your last one," she quipped.

"Ice cream."

"Great idea."

"And chocolate sauce."

"Even better."

"And you getting out of these clothes."

She sat up and unbuttoned the top few buttons of her blouse. "You're batting a thousand now, darling."

Logan rose from the sofa. "Meet me upstairs," he said.

Robin rushed upstairs as Logan prepared ice cream sundaes that they weren't going to eat from a bowl. This had been a tradition they'd started on a July afternoon in New Orleans. They had been walking back from the grand opening of Ice Cream 504 on Jena Street after an alumni cookout at Xavier. The small batch of homemade ice cream had been bursting with flavor, but since it was super humid and hot outside, Robin's strawberry sugar cone had started melting and Logan licked the cream from her finger. His tongue against her skin made her so hot that she had been ready to strip naked on the sidewalk and make love to him. Logan had felt her desire and they'd ducked in an alley where he'd drizzled melted ice cream across her bosom. As he licked the sweet cream from the tops of her breasts, Robin had melted like her ice cream. They couldn't get home fast enough to make love. Now anytime ice cream was mentioned, the couple knew that it wasn't about going to get scoops and cones.

Robin stripped out of her clothes and then ran her hand across the down comforter on the bed. It felt good to be home. Good to be in her bedroom, knowing that she was here for good now and this was and always would be her home.

Logan's love hadn't changed. Her heart hadn't been broken. She was safe to love her husband and not worry that another woman had replaced her. Maybe she believed it because she had allowed herself to believe that she'd lost him because she had lost herself.

She eased onto the bed and smiled. Moments later, Logan walked in with a tray of ice cream, chocolate chips, and whipped cream. "Didn't have strawberry," he said as he nodded toward the bowl of vanilla ice cream.

"We can make do," she said with a wink.

"Absolutely," he said as he crossed over to the bed and set the tray on the nightstand. Logan eased onto the bed and pulled naked Robin into his arms. She stroked the back of his neck as he ran his tongue across her bottom lip.

"I swear you're sweeter than any kind of ice cream." He reached for the bowl of ice cream and spooned up a scoop. He smoothed the cold treat across her breasts and she shivered with delight. Logan teased her nipples with his fingers and the ice cream. Robin's body responded to his touch as if she was in a sensual trance. When his tongue replaced his finger, she moaned like a saxophone hitting a high note. Logan reached for the can of whipped cream and drew a line of the cream down the center of her stomach. Then he sprinkled the chocolate chips on top, making her his sweet treat. Logan licked the cream away slowly as she arched her body into his kiss. Easing down her body with his tongue, Logan made Robin writhe under his touch. Once he reached the valley of her thighs, she was trembling with the anticipation of feeling his lips against her throbbing pearl of desire.

But Logan had other plans, slipping his finger inside her as he reversed course and licked the remainder of the cream and chocolate chips from her torso and breasts. As he licked, he pressed his finger in and out. She felt as if she was going to explode with each lick and thrust of his finger.

"Oh . . . oh, Logan," she moaned as he took her nipple between his teeth.

"Ready for some more?" he whispered.

"Need. You. Inside."

He winked at her as he reached for more ice cream, then traced her lips with the melting cream. Logan kissed the sweetness away as he toyed with her femininity. She shivered as he nearly brought her to a climax with his finger. She pressed her hand against his chest and pushed him on his back.

"My turn," she said as she took the spoon from his hand and dipped it in the bowl. She spooned the melting cream across his hard cock. In a swift motion, she took the length of him into her mouth, slurping the sweetness off his sensitive muscle as he ran his fingers through her hair.

"Damn, baby," he moaned. Robin didn't stop, giving him a taste of his seductive medicine and bringing him so close to a climax with her hot mouth. Logan pulled back from her, gritting his teeth. "Ugh, you win. You win."

"Not yet," she said as she mounted his erection. Robin wrapped her arms around his neck and treated him to a slow grind. Up and down, up and down. Logan thrust forward and Robin matched his energy, giving as good as she got. Logan flipped her over and buried his mouth in her neck. They ground against each other, falling into a sensual rhythm. As they reached a thunderous climax, Robin closed her eyes and whispered how much she loved her husband. Logan kissed her sticky cheek.

"I love you too, boo."

Despite how sticky they were, Logan and Robin lay in each other's arms, basking in the afterglow of their lovemaking. "This is going to be hell to clean up," she said.

"You're the one who loses it over ice cream."

"Um, ice cream and your tongue," she corrected. "You know I can't eat strawberry ice cream around other people, right?"

"Good. Because that's my treat. We need to go visit New Orleans this summer and buy the whole lot of Ice Cream 504's strawberry flavor."

"Then drive slow back to the hotel and see what we can do in the car with that melted ice cream."

"You mean how many times we can do it in the car on the way to the hotel."

She kissed his chin and rolled her eyes. "We should probably get in the shower."

"Not yet. I just want to hold you," he said. "This feels like heaven. Sticky, but heaven."

Robin closed her eyes and exhaled slowly. He was right, it was heaven to be in his arms.

Chapter 23

Kamrie read the summons for the third time in the three hours since that little punk on a bike rolled up to her and said she'd been served. Logan and that woman had a nerve. They wanted to take her to family court to prove that he wasn't Jean's father. This was not a part of the plan! How was she going to keep the true paternity of her son a secret? What if that bitch in Atlanta found out about Jean? Would she try to take him away?

"This can't be happening," she muttered as she paced back and forth. According to the papers, the case was going to head to court in two weeks. How was she going to get out of this?

"I could go back to Atlanta. I can't . . ."

"Kamrie?" Dr. Carter asked as he walked into the break room. "Are you all right?"

"No, I'm not. Your little plan got me sued and put under investigation here!"

"Shh," he said. "We can't have this discussion here."

"Then where, Dr. Carter? I did what you asked and what do I get? Served a family court summons."

"That's good. Now Dr. Baptiste will be in the court

documents. His name can be linked to your story and anything else he says will be tainted by the scandal."

"And what about me? My son?"

Carter shrugged. "Kamrie, this is bigger than you. I thought you understood that."

"I understood that I was going to be rewarded. I understood that you were supposed to . . ." She stopped talking when two nursing assistants walked in.

"We can finish this later, Nurse Bazal," Dr. Carter said, then turned on his heel. As she watched him walk out of the room, she realized that she had been played and this was going to be the last time.

Logan watched Robin smooth cocoa butter on her shapely legs. He loved her legs and the way cocoa butter made them shine. "What?" she asked when she caught his gaze.

"Just admiring my wife. My beautiful, brilliant wife." Logan crossed over to her and planted a kiss on her forehead. "What are we going to do tonight, and don't say watch HGTV."

"I have an idea. New Year's Eve is a few days away. Let's go to New Orleans and pretend we don't have a huge court date in two weeks."

"As great as that sounds, do you think that's a good idea?"

Robin sighed. "I just want to get away from all of this. We have so much going on right now and I want to just forget for a little while."

Logan took her face in his hands. "And when did we start running from our problems?"

She rolled her eyes. "Fine. But let's get out of the house tonight. Go catch a movie or something."

"You and I in a dark movie theater? I like that."

She elbowed him in the side. "You're a mess, Dr. Baptiste."

Logan laughed. "I remember the first time you called me that. I knew I was going to make it through medical school because I loved the way you sounded when you said *Dr. Baptiste.*"

Robin closed her eyes as if she had been taken back to the day when they talked about their futures. Her law school dreams and his acceptance to medical school. "Yeah, I remember telling you that you'd better hope I got into law school because I was going to handle your malpractice cases after you called yourself stitching my finger when I cut it making those steak fajitas."

Logan reached for her hand. "Can't even see a scar. I did a brilliant job."

She rolled her eyes. "Let me get dressed."

"Don't let me stop you, I was enjoying the show."

Robin chuckled as she reached for her blue and white leggings. "Well, if you can watch, you can help. Pass me my shirt."

"How about no?" Logan pulled her into his arms. "You look so much better without it."

"I thought we were getting out of the house, doc?"

"Seemed like a good idea when you said it at first, but now . . ." He captured her lips in a slow kiss. Robin melted against his chest and moaned as his tongue danced across her bottom lip.

"Lo . . . gan," she moaned.

Before he could reply, the doorbell rang. "Damn it," he muttered. "Are you expecting a package or something?"

She shook her head as he dropped his arms. "And since you're dressed, you have the honor of seeing what Liam wants."

"If it's Liam, I'm going to punch him in the face," Logan quipped as he headed for the stairs. When Logan got to the door, he was shocked to see Kamrie standing on his front steps.

"Shit," he muttered as he cracked the door open. "What are you doing here?"

"We need to talk."

"You can't be here. We'll talk in court."

"Logan, you need to know what's going on and . . ."

"Leave." He attempted to close the door and she stuck her foot inside before he could close it.

"You need to listen to me!"

"Logan," Robin said from the staircase. "What the hell is going on here?"

Robin wanted to rush to the front door and claw Kamrie's eyes out. Why was this lying bitch at her house? She closed her eyes, took a breath, then crossed over to her husband. "Why is she here?"

"Because I need to talk to both of you," Kamrie said.

"Is your attorney present? Otherwise, we don't have anything to talk about."

"No? Do you know that Dr. Carter is setting you up and he's hoping that your little lawsuit will discredit you at the hospital?"

Logan shot Robin a look. "Should we hear her out?"

"She should get out!" Robin exclaimed.

"We're all victims here," Kamrie said.

Robin's body tensed. Did she really say that? "You started this with your lies."

She shook her head. "This is bigger than that, and if you can put aside your anger, we can fix this."

Robin squeezed the bridge of her nose and counted to ten. She wanted to punch her in the face. Wanted to knock her out and stomp on her as if she were the first embers of a forest fire. "You broke whatever needs to be fixed, so don't come here acting like you're trying to help."

Kamrie rolled her eyes and slapped her hand on her hip. "I'm trying to help and . . ."

"Get the fuck out of my house!" Robin yelled. "You don't get to start the fire and bring the water to put it out."

She smirked at Robin, and Logan grabbed Robin's arm. She hadn't realized how close she'd come to actually punching Kamrie in the face.

"We're going to deal with this in court," Logan said. "There's nothing we can do here."

"So, you want this to go public and you want people to put these shady puzzle pieces together and drag your name through the dirt?"

"You know this all started when you lied about my husband being the father of your child."

"If that's what you need to believe. But you saw the DNA test."

Robin broke free from Logan's grasp and pushed Kamrie against the door. "I'm done being nice to this delusional bitch! You may not admit it now, but we know that DNA is a fraud."

"When this case goes public and Logan's name is attached to this sexual harassment and assault, how much

are you going to cry then? Are you going to walk away
like you did before? Logan deserves better."

Robin slapped Kamrie as hard as she could and didn't
care if she left a mark or not. How long had she wanted
to do this, and this tramp deserved it. Logan quickly
stepped between the women.

"Stop, stop!" he exclaimed. "This is the last thing we
need."

A couple who had been jogging was staring at their
front porch. Robin waved at them and moved away from
Kamrie. "She's not coming in this house because she
won't tell the truth and this is all her fault! There is nothing she can say or do to fix the mess she caused."

"What was I supposed to do when my son's father
won't acknowledge him or help me take care of him?"

"That's the hill you want to die on?" Robin snapped.
"You still want to pretend that Logan is . . ."

"Robin," Logan said quietly. "I know this is tough and
the last thing we expected to be doing right now."

"Don't try to handle me right now," she growled. "I'm
tired of this bitch and it's such a coincidence that she gets
served and then she wants to come here with bombshells.
I'm not here for this bullshit."

Kamrie glared at Robin. "I ought to call the police and
have you arrested for assault."

"Do it and I'll have you arrested for trespassing."

"Robin," Logan whispered. "Please . . ."

She whirled around and looked at him. "Don't tell me
to calm down and don't try and make an excuse for this
waste of flesh."

"Not going to do that, but keep in mind that there are

cameras everywhere and the last thing we need is to cause a scene."

Robin pointed at Kamrie. "She needs to go."

Logan nodded. "We'll deal with this in court," he said.

"Fine, it's your mistake. I was trying to help," Kamrie said. "Dr. Carter is going to have a field day with you and I'm going to cheer for him. Stupid."

Robin lunged at her again, but Logan was able to hold her back. "Let her go, babe. Just let her go."

Once Kamrie got into her car, Robin screamed like a mythical banshee. "I'm going to pray for forgiveness, but if she falls off the face of the earth I wouldn't cry."

"I know."

"Who does that? Who creates all of this turmoil and then claims she wants to help?" Robin pushed away from Logan and stormed inside the house. He followed her and touched her elbow.

"Robin, baby, let's just deal with this in court."

She nodded, realizing that all of those times she saw Logan and Kamrie together she was watching a woman put on a show and she almost let those lies pull her marriage apart. She had played the fool Kamrie wanted her to be. Tears of anger and disappointment filled her eyes. Logan wrapped his arms around her shoulders.

"Babe," he whispered.

"I can't . . . Let's get out of here. We can drive to Charleston and spend a few days with Dad. I just want to get away."

"All right, I'll pack a bag for us and we can get going."

Robin looked at her watch. "Maybe it will be smarter to leave in the morning."

"Whatever you want to do, I'm with it," he said, then kissed her on the neck.

"Great, because we're going to the liquor store right now," she said.

Logan fought back his laughter because his wife was a lightweight when it came to hard liquor. If she wanted a drink, she had to be in a mood. If she wanted a stiff drink, he hoped that it would give her a little bit of peace. Seeing Kamrie had to have thrown her for a loop, but Logan didn't want them to go back to the days when she would see her and question his love and fidelity.

"Logan," Robin called out, "I'm sorry I lost control."

"It's all right. I mean it was bound to happen and I'm glad no blood was shed."

"Mine or hers?"

"Both, actually. The last thing we need is for her to have another false allegation to throw at us."

Robin took a deep breath and ran her hand across her face. "I'm so tired of this shit."

"I know. I know." He took her into his arms and held her as she silently cried.

"I can't believe I thought you would've been with a woman like that," she said after her tears stopped.

He stroked her hair. "It's okay. We're going to get through this. And we're going to do it without getting drunk. Because you know you can't handle your liquor."

She laughed hollowly. "But we have to get out of this house."

"You know what we haven't done in years?"

"What?"

"The tacky lights tour. We've still got time before they shut them off. And we can get out of the house and think about some happy things."

She took his face in her hands. "You are a genius."

Logan brushed his lips against hers. "Let's go."

Chapter 24

The next morning, Logan and Robin took the long ride to the Richardson Bed and Breakfast in Charleston. Robin had offered to drive but Logan assured her that he'd be fine driving.

"At least I'm going to see Pops without worrying about him being ready to slap the taste out of my mouth for hurting his daughter," Logan said as he took the keys from Robin's hand.

"True, and I hope Alex and Yolanda haven't told him stories about what's been going on here. They both have a history of stretching the truth to suit their needs."

Logan laughed. "Not your sisters."

"Whatever. There's a reason why I've always been known as the peacemaker. And as quiet as it's kept, I'm Dad's favorite."

Logan laughed again. He'd heard this story from each of Robin's sisters over the years. And Sheldon told him who his favorite was, all of them. Alex was his strong-willed daughter who knew more about business than life. He couldn't run his company without her and he knew she'd be the one to keep the bed-and-breakfast strong for years to come. Then his other favorite was Robin, the level-headed daughter who knew what she had to do to keep the peace in the family. She knew how to calm her sisters when the fights started and got them to see things from the others' perspectives.

Then his other favorite was his wild card daughter, Yolanda. Her speak-first-and-think-second nature may have gotten her in trouble at times, but she was always going to live by her own rules and if anyone—family or not—tried to challenge her, there would be hell to pay.

And finally, his baby girl, Nina, held a special place in his heart because she reminded him so much of his wife. Nina loved hard. Nina always turned a no into a yes and she was fiercely independent. Since his daughters were so different it was easy for them to be his favorites, but Sheldon was never going to tell them that.

"Sure you are, babe," Logan quipped as they started toward South Carolina.

Once they arrived at the bed-and-breakfast, the sun was beginning to set on an unusually warm winter day. Robin pointed to her father's empty parking space.

"I wonder where he is," she said as Logan parked the car.

"Did you tell him that we were coming?"

She shook her head.

Logan shrugged. "Maybe he's on a date."

"Please, you didn't hear Alex's head explode, did you?" Robin laughed, then shook her head. "And my phone hasn't been dinging from text message alerts."

"Would you be mad if Pops was out with a woman?"

"Do you want to start a fight with me?" Robin pulled her phone out of her pocket and called Alex.

"What's going on?" her sister said instead of hello.

"Logan and I just got into town. Where's Daddy?"

"Why are y'all here?"

"That's quite the welcome, sis," Robin quipped. "We just needed a break and . . . Where is Daddy? Logan seems to think he's on a date."

Alex laughed so loudly that Robin had to move the phone away from her ear. "Daddy's golfing."

Robin stuck her tongue out at her husband. "He's playing golf."

"That's what he told y'all," Logan said with a laugh.

"Anyway," Robin said, returning to her conversation with Alex, "we're in the parking lot and you need to let us in."

"Do I? Are you sure everything is all right?"

"Yes," Robin replied with a sigh. Logan gave her thigh a comforting squeeze.

"Fine, I'm coming out."

Robin ended the call and she and Logan exited the car. It was about twenty degrees warmer in Charleston than it had been when they left Richmond. She took a deep breath and inhaled the salty air. "Feels good to be home," she said.

"Ever think about moving back?" He reached for their bags, then turned toward the ocean. "It's warmer, your family's here, and . . ."

"I don't want to think about moving back now because it's going to feel as if we're running."

"We're not running, but haven't we had enough stress in our lives? Coming to Charleston would kill 90 percent of it."

Robin was about to respond to him when she saw Alex coming their way. "We'll talk about this later," she said.

Alex joined the couple and gave her sister a tight hug. "Please tell me you're not here to throw him in the ocean and you need an alibi."

"I can hear you, Alex," Logan said.

"I know," she said, then shrugged her shoulders. "Seriously, though, what brings you guys to town in the middle of the week?"

"Can we go inside and have some coffee or something before you start with the third degree?" Robin asked.

"Okay."

"Where's Yolanda?"

Alex shrugged again. "I think she and Charles went to Charlotte to check out the security for her new store and at Nina's place. She's going to be staying there while she gets the business up and running. Which, I have to say, doesn't make sense to me. She was successful in Richmond."

"I was surprised when she closed the store as well," Robin said. "She said there were too many boutiques and they were basically selling the same stuff."

"Yeah, but Daddy invested a lot in . . . I'm minding my business," Alex said. "According to our younger sisters, I'm too judgmental."

Robin and Logan exchanged a look as Alex walked them over to the family area of the bed-and-breakfast. They walked in and headed for the seating area.

"Whatever," Alex said. "When I take this vacation, none of y'all better call, text, or e-mail me."

"The more you talk about it, the less I believe it's going to happen," Robin replied.

Alex rolled her eyes. "Anyway, what are you two doing here? Just wanted to come see the ocean to ring in the new year or is there another scandal brewing?"

"You're not judgmental at all, Alex," Logan quipped.

"Maybe I was about to catch a case because that ignorant . . . We needed a break from everything. We have a court date in two weeks to disprove paternity and now she's in the media with sexual assault allegations."

"What?" Alex exclaimed. "Does that woman have any morals?"

"Clearly the answer is no. But here's the kicker. She claims . . ."

"Babe," Logan said. "If Kamrie is telling the truth about anything, it's that Dr. Carter is trying to get her to spread the lies to discredit me."

Robin rolled her eyes. "She is a problem and now she's trying to act like she's a fucking solution." She started pacing back and forth. Logan nodded toward his wife.

"And this is why we came to visit," he said.

Alex shook her head. "Bourbon tea?"

Robin clasped her hands together and nodded. "And that is how you should greet folks. Bourbon tea is always a great hello."

After a few moments, Robin finally sat down while Alex made the potent tea and heated a tray of chocolate chip cookies. "I'm sorry," she said as she leaned her head on Logan's shoulder.

"You have nothing to apologize for. And your reaction to everything that's going on is why I suggested moving."

"And it's still running. Logan, let's not forget that we both have careers in Richmond. I love Charleston, but I don't want to give up everything that I worked for because these people are spreading lies about you. And you can't want that either."

"You know what else I don't want, my wife to have a heart attack because she's stressed out all of the time. No matter what happens in a couple of weeks, this is going to follow us and we're going to be the focus of gossip and innuendoes."

"How is that different from what's going on right now?"

"Robin, it was just a suggestion."

She expelled a frustrated sigh. "I don't want to fight with you."

"Oh, we're not fighting at all, Robin. We've done enough fighting, baby."

"What do you want to do? Because this is your reputation and your future."

Logan stroked her cheek. "I don't know what I want to do. I want to save the patients at the hospital and make sure they are being treated with safe drugs. I want to clear my name and I want my wife to love me forever."

"We can do all of that. And we don't have to run away to make it happen." She leaned in and kissed him softly. "And I'm behind you, no matter what. So, you already got your wife loving you forever."

"Thank God for that," he said.

Alex returned to the sitting room with the bourbon iced tea and cookies. "Everything cool in here?"

Robin nodded as she took the cookies from Alex's hand. "We're good," she replied.

Alex set the glasses on the table in front of the settee where Logan and Robin were sitting. "I've got a couple of reports to write, so I'm going to head over to the office for a little bit." She tossed Robin a key. "If you two start feeling some kind of way, go to your room."

"Subtle, sis," Robin quipped.

"She has a point, though," Logan said as he kissed Robin's cheek.

"Eww," Alex said. "I'm out. I'll let Daddy know y'all are here so we can get together for dinner. And Nina and Clinton are coming back New Year's Day if you two want to stick around."

"I really need to talk to her. I still feel some kind of way about how I acted at her wedding," Robin said wistfully.

"You didn't do anything wrong," Alex said as she headed out the door. Once they were alone, Logan reached for Robin's hand.

"If anyone put a cloud over your sister's wedding, it wasn't you. Remember that."

Robin sighed and leaned against her husband's chest. "I know, but it feels that way."

"Don't think about it like that. I hate that I didn't get to see little sis walk down the aisle and give that guy a warning about how the Richardson sisters really roll."

"How about a warning about not hurting my sister so he can live to see their fiftieth anniversary?"

"And I rest my case. You know, when I showed up here, I really thought Yolanda and Pops were going to shoot or stab me."

"Yolanda wanted to," Robin said. Logan started to laugh. "Babe, I'm not joking."

"Why am I not surprised?"

"Everybody was mad as hell and . . ."

Logan leaned in and kissed her gently. "That's the past and we're not going to dwell on it. I want you to consider what I asked you before."

"Moving here?"

Logan nodded. "There is so much we can do with a fresh start. Not just because of the lies Kamrie told, but because this is a great place and I know you wouldn't mind being closer to your family."

"You make it sound so easy. But it still feels like running to me. I'd love to be closer to my family and get away from all of this bullshit. But the truth is, I can be happy anywhere as long as we're together."

"It is." Logan held her closer to his chest. "Why don't we head to your bedroom and relax?"

"Just relax?"

"Clothing optional," he said with a wink.

"You are always trying to get me into bed these days," she quipped. "You're lucky I'm into it."

Logan and Robin headed to her room holding hands and smiling. She opened the door and inhaled the fresh scent of lavender that greeted them. Despite the fact that Alex was the only one who lived in the family wing now, all of the rooms were always kept clean and fresh for visits.

Logan crossed over to the full-sized bed and sat down, then opened his arms to his wife. "You're beautiful when you smile like that."

"Well, you make me smile, so keep doing what you're doing." Robin fell into his embrace. Logan kissed her soft and slow. Then he slipped his hand between her thighs. Robin moaned as he stroked her through the fabric of her leggings. He made her throb, made her weak for his touch. Their kiss got wetter, hotter, and deeper as Logan lay back and Robin mounted him.

In this moment, nothing else mattered and it felt like the world outside didn't exist. There wasn't a pending case, a hospital out to ruin them, or anything that would come between them. It was just Robin and Logan. Their love, their need and desire. Logan lifted her shirt and ran his fingers across her belly. His touch sent ripples of desire down her spine.

"Logan," she moaned as he tweaked her nipples. She unbuttoned his shirt and ran her hand across his chest. Logan smiled when she reached for his belt.

"You're going to be aggressive, huh?"

She shrugged as she unbuckled his belt. "Stop acting like you don't like it."

"Don't think I'm complaining."

Robin slid his pants down his hips and then pulled his boxer briefs off. She stroked his hardness until he moaned. Then she took him into her mouth, slowly sucking and licking him into near submission.

"Oh shit," he exclaimed as she took him deeper down her throat. Logan wanted to pull away, wanted to drive into her, but Robin wouldn't let go. Lick. Suck. Deep throat.

Logan exploded and Robin swallowed his desire, then locked eyes with him.

"Damn," he muttered. "Damn."

"And what were you saying about me being aggressive?"

"Keep it up," he quipped.

Robin rolled over on her side and Logan eased closer to her and drew her into his arms. "You know I'm going to have to redeem myself and find some ice cream to make you weak."

"Yeah, we're not going to do that here. You'll have the whole property hearing me scream. Let's have that ice cream social when we win this case." She pressed her round bottom against him and Logan was instantly aroused.

"So, um, you see what you're doing to me, right?"

"No, but I definitely feel it." Robin turned around and faced him. She pulled her leggings off.

Brushing his lips against hers, Logan pulled her closer to his chest, then captured her lips in a steamy kiss that made her quiver. She threw her leg across him and Logan slid into her wet valley. Robin gripped his shoulder and called out his name. He thrust deeper. Harder. Robin matched him with every stroke, every thrust.

Sweat covered their bodies as they rocked to a rhythm of their own. Robin's moans filled the air as she reached an explosive climax. Logan's explosion followed. Holding on to each other, they drifted off to a satisfied sleep.

Chapter 25

Robin woke slowly, and when she turned her head, she locked eyes with her husband. "I was wondering if you were going to wake up," he said, then kissed her forehead.

"Guess I was a little tired. Had an amazing workout."

"You definitely put in work."

"Then why are you awake?" she quipped.

"Because I still have to make sure I'm not dreaming when I feel you in my arms."

Robin's cheeks heated and she kissed him softly on the cheek. "It's never going to be just a dream," she said. "What time is it?"

Logan glanced at his watch. "Time to eat."

Robin stretched her arms above her head. "That means Alex is going to be knocking on . . . "

As if on cue, there was a knock at the door. "So predictable," Robin muttered, then called out, "Just a minute."

"Hurry up and open the door," Yolanda said.

Robin bounced out of the bed and grabbed her robe from the closet. She could've sworn Alex had said Yolanda was in Charlotte. Once she'd covered her body with the plush robe, she cracked the door. "What are you doing here?"

"Bigger question, what are you doing here? And is that Logan or—"

"Who else would it be?" Robin snapped.

Yolanda shrugged. "Can't tell with y'all these days. Are you two going to come to dinner?"

"Yeah. Everything all right with you?"

She nodded. "See you at dinner."

Robin looked over Yolanda's shoulder to see if Charles was around. When she didn't see him, she wondered if her sister's drama was over.

After closing the door, she turned to Logan, who was getting out of the bed and reaching for his boxer briefs. "Guess it's time for dinner."

"Why would Yolanda think you'd have someone else in here?"

"Because my sister is a drama queen. And I don't think she's forgiven you yet. Yolanda isn't the forgive and forget type. She'll come around, though."

Logan ran his hand across his face. "This is going to be life now? People second guessing me because of all of these lies?"

"When we have our day in court, everyone is going to know the truth. And remember, we're here not to think about all of that."

Logan nodded as he headed toward the bathroom. "Want to join me in the shower? We can save water."

"Um, I'm sure that's not all that we're going to do," she said as she dropped her robe and went into the bathroom with him.

By the time Logan and Robin joined the family for

dinner, dessert was being served. "Well, well," Yolanda said. "Look who finally came up for air. Making up for lost time?"

Alex rolled her eyes and shook her head. "Yolanda, you are so . . . I'm not even doing this with you today."

"Where's Daddy?" Robin asked.

"He's staying over at the golf course tonight. I told him you and Logan were here and he said he'd be back in the morning. So, you two can't leave right away," Alex said, then turned to Yolanda. "You, on the other hand, why are you here without Charles?"

"Because this is my family home and if I want to visit then I can do it."

"And your security detail is just on break?" Alex asked. Robin was interested in the answer as well. Logan stroked the back of his wife's hand as if he was reminding her that he was there.

"I got tired of being watched, especially when . . . Can we just eat this cake and call it a day?"

Robin wanted to ask her sister what was going on, but she let it go. Unfortunately, Alex didn't.

"You slept with him, didn't you?" Alex exclaimed.

"My God," Yolanda snapped. "Have you actually slept with anyone in the twenty-first century?"

Logan and Robin exchanged uncomfortable glances. "Can we not argue?" Robin said. "You two know the rules, no arguing at the dinner table."

Yolanda rolled her eyes and Alex sucked her teeth. "Daddy's not here and that's a rule to keep Alex's mouth shut," Yolanda said.

Alex slammed her hand on the table. "I'm sick of

walking around on eggshells because you're in trouble again."

"Again?" Yolanda said. "I'm sick of you judging me."

Robin shook her head, trying to understand what was going on between her sisters. Now, she knew Yolanda and Alex argued often but this was harsh for them. "What in the hell is this all about?" Robin asked.

"Nothing," Yolanda said. "But I'm tired of everybody telling me what to do and how to live my life."

Alex rolled her eyes and groaned. "Then grow up."

"Alex," Robin cautioned. "Stop."

"No," Alex said as she rose to her feet. "We are always pussyfooting around Nina and Yolanda. But at what point do . . . "

A door slammed and Yolanda yelped. "Who left the door unlocked?" she asked quietly.

"I'll check it out," Logan said. Robin couldn't help but wonder if he was happy to get away from this argument. She started to go with him because she definitely wanted to get away from her bickering sisters. Instead, she looked from Alex to Yolanda.

"I don't know what's going on right now, but I know I've been fighting for a while and I'm tired of it. Can you two get your shit together and calm the hell down?" Robin snapped.

Alex opened her mouth to say something, but then Logan walked into the dining area with Charles.

"Have you lost your damned mind?!" Charles boomed when he saw Yolanda.

"Here we go. I'm not the one who's acting like I broke the law because I have feelings that can't be turned on and off like a light switch."

"You do realize that you're still at risk. And it's my job to protect you."

Yolanda leapt to her feet and got in his face. "I made it here and I'm still alive."

"And it's my job to keep it that way. You want to do this here or can you be an adult and have a conversation with me in private?"

Alex and Robin watched them and wanted the two of them to continue. Robin was slowly putting things together. Yolanda and Charles had crossed a line and he wasn't happy about it. She still didn't know enough about why her sister needed a bodyguard, but Charles did seem like he wasn't going to let any harm come to Yo-Yo, even if she didn't appreciate it.

"I really don't want to talk to you," she said.

Charles nodded and then took hold of her arm. "Being that I work for your father, you don't have a choice. Can we please go someplace private?"

"Her room is available," Alex suggested.

Yolanda glared at her sister, then turned toward the door with Charles close on her heels.

Robin and Alex shook their heads as the two left the room. Logan sat down and toyed with his cake. "Never a dull moment around here," he said.

"You hush," Alex said. "You're just back on the good side of the family."

Robin crossed over to her husband and gave him a kiss on the cheek. "We should've stayed in bed."

Alex headed for her office after she finished her slice of cake and more whining about Yolanda's actions. Robin and Logan tuned her out and played footsie under the table. After Logan and Robin cleared the table, Logan suggested they leave Yolanda and Charles to fix their own affair and the two of them decided to take a walk on the beach. With the sun setting and the wind picking up, Logan had an excuse to hold his wife closer to him. Robin didn't mind. She relished the feeling of his warmth as a cool breeze blew over them.

"Yolanda and Alex are always going to be oil and water, huh?"

"Until they need each other," Robin said. "I wish I knew what was really going on with Yolanda and Charles."

Logan shrugged and stroked her forearm as she shivered. "Have you talked to her, without Alex around?"

"No. They have been so focused on my issues. I just need all of us to be happy. Am I wrong to have that in my heart?"

"Not at all." Logan brushed his lips across her cheek. "I'm sorry if I caused any arguments with you and your sisters."

Robin placed her finger to his lips. "We were all wrong. No one more than me. Logan, I'm sorry I didn't trust us and our love."

He stopped walking and turned to face her. "We're past that and it's never going to happen again."

She brought her hand to his cheek and smiled. "You're right. And after we see Daddy tomorrow, we're going home."

"Why? I thought we were going to ring in the New Year here?"

She shook her head. "Whatever is going on with Alex

and Yolanda is something I don't want to be involved with."

"Then let's get out of this wind and warm up. Then we can go to another hotel and get away from the family drama."

"There's probably not another vacancy in this city. And we can't leave. I've got to . . ."

"Relax. Your sisters always fight and figure it out. We need this little break." Logan kissed her gently. "When we get back to Richmond, the real fight begins. I want to have a little bit of joy with my boo before life comes at us again."

"When you put it like that," she said with a smile, "I guess we can have our New Year's celebration here and put off the real world for another few days."

"And you're going to stay out of whatever Yolanda has going on. I believe Charles can handle it."

"Clearly you don't know my sister. She won't be handled."

"If you say so," he replied with a smile. "You think we can sneak some hot chocolate into your room tonight?"

"Absolutely, and cookies, too. I'm sure that cake is long gone by now," she said with a wink.

"Alex took it to her office?"

Robin nodded. "What she does when she's stressed is eat, work, and then work out. She needs a vacation, and soon. She keeps talking about it."

"Let's go back inside before we catch a cold."

"And have to spend the rest of the time we're here together in bed, wrapped up in a blanket and . . ."

"Sneezing, nose running, and fevers?"

"Point made." Robin took off jogging toward the bed-and-breakfast. Logan was close on her heels.

"Hey, hey, I thought I was the athlete here," he said once he caught up to her.

Robin laughed. "You know what I did these last six months when I was frustrated? I worked out. I can probably take you on the basketball court now."

"Is that a challenge, woman?"

She faced him and grinned. "It is."

"Name the time and the place and it's on."

Robin opened the door and smiled. "We can go to the MUSC Wellness Center after breakfast."

"So, that means you need to get a good night's sleep to be ready, huh?"

"Yeah, so keep your hands to yourself!"

They headed for the kitchen and made hot chocolate while munching on cookies. Robin found a bottle of red wine and poured some in the hot chocolate.

"Really?" Logan asked.

"I saw this on the Internet and I've been dying to try it," she said as she stirred the liquid. Then she poured the spiked cocoa into their mugs. She watched as Logan took a sip.

"This is good," he said.

"I know, right?" she said as she took a huge sip of her own. "Maybe I should give Alex and Yolanda a big cup of this."

"Later. You need to go to sleep and get ready for your beatdown tomorrow."

Robin took his chocolate chip cookie from his hand. "Keep talking."

"Want to make a wager?"

"What are you willing to lose?" she quipped.

"Hmm," he said as he broke the cookie in half. Before he could answer, Logan's cell phone rang. He had to give up his half of the cookie and answer. When he saw it was Liam, Logan felt a wave of dread sink in his stomach.

"What's wrong?" Robin asked when he answered.

Logan held up his finger and turned his attention to the phone call.

"Liam, say that again," Logan said, his voice taking a deep timbre.

"Dr. Carter was arrested. Seems as if there was more than one investigation going on at the hospital about those dangerous drugs," he said. "Have you seen the news?"

"I'm actually in Charleston with Robin."

"Well, if you two are ringing in the New Year down there, you're going to have a lot to celebrate. One of the patients who died after being treated with the Cooper Drug cocktail was the niece of Senator Dale McKinnon."

Logan gasped. "That was my patient. She had a kidney transplant."

"Yeah," he said. "I found out during my investigation that the McKinnon family was thinking about adding you to their lawsuit. So, I let them know about the allegations about Dr. Carter and his partnership with Cooper Drugs. Once the government got involved, the arrest happened."

"Great, but how do I prove that I wasn't involved with this?"

Liam laughed. "Easy. I've given a lot of my investigation reports to the McKinnon family, and you're in the clear so far."

Logan released a sigh of relief. "Now if everything else can be this easy."

Robin stared at her husband, wanting to know all of the details of what was going on.

"At least you're going to have a better New Year than Christmas. Tell Robin I said hello."

Logan ended the call with his friend, then pulled Robin into his arms and spun her around.

"What is going on?" she asked.

"Dr. Carter is in jail and the Cooper Drugs conspiracy is coming to light."

She smiled and stroked his cheek. "That's what you wanted, right? How did all of this happen?"

"The wrong patient died," he said bitterly. "Thank God Liam was around to provide the right information or I would've been in the middle of a malpractice lawsuit."

"And you still want to go back to that hospital?"

Logan shook his head. "I don't know what I want anymore. Well, that's not true. Right now, I want to take our lukewarm chocolate into the room and go to sleep with you in my arms."

"That sounds like a great plan," she said as she reached for her mug. "And guess what?"

"What?"

"It's still hot."

Chapter 26

The next morning, Robin and Logan woke up feeling lighter than they had in months. Though she would've been content lounging in bed all day, Robin knew they had to have breakfast with her father. And then there was the basketball challenge.

She was not planning to lose. As she attempted to rise from the bed, Logan wrapped his arm around her waist. "It's too early for all this movement," he said, his voice thick with sleep.

"I know what you're trying to do and it's not going to work." She moved his hand and smiled. "Still going to kick your butt on the court."

"If we were talking about the court of law, I'd be afraid. But the basketball court? You really don't stand a chance." Logan turned over on his side and watched Robin's fluid movements as she rose from the bed and grabbed her robe. "What happens if I let you win?"

"Let me win?" She laughed and dug in her bag for a pair of black leggings and socks. "You should consider what happens if I let you win. Have you seen my perimeter shot?"

"Really, Stephen Curry?" Logan laughed.

"He asks me for tips," Robin quipped. "Let's get this breakfast in and then you can take your loss like a grown man."

Logan stood up and crossed over to his wife. Drawing her into his arms, he brushed his lips across her neck. "If you want to forfeit, I won't hold it against you."

She giggled and tweaked his nipple. "You wish."

"I'm not going to take it easy on you. Just remember you started it." Logan winked at her before dropping his arms from around her. After they got dressed, the couple headed to the dining room, where Sheldon was sipping coffee and reading the local paper. Robin smiled because her dad was probably one of the last people in the world who still read the physical newspaper.

"Morning, Daddy," Robin said as she crossed over to him and gave him a kiss on the cheek.

"Good morning," he said, then glanced at Logan. "I'm glad to see you both."

Logan nodded at his father-in-law, happy to see that he wasn't in danger of being tossed out of the bed-and-breakfast this time. Robin and Logan sat down with Sheldon, who folded his paper and turned his attention to the couple.

"Now, you know I have questions," he began. "Because y'all weren't a happy couple the last time I saw you to-gether."

Robin nodded. "I took your advice, Daddy. I actually listened to my husband."

Sheldon looked at Logan. "So, all of this was bullshit?"

"Yes, sir," Logan replied. "Pops, you know how much I love Rob and I would never betray her so viciously."

Sheldon smiled broadly. "That was my sincere hope. And I'm glad I was right. What's next for you two? I'm guessing that the woman spreading those lies isn't going to just back off because you and Robin are back together."

"We're going to court to prove Logan isn't her child's father. Remember Liam Jones, who went to Xavier with us, right?"

Sheldon nodded. "Big Willie." He was the only person Liam allowed to call him William or any variation of the name he hated.

Logan couldn't help but laugh and make a note to tell his friend that Sheldon still called him by that name.

"Well," Robin continued, "he found out some real information on Kamrie and who the legitimate father of her child is. We're going to take his findings to court and get her off our backs."

"Some people aren't going to believe the truth," Sheldon said. "How are you two going to deal with that?"

Robin and Logan exchanged looks before shrugging. Robin knew what she wanted to do but Logan still had concerns about patients at the hospital. She hoped that Dr. Carter's arrest would spur him to think about private practice.

"We're still trying to figure that out, Pops."

"Why are y'all dressed like you're about to go running?"

Robin laughed. And Logan cleared his throat before saying, "Your daughter thinks she can take me on the basketball court."

"Oh my goodness, both of you realize that you aren't

as young as you thought you were. You ought to consider golf."

"Golf?" Robin questioned. "I've never known you to take an overnight golf trip in Charleston."

Sheldon downed his coffee, then rose to his feet. "Stay out of grown folks' business. I'm going to the office."

Once Sheldon was out of earshot, Logan broke out into laughter. "I told you Pops had a girlfriend."

"Shut up, Logan," Robin said as she reached for the coffeepot. A few moments later, Alex walked into the dining area.

"Morning," she said through a yawn.

"You okay?" Robin asked.

Alex fanned her hand. "Stayed up too late working on some proposals."

Robin raised her right eyebrow and leaned in to her sister. "Does Daddy have a girlfriend?"

Alex rolled her eyes. "Please, all he does is golf and worry about his younger children."

Logan laughed. "Golf is what they're calling women these days?"

Alex glared at him. "You really think you're in a position to be making jokes?"

Robin shook her head. "Don't do that."

"I think if Daddy was seeing somebody, I would know."

"Okay," Robin said as Roberta walked into the dining area with a platter of eggs, grits, fresh fruit, and raisin toast.

"Robin, give me a hug. You left so soon after Nina's wedding, I didn't get a chance to say good-bye."

Robin hugged the family's longtime cook. "I'm sorry that I missed you. There was a lot going on at that time."

Roberta turned to Logan and smiled. "How are you, doctor?"

Logan returned her sweet smile as he gave her a hug. "Glad to see you two together."

Robin beamed. She was even happier to be with her husband. But he was going to lose this basketball game.

"Miss Alex, how are you this morning?" Roberta asked.

"I'm looking forward to this evening so I can go to sleep. But thank you for this spread."

"Any time. Thanks for letting me know our vegetarian would be joining us this morning," Roberta said. "But I do have bacon and sausage."

"Aww, Roberta," Alex said. "You are a godsend and I hope you didn't go to extra trouble."

She waved her meaty hand. "Got to feed the guests, too, since you and Clinton have this place packed for the New Year."

Alex laughed. "Yes, we do. But I don't want to see you here New Year's Day. We have someone else to feed the guests. I know you have that major church service and dinner."

"One year you're going to come so I can introduce you to some nice, God-fearing men."

Robin coughed to cover her laughter and Logan stuffed a piece of pineapple in his mouth. Alex didn't respond and Robin knew it was out of respect for Roberta. Anyone else would've gotten cursed out until New Year's Eve for making such a statement.

Roberta patted Alex's shoulder and then headed for

the kitchen to bring out the meat. Alex looked over at Logan and Robin and shook her head. "Glad you two got a good laugh in," she quipped. "Are y'all going for a run or something?"

"I'm about to show your brother-in-law that I've got skills on all courts," Robin replied.

Alex sipped her coffee and shook her head. "Glad he's a doctor, so he can patch your clumsy butt up."

"Funny. I've been a lot more active these days. Is Yolanda still here?"

Alex shrugged. "I'm not extending any more energy into the woes of Yolanda Richardson." She reached across the table and filled her plate with eggs and toast. As if she felt that she was the topic of conversation, Yolanda strolled into the dining area, dressed in a purple jumpsuit and a pair of matching sneakers.

"Good morning, family," she said with gaiety in her voice. "Did I miss Daddy?"

Robin nodded. "He's in his office."

Alex picked up the newspaper that Sheldon had left on the table and proceeded to ignore her sister. Yolanda didn't seem to care about Alex's little show. Before Robin could ask where Charles was, he appeared in the dining room like a ghost. How a man that big moved in silence, Robin would never know.

Charles nodded to the table before taking a seat beside Yolanda. Robin was surprised to see her sister fix him a plate of food, but she kept her mouth shut. Patting Logan on his knee, she smiled and asked, "You ready for this beatdown?"

"I'm going to get some bacon and then I'll try to take it somewhat easy on you," Logan quipped.

"What are y'all talking about?" Yolanda asked.

"Your sister wants to play ball this morning," Logan said with a smirk.

"I almost want to see that," Yolanda replied with a laugh. "Where is this epic battle taking place?"

"MUSC Wellness Center," Robin said. "And we're not accepting guests. Logan doesn't want there to be any video of him getting beat by his wife."

Alex laughed and set her coffee cup next to her empty plate. "Even I know you have no chance."

Yolanda rolled her eyes. "I have faith in you, sis. After all, it's not like Logan is still in college basketball shape, and you look like you're trying to audition for a Marvel movie. If I were a betting woman, I'd totally put my money on you."

"Thank you for having faith in me," Robin said, then stuck her tongue out at her husband.

"This is cute," Logan said. "We'll see how she feels when she takes this L."

Roberta returned to the dining room with the breakfast meats and a big hug for Yolanda.

After Logan ate his fill of sausage patties, bacon, and eggs, he and Robin were ready to play. They took the quick drive to the Wellness Center. Once they arrived, Robin started stretching to warm up. Logan couldn't take his eyes off her body as she did a few dozen squats. The moment she started doing lunges, he wanted to call the game off and head to the sauna and get naked with her.

"What are you looking at, Baptiste?" she said, breaking into his lustful thoughts.

"Thinking about how I'm going to post you up. What are we playing to?"

"Ten."

Logan laughed. "Ten it is." He grabbed a ball from the rack near the door. He dribbled the ball, remembering how he used to warm up in college. Robin crossed over to him and smiled.

"I brought you here for more than one reason," she said as she shifted her weight from left to right.

"Really?" He tossed the ball in the air and caught it.

"You could work here. MUSC has a great reputation with transplants and . . ."

Logan bounced the ball against the wall, caught it and gave his wife a sideways glance. "I think I'm done with hospitals. When we get back to Richmond and see the fallout from Carter's arrest, I'm going to look into my own practice. Then I can make the best decisions for my patients without wondering who's getting a payoff to pump them full of drugs that don't work."

Robin punched the ball from his hand and dribbled down the court. She moved so fast that Logan was slow to respond. When she threw up the shot and made it, Robin did a shoulder shimmy. "Two nothing," she said. "You'd better get on your game, Baptiste."

"You know you're cheating, right?"

She tossed the ball to him. "I call it outplaying you."

Logan palmed the ball and held it up as Robin attempted to jump and knock it loose. But he had height on her. He took a shot from beyond the three-point line. "Three-two," he said with a wink.

Robin took the pass from Logan and dribbled around

him. He knew he should've been playing defense, but he couldn't get past the way her ass bounced as she ran and shot the ball.

"Five-three," she said when her shot went through the net. "Where's the defense, baby?" Robin tossed the ball back to him. Logan threw it over his shoulder and scooped his wife up in his arms.

"You win," he said. "Now, let's get out of here." He captured her mouth in a steamy kiss and Robin moaned in delight. When he broke the kiss, she nodded.

"Yeah, let's go."

Chapter 27

Robin and Logan had a quiet New Year's celebration with the Richardsons in Charleston. Yolanda and Alex mended their fences before midnight and they all had a peaceful toast with some of the guests and their father. But as the clock hit 12:01 a.m., Robin couldn't help but think about the reality that was waiting for them in Richmond. The court case, the fallout from the scandal at the hospital. Part of her wished that she could just bottle this feeling and pull it out when they needed peace again.

When they got back to Richmond, Robin could've sworn that time sped up. The days before the paternity case were blurs. Even though she worked on other cases, all she could think about was clearing Logan's name. The months of pain and hell that Kamrie had put them through with her lies.

Luckily, with the arrest of Dr. Carter, the story about sexual harassment at the hospital disappeared from the headlines. Robin was glad because she was going to sue anyone who said Logan Baptiste's name in conjunction with that lie. One gossip blog tried to tie the paternity case and the hospital's issues together, but it didn't gain traction. Robin also sent the owner of the sleazy website a cease and desist letter that must have scared him because the piece disappeared.

Today, though, nothing was going to disappear. She and Logan were going to have to face this woman in court. She walked over to the coffeemaker in her office and fixed herself another cup. Logan was on his way to the office so they could go to court together. She couldn't help but think about how his meeting went with the hospital administration. Would they try to talk him into staying or accept his resignation because of the hell they put him through? She drummed her fingers on the side of the mug and tried to imagine a future where she and Logan could get back to their peace.

"Boo," Logan said when he walked in the office. The sound of his voice startled her and Robin nearly dropped her coffee. "I think you might need to switch to decaf."

"Don't even joke like that. I was just thinking about all of this shit and how it'd better come to an end today."

Logan crossed over to his wife and took her coffee mug from her hand. "Well, I no longer work for Richmond Medical. So, that came to an end today."

"What? Did they take it well?"

Logan shrugged. "I got hush money or, as they call it, a severance package. This is going to be the nest egg I'll need to start my practice here and maybe in Charleston."

Robin smiled broadly. "So, that means I can finally be one of those doctor's wives like on the reality shows?"

"No," he quipped. "You've still got to work. But we can spend more time with Pops and figure out who his girlfriend is. My money is on a church lady that Roberta introduced him to."

Robin thumped him on the shoulder. "My father does not have a girlfriend."

Logan kissed her on the forehead. "Whatever you say."

"Anyway," she said. "Don't you think we need to focus on something more important?"

"Trust me, I'm focused."

Robin leaned against his chest and sighed. "Hopefully, this all ends today. Have you heard from Liam yet?"

"He should be here soon," Logan said. "Can you calm down?"

She shook her head. "This is a different case because this is so personal. When I think about all of the time she took away from us, I just want her to pay and suffer like I did. Like we did. It's not fair that she used an innocent child like this. Kids aren't pawns, and she played him in this dirty chess game. And for what?"

"She picked the wrong doctor this time. I wasn't tempted to risk our happiness with her and . . ."

"I just want to know how she found out about my . . ."

Logan stroked her cheek. "That's another reason I got the package I got from the hospital. Kamrie and one of her nurse friends accessed your medical records without authorization. Even though you didn't have your surgery at RM, you were still in the hospital's system."

"I ought to sue the . . . You took the money and I can't sue now, right?"

"That's up to you. I can't sue them, but they weren't my records."

She shook her head. "I'll file a complaint with the medical board." Robin glanced at her watch. "If Liam doesn't hurry up, we're going to be late for court."

Robin's desk phone buzzed. "Mr. Jones is here," her assistant said.

"Thank you. Please send him in."

Logan and Robin broke their embrace as the door to her office opened. "Hey, hey," Liam said as he handed Robin a file folder. "Ready to take this woman down?"

"Let's hope it happens that way," she said as she skimmed through Liam's reports.

Kamrie sat on the bench outside of the courtroom and smiled at her son over the video call app on her phone. The little boy cooed and reached for the babysitter's arm. "Jean, are you being a good boy? Mommy loves you," she said softly.

The little boy pointed at the screen and smiled. Kamrie returned his sweet smile, then blew him a kiss. "I love you, little boy," she said. "Everything I'm doing is for you. Shannon, I'm going into court soon and I'll pick Jean up when we're done."

"Okay. I can keep him until three but then I have to go to work," Shannon said.

Kamrie nodded and ended the call. She took a deep breath and tossed her head back. Today was going to ruin everything she'd been working for. She wanted to give her son the life she never had. Wanted to make sure he didn't have to struggle as she had growing up. What if she hadn't bought the dreams that being a doctor's wife would change her life? Things may have been different. But she envied those women. She'd watched those wives at holiday parties, dripping in diamonds, wearing the top fashions, and doing nothing. Always talking about their volunteer work and lives of leisure. She deserved that lifestyle. How many years had she and her mother suffered and struggled? There was no way that she was going to make her son suffer the way she had because a man left her holding the baby bag. Granted, Logan wasn't the man responsible for her pain, but he shouldn't have given her the mixed signals. No one is that nice.

Those smiles, words of encouragement. He was everything that Thomas was in the early days. But Thomas was too much of a henpecked husband to leave his wife and follow his heart. Why would he say he loved her and then let that bitch run her out of town?

Kamrie wasn't going to be her mother. Maybe that's why she went after Logan. But this court case was going to ruin everything. And Dr. Carter's arrest had her looking like a fool at work. She couldn't name Logan as the man who had sexually harassed her now because of his resignation and the fact that the court was probably going to order a DNA test. But that new DNA test would expose the truth and ruin everything.

"Too bad you're not here to go to prison," a voice said from behind her.

Kamrie turned around and saw Valerie Adams standing there. "What are you doing here?" She stood up to face the woman who'd ruined her life in Atlanta. The city she'd loved.

Valerie glared at her and folded her arms across her chest. "I knew you were a fool but I didn't take you for a damned idiot. You and I know that my husband is the father of your child."

"And you told me that he'd never be a part of Jean's life."

"Those are still facts. But for you to try and ruin a

man like Dr. Baptiste with a bunch of lies? What do you think is going to happen when you walk into that courtroom and real tests are done? Do you know how lucky you are to still have a medical license?"

"My son isn't going to suffer because you are banning his father from seeing him and taking care of his responsibilities."

"Did you sic that private investigator on us? Are you trying to embarrass me and my family? What's your endgame? Thomas isn't going to leave me. If you want a quiet settlement, I'd be open to it. But my husband is not . . ."

"Valerie," Thomas said as he rushed toward them. "Stop it."

"What are you doing here?" Valerie demanded. "I told you I was going to handle this."

"There is nothing for either of you to handle," Kamrie snapped. "You are Jean's father and you let her keep you from our child." Angry tears fell down her cheeks.

"Then why did you say this other man was his father? What did you want me to do?" Thomas asked.

"Be a man, you son of a bitch!"

Valerie closed her eyes and shook her head. "Can we go somewhere private and talk about this?"

"What am I supposed to do about this court case?" Kamrie asked. "I can't just not show up."

"And I can't have my husband's misdeeds going public. You need to call Dr. Baptiste's lawyer and tell them you are not contesting their case and you want to withdraw whatever lies you've told."

Kamrie narrowed her eyes at Valerie. "And what do I get if I do that?"

"Kamrie," Thomas said. "I'm willing to be there for our son, but I can't do it publicly."

"But," Valerie interjected, "we're going to pay for the child's needs as well as your silence. Just not in Atlanta."

"Then how will my son have a relationship with his father?" Kamrie asked.

Valerie shot Thomas a glaring look. "I don't mind Thomas spending time with his son. We can easily tell people that the little boy is his nephew."

"I'm not going to lie to my son—"

"What are you doing now, bitch?" Valerie snapped.

Kamrie stopped herself from lunging at her and scratching her eyes out. But being that there were deputies and other security guards around, she knew it wasn't the time or the place.

"Kamrie, I'm not leaving my wife, but I want to see my son grow up."

"And what happens when she tells you that you can't?" Tears welled up in her eyes and her knees went weak. Thomas rushed to her side and grabbed her before she hit the floor. The look he gave her told Kamrie that things weren't over with them. Maybe she should take their offer and call Logan and his wife.

Valerie didn't say a word as she saw the electricity between her husband and his mistress.

Robin sat quietly as Logan drove to the courthouse. Her mind was full of cases where men had been held responsible for kids who didn't belong to them. What if the judge did the same thing to Logan? Should they ask for shared custody of the little boy despite what Liam's investigation discovered?

She was sure Kamrie was going to fight them on everything. Why wouldn't she? She had been spreading these lies for months. She had no reason to stop today.

"You okay over there?" Logan asked.

"Nope, I'm not okay. I won't be okay until this is over and this woman is out of our—" Robin's phone rang and she dug it out of her purse. "Robin Baptiste."

"Mrs. Baptiste, this is Kamrie."

"What do you want?"

The woman sighed into the phone. "I'm calling to tell you that I'm not going to contest the paternity hearing. Logan isn't Jean's father and I don't want to drag this out."

"What?"

"I made a mistake. And I don't want this to go public or have my son suffer."

"What kind of game are you playing?" Robin snapped.

"I'm not playing a game. Not anymore," she said, her voice low. "I'm sorry for what I did to you and Logan."

"Sorry? You think that's enough?"

"What more do you want from me?" Kamrie snorted. "I'm giving you a gift. Stop being a bitch and accept it."

"You . . . I don't know what you expect me to say. But I got your bitch. You need to watch how you speak to me."

Logan shot her a quick look as he pulled into the parking lot of the courthouse.

"What do we have to do to get this case dismissed?" Kamrie asked.

"We just got here. We'll go speak to the clerk. And I will tell you this, don't you ever try to come after my family again. I promise you, it won't be settled in court next time."

Robin ended the call and took a deep breath. Then she pumped her fists and banged on the dashboard.

She screamed and stomped her feet. Logan slowed the car and turned to his wife.

"I'm almost afraid to ask, but what was that all about?" he asked.

Robin's eyes gleamed with joy as a slow smile curved her lips. "That was Kamrie. She said she isn't going to fight the case and she admitted that you aren't her son's father."

Logan grunted. "I'm willing to bet that Carter's arrest is the root of her change of mind."

Robin shrugged, then opened the car door. "I don't care what it is. I'm just glad this is finally over."

Logan stepped out of the car and crossed over to his wife. "This is over and we're about to have a new beginning." Drawing her into his arms, he gave her a sweet kiss. Robin felt at peace for the first time in months and she couldn't have been happier.

Epilogue

Robin walked toward Logan on the shores of Folly Beach. Her yellow halter gown blew in the gentle breeze and she was glad that she'd opted to pin her hair up. It didn't hurt that Logan loved that style on her either.

She held a bouquet of yellow lilies against her chest. She knew that she was stepping closer to her future. She was about to renew her vows to the only man she'd ever loved. The man who would always hold her heart. A year ago, she would've never believed that she and Logan would be together. She had tried to pretend she could live without him. Had believed that her life would've been better without him.

It was a good thing that she was wrong and her husband wasn't going to let her go.

This time she needed to make sure she stuck to the words that they were about to share. Robin was going to believe in her husband. He'd already proven to her that he had her back no matter what. That she was enough for him and everything he'd ever wanted. And Logan meant that much to her as well. She inhaled the salty sea air and smiled. The crashing waves signaled a new beginning and she was ready for it.

Robin glanced at her sisters and their smiles warmed her heart. Seeing Nina being held by Clinton made her believe that they all deserved a happily ever after. Even Alex seemed happy as she looked at her. That was a real smile on her face. Yolanda didn't seem as upset to have Charles with her, and Robin noticed that he was holding her hand and not in a come-with-me-if-you-want-to-live way. Something was going on there, but she was going to get to the bottom of that later.

Robin focused her glance on Logan. She drank in his image: white linen suit, no shoes, and a huge smile. She wanted to run into his arms, but she followed the rhythm of the crashing waves. They had the rest of their lives to be together forever.

And Logan was going to start his private practice in July. He was going to have an office in Richmond and one in Charleston. Robin was happy to know that she and her husband were going to be spending more time together and with her family. When she reached him, Logan reached his hands out to her and pulled her against his chest.

"You're going to smash my flowers," she whispered.

"That's not all I want to smash," he replied in a lower voice.

The reverend cleared his throat. Clearly, they hadn't been as quiet as they thought. "Sorry," they said, then laughed.

"Since you're already married, I guess it's all right," he said. Robin turned to Nina and handed her the lilies. Then she and Logan joined hands.

"Dearly beloved, we're gathered here on this day that the Lord has made to renew love. To celebrate love and to reunite Logan and Robin Baptiste in love."

Logan stroked Robin's cheek and mouthed, "I love you."

Warm tears of joy slid down her cheeks.

"Marriage is more than a beautiful wedding. Marriage is about the in between. The ups and the downs, the highs and the lows. It takes two people to make the decision to make a marriage work. With love, faith, and dedication, marriage is an everlasting commitment."

Murmurs of amen and yes rippled through the small crowd. "Now, I want everyone standing here on this beach to take a vow. We have to vow to protect and pray for this couple. We have to keep them lifted in the Lord."

Logan and Robin looked out at the faces of their family and friends. Robin could've sworn she saw Liam wipe a tear away from the corner of his eye.

The reverend turned to Logan and Robin. "The couple has written vows that they'd like to exchange. Logan, go ahead."

Logan kissed Robin's palms. "Robin Richardson Baptiste, I knew I loved you the first time I saw you. I just didn't know how I was going to get the smartest girl at Xavier to see more than a basketball player. But you did. And you gave me something that I didn't know I'd been yearning for. You brought me into this family. And you loved me unconditionally. I will never love anyone as much as I love you and I plan to spend my entire life showing you how much I love you."

Robin fought back her tears after she listened to Logan's vows. She could barely find her voice to say her vows back to him. Logan stroked her cheek. "Take your time, baby," he said.

She took a cleansing breath. "You are the man of my dreams. I close my eyes and see your face. And I've been blessed to wake up to your face for all of these years. Half of my heart is with you. And I know that you're going to protect my heart, because you have since the day I told you that I loved you. You've been there for me when I was at my lowest. You made sure I felt safe, comforted, and protected. With you by my side, I know that we can weather any storm. And we have. I look forward to the next hundred years of being your wife."

Logan leaned forward and kissed her on the forehead.

"If you two will join hands," the reverend said.

Robin smiled at Logan as they held hands. "What God has joined together, let no man put asunder."

Logan pulled Robin into his arms and kissed her with a slow and deep passion that made the family cheer. Breaking the kiss, they looked at each other and Logan winked.

"Are you ready?" Robin asked.

"Let's do it," he replied.

The couple took off running into the ocean and splashed around like a couple of kids. "I love you so much," Robin said.

"I love you even more."

**Don't miss the first book
in the Richardson Sisters series . . .**

OWNER OF A BROKEN HEART

**The four very different Richardson sisters have one
thing in common: their fierce loyalty to their family
and pride in the historic bed and breakfast they
own. But unexpected desire will challenge them in
ways they never imagined . . .**

Sportswriter Nina Richardson had the perfect life
away from her family's famous shadow. But a social
media blowup and rejection by her boyfriend brought
her back to their peaceful Charleston, South Carolina
B&B to figure out what went wrong.
So there's no way she's going to trust the crazy-hot
sparks flying between her and handsome new employee
Clinton Jefferson. It's just reckless, rip-his-clothes-off,
one-night-and-forget-it lust—right?

Fresh from working for the Richardsons' biggest rival,
Clinton wants to show his modernization ideas aren't
sabotage or a gimmick. Getting involved with the
rebellious Nina means trouble for sure—but he can't
resist showing this stubborn, fiery woman how she
should be loved. But false accusations and Nina's
returned ex shake their passion—and fragile trust—to
the core. Now between cascading obstacles and
conflicting loyalties, can Clinton and Nina untangle
what they really want in time?

*Available from Kensington Publishing Corp.
wherever books are sold*